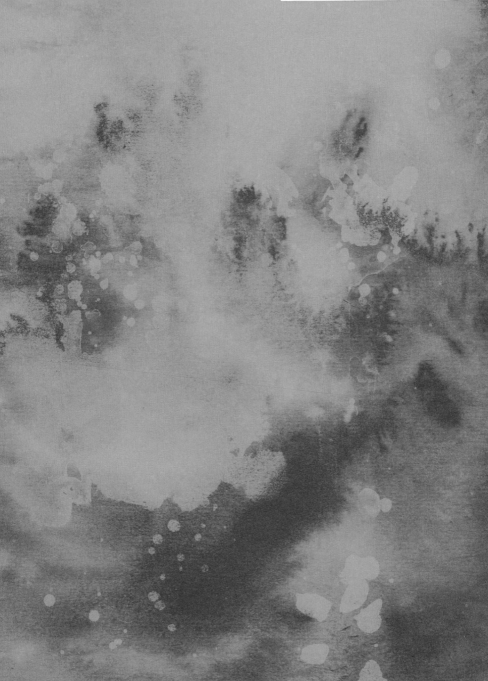

Praise for *Strange Alchemy*

"With whip-smart, instantly likable characters and a gothic small-town setting, Bond weaves a dark and gorgeous tapestry from America's oldest mystery." – Scott Westerfeld, #1 *New York Times* bestselling author of the Uglies series

"Bond takes some reliably great elements – a family curse, the mark of Cain, the old and endlessly fascinating mystery of the Roanoke Colony – and makes them into something delightfully, surprisingly new. How does she do that? I suspect witchcraft." – Karen Joy Fowler, *New York Times* bestselling author of *The Jane Austen Book Club*

"This haunting, romantic mystery intrigues, chills, and captivates." – Cynthia Leitich Smith, *New York Times* bestselling author of the Tantalize series

STRANGE
ALCHEMY

GWENDA BOND

Switch Press
a capstone imprint

Strange Alchemy is published in 2017 by Switch Press,
A Capstone Imprint
1710 Roe Crest Drive
North Mankato, Minnesota 56003
www.switchpress.com

Library of Congress Cataloging-in-Publication Data is available on
the Library of Congress website.

ISBN: 978-1-63079-076-9 (paper over board)
ISBN: 978-1-63079-099-8 (reflowable epub)

Summary: On Roanoke Island, the legend of the Lost Colony still haunts the
town. And when 114 people suddenly disappear from the island in present day,
it seems history is repeating itself.

Designer: Kay Fraser

Image credits: Shutterstock: SSokolov (forest), cover and inside, run4it (texture),
cover and inside

Printed and bound in China.
010350F17

For my parents (principals but never fascists)
and
for Christopher (my partner-in-crime)

For what we sometimes were, we are no more;
Fortune hath changed our shape, and destiny
Defaced the very form we had before.

— Sir Walter Raleigh, *Petition to the Queen*

MIRANDA

I am a Blackwood, and in this town, on this tiny island, that means taking whatever escapes are offered. I cock my head back and pretend to be in two places at once. Here, in the wings of this outdoor theater, half-listening for my favorite part of *The Lost Colony*, and there, as far away as the stars, light-years above it all. The night sky is as familiar as the constellation of calluses that dot my palms. As familiar and set as everything in my life.

I used to think I could get away for real. I was younger then . . . stupider or more innocent, depending on your point of view. The first time I checked the back of my closet for a portal to another world I was eleven. The year Mom died. After the closet, I tried other places. I wandered small patches of woods, seeking doors hidden in the twisted trees, and peered into mirrors searching for reflections that weren't mine. No wonder the kids at school decided I was a freak. No, that's not fair. They would've decided that anyway. The Blackwoods are cursed, after all — the unluckiest family on the island.

Escape is a romantic notion. I'm too practical to believe in it now. I no longer hope to step over a secret threshold and leave Roanoke Island behind forever.

And yet here I am, staring at the stars.

It's almost funny that I'm unable to escape a place that's famous *for* people vanishing. Roanoke Island, the site of the first English colony in the Americas, where 114 men, women, and children went missing without any explanation, save for a single cryptic carving left behind on a tree. Disappearing completely is some trick to pull off, even hundreds of years ago when the country was still almost entirely wild places.

"They've survived!"

The bullish voice of the actor who plays Governor John White snaps my attention back to the stage. The line signals his return to the colony after his trip to England. The set's faux oak tree, hollow boulders, and packed dirt floor pass for an abandoned settlement, except for the shining spotlights.

Surrounded by sailors, White gasps — hamming it up — as he points to the oak on the far side of the stage. The simple cloak around his shoulders flies out with the gesture. I can't see the word from here, but of course it's the famous *CROATOAN* carved into the bark in desperate, crooked letters.

White, overacting like crazy, shouts: "My granddaughter, I will see her beautiful face!"

I exchange a look with Polly, my boss and the stage manager, the one who lets me stand here in exchange for my intern scut work. She's the closest thing I have to a friend — well, besides my dog, Sidekick.

Polly shakes her head, her prematurely gray ponytail swishing. We both know Director Jack, aka His Royal Majesty, will give John White a scathing note on his over-the-top performance later.

For now, the governor, along with the sailors in the background, freezes. The lights dim. The final reveal is cued up.

It's sticky humid out here, but a small shiver runs through me. The same one I always feel when I think about the colonists. Every time I watch the show, I wonder how or where they ended up. The standard theories involve bad endings and tragedy. But the reality is, the truth died when they did. We'll never *ever* know what happened to them.

A single low spotlight draws my attention back to the stage. The beam fixes on a solemn young blond girl as she wanders, ghost-slow, through the frozen men. Her face is chalk pale.

His Royal Majesty's biggest change to this year's show was making Virginia Dare — the first English child born in America — the show's deadpan narrator. The actress, Caroline, is a local kid, seven, and a holy terror mean-girl-in-training. But the casting works.

I lean forward to see how the scene's going over for the crowd. We aren't sold out tonight, but the curving rows of the amphitheater are still nearly full. Twelve hundred people sit, riveted and silent, as Caroline haunts the stage.

And then I spot something off . . . a shadow at the back of the audience. One moment everything's normal, the next this giant shadow is there, hovering in the air.

It's definitely not part of the show.

The floating darkness grows and grows and then resolves into a recognizable shape — an immense, old-fashioned black ship. The kind of ship that was used by colonists or pirates. Odd gray symbols bloom on each of three billowing black sails, the shapes a mix of straight lines and arcs, a half-moon curving above a circle at the top. The sailcloth ripples in a wind I don't feel on my skin.

I blink. And again.

The ship is still there.

I raise my hand, and my hand is *in front of* an immense black ship with tall black sails. The ship glides forward, swallowing the audience row after curving row.

In a few seconds, half the audience has disappeared beneath it. No one reacts.

My breath catches in my throat as the ship moves steadily closer.

I turn to Polly, and she smiles with the normal relief of reaching the end of the night. A smile with no hint of concern.

The ship is heading straight for the stage now. Those odd symbols shift on the sails in curving and slashing lines. The black monster gathers speed, faster and faster.

When little Caroline hits her mark at center stage, there are only a dozen feet separating her from the ship. She gives no sign of seeing it either. She might be a brat, but she's also only seven years old.

"Look out!" I finally point and stagger forward onto the stage. Caroline opens her mouth to speak, and I throw myself at her, shielding her small body with my arms.

There are a few shocked cries. I close my eyes and wait for the impact.

It never comes.

Murmurs and questions from the crowd reach my ears, but nothing else.

Caroline squirms in my arms. I open my eyes, and the massive curving prow looms above us, unmoving, throwing a heavy shadow over Caroline and me. Then — between one blink and the next — it vanishes.

The spotlight is suddenly blinding in my face, and I squint, not used to the bright heat. I glance over my shoulder as I hold wriggling Caroline tight.

Governor White glares murder at me, but none of the men break character. They're supposed to remain frozen until the lights go down, and they are.

Caroline says, "Let me go, *Blackwood.*"

I don't understand her meaning right away, don't understand what's happening. Until Caroline grabs a handful of my hair and yanks hard.

"*Ow.*"

And that's when I realize — the show isn't over.

I interrupted the performance because a giant ship appeared. A giant ship no one else seems to have noticed.

From the side of the stage, Polly gives a low command. "Miranda! Get. Over. Here."

That's what gets through to me. I've disappointed Polly. Let her down.

I release my hold on Caroline and hurry from the stage.

Polly takes my arm. "What *was* that?"

On stage, Caroline looks like an angry ghost, her face pink instead of pale. Polly brushes at the sleeve of my T-shirt where the girl's stage makeup rubbed off onto it.

"I'm so sorry," I tell her. But finding the right words proves difficult. "I don't know . . . I thought I saw . . ."

"What?" Polly asks.

A phantom ship, coming right at us, I think. But I can't say *that.* I don't believe in phantom ships. I'm the practical one, the steady one, the one who takes care of things in the Blackwood household. Someone has to. "Nothing. It was nothing."

Polly frowns but stays beside me while rosy-cheeked Caroline manages her last lines:

"The one hundred and fourteen men, women, and children of the Roanoke colony remain lost, their fate unknown. A mystery trapped in time."

At last, the spotlight dies.

*

Backstage, His Royal Highness — also known as our director, Jack — stalks back and forth in front of the cast and crew. He's backed by a life-sized model ship that can't help but remind me of the one I — and I alone, apparently — saw. Normally Jack doesn't bother me. He's short with a square jaw and golden-brown hair. If you passed him on the street you'd forget about him as soon as he was out of sight. *Unless* he trained his outsized dictatorial personality your way. Tonight I barely hear the sloshing waters of the Roanoke Sound behind Waterside Theater as I wait, my heart pounding in my ears, for the director to start talking. This hastily called meeting is mainly for my benefit, and every member of the cast and crew knows it too.

"I had to ask someone your name, you know," the director finally says, stopping in front of my section of the crowd. "Who, I asked, is the girl who decided to become the first person *ever on my stage* to disrupt a show in progress? The answer? Miranda Blackwood."

Leah from costumes sits on the ground in front of where I'm standing. I'm looking down and so I see her flinch at my name. Polly's roommates, Gretchen and Kirsten, are beside Leah, and they exchange a whisper that only ends when Jack looks at *them.* Behind me, Polly puts a reassuring hand on my back to shore me up.

Jack continues. "I was told that I should have expected no less from an infamous Blackwood, even a lowly intern."

I cringe but only inwardly. Outside, I remain calm, collected. I've heard it before — not at the theater, not often. That's only because Jack and Polly, like most of the actors and a significant number of the crew, aren't from the island. The few locals here know all about the infamous curse. We're the unlucky Blackwoods of Roanoke Island, supposedly going all the way back to the time of the lost colonists — there's no record of a Blackwood among the settlers, but why let details get in the way of a good rumor?

Jack makes a flamboyantly dismissive gesture. "Never trust a Blackwood; they're bad luck. That's what they told me. It sounds like superstitious hogwash, but the theater loves superstitious hogwash. I'll be consulting with the stage manager about your future employment —"

"Miranda is an excellent employee, Jack," Polly interrupts. "She's been with us for three years. She's willing to sand wood, help with construction, pitch in with costumes. I'm sure she had a good reason for what happened. I'll speak with her."

Her sticking up for me makes my eyes sting. Polly knows I won't be back next year. Senior year starts soon, and after graduation I'll have to find a year-round job that will pay more bills. No more doing whatever needs doing to make the show's version of history — complete with musical numbers — come alive for the tourists.

"I'll take that into consideration when we talk. Tomorrow." He broadens his attention to encompass everyone else. "The rest of you get an A plus for not breaking character. The fact we finished despite the interruption means no ticket exchanges or refunds. Which is the only reason, Miss Blackwood, that you're not already fired. You can thank everyone in the final scene for that. And you should."

His eyes gravitate back to me. He waits.

"Thanks, everyone," I manage.

"Dismissed," Director Jack says.

The rest of the group is instantly chattering, but no one says anything about a big black ship with billowing sails. But I *did* see it. Didn't I?

"See you later," I mumble to Polly, heading for the path through the trees to the parking lot. I need to get out of here.

"I hate for you to go straight home after that," Polly says, following me. Kirsten and Gretchen nod at her on their way past but don't offer to wait. I assume they're headed home. The out-of-towners all live at Morrison Grove, just up the coastline. "Come out to the Grove, and I'll sneak you a margarita. We can talk, okay?"

I bite my lip. I have to ask, to make sure. "You didn't notice anything . . ."

"Anything?" Polly prompts.

"I don't know . . . odd?"

Polly frowns. I've never seen her frown so much. "You mean besides what you did?" she asks.

Yes. "Was there anything else?"

Polly's response is careful. "No. I didn't notice anything else odd. Did you?"

So I really *am* the only person who saw the ship. "Probably not. I better go on home."

"Sure?" Polly waits, giving me a chance to say more. When I don't take it, she shrugs. "Okay. Be careful. We'll figure this out." She gives me a hug, then splits off with a wave, in a rush to catch up with Kirsten and Gretchen.

I watch them go. So much for the theater being my great escape. The people who work summer stock have always treated me like they treat each other. Normal.

That's over.

It was going to end anyway, but that doesn't mean I was ready to have all my good memories of this place cast into the shadow of a dark cloud. I wasn't ready to not fit in here.

The sensation of losing normal status — of no longer being treated the same as everyone else — is all too familiar. The other kids at school didn't truly decide to turn on me until I was thirteen. My mom was dead, which was bad enough, but then the new police chief's kid, Grant Rawling — radiating cool like all new kids do — humiliated me in front of everyone. I don't even think he did it on purpose. It doesn't matter. What mattered was he gave the others the confirmation they needed that I will never be like them.

The instant I hit the pavement of the mostly deserted parking lot, a pickup truck roars alongside me. A dozen Tarheels stickers cover the bumper and back window, and I know instantly who it belongs to — Bone, my sad-sack nemesis and the only other intern at the theater this summer. Basketball is the closest thing North Carolina has to a state religion, and Bone — so called because he's basically skin and bones — is a devoted member of the faithful.

My night just keeps getting better.

Bone rolls down the window.

"What?" I snap, waiting for some insult.

Unlike me, Bone doesn't work at the theater by choice. His rich kook of a dad — a conspiracy theorist who's obsessed with the lost colony — forces him to. This doesn't usually get to me. Life isn't fair. I know that. The fact that I hallucinated

9

a phantom ship and Bone's doubtless about to remind me yet again of my family's reputation, well, *that* gets to me.

Bone's elbow juts out the window. "Like father like daughter, I guess. Screwing up just runs in your family. Sorry about your Blackwood luck."

"Sorry you're a jerk."

"I'm going to hang out with some friends. Where are you going? To pick up your dad?"

He means from whatever bar Dad's installed himself at tonight. I raise my hand and make a shooing motion. "Leave, begone, scram."

He hesitates, stumped for a comeback. Finally, he says, "I will," and roars away.

I reach my beloved car, Pineapple, and climb into the driver's seat. I turn the key, and Pineapple starts up. I pat the dashboard gratefully. "Thank you for not roaring."

I bought Pineapple with my first few hundred bucks of paychecks. The original make is impossible to determine, and I've never had to figure it out. I never signed on the dotted lines of any insurance or registration papers. Dad claims that forms and laws are for other people. Respectable people. I just assume the town police must feel too sorry for me to bust me.

I drive out of Fort Raleigh, the plastic hula girl stuck to Pineapple's dash wobbling seductively with each turn. Downtown Manteo, the island's main drag, is packed with tourists on this warm summer Wednesday. The town center resembles a perfect model of itself, preserved Victorian houses and Colonial-style storefronts with the sound's peaceful waters as scenic backdrop. Gelato shops and fancy restaurants are tucked next to pricey B&Bs that offer tickets for fishing expeditions and dolphin spotting.

My street is off a more remote stretch of highway, a small pocket of cheap, mostly rental houses shoved where the tourists will never see. A different kind of lost colony.

I pull into my usual spot at the curb and get out. Walking quickly, I cross the patchwork yard to the house. I grip my keys as I go so their teeth stick out through my fist. Dad showed a rare flash of concern when I started at the theater, and made me promise this little action whenever I'm outside at night alone. I'm not worried, but I do it because he asked me to.

The porch light is off, making it hard to see the white paint on the house, which has been flaking for years. I test the front door.

Locked.

Just then the best golden retriever in the world lopes across the yard to join me. I reach down to scruff the fur under his neck. "Hey, Sidekick. Hey, pretty boy."

Sidekick showed up a couple of years ago out of nowhere. He got his name because sidekicks are usually the characters I like most. Streaming TV binge-a-thons are my main escape besides the theater.

I release my death grip on the keys and fumble at the lock. As I struggle with the door, I manage to drop both my bag and the keys. *Clunk.* With a sigh, I bend to pick them up. Dad must not be home, or surely he'd have heard me out here by now.

Grrrr . . .

Sidekick's low, angry growl makes me jump. His yellow head whips toward the street. His body stretches tight from nose to tail as he lets out a warning bark.

I freeze. He rarely barks. And never like this.

Then the others start.

Every dog in earshot bays and howls in a riotous symphony devoid of any melody. Sidekick's neck cranes to the sky, more wolf than happy golden retriever.

I refuse to look up, afraid of what they're barking at, afraid of what I'll see. I jam the key into the door's lock and twist hard. The knob spins, and the door gives. I kick my bag inside. I hesitate, halfway in, holding the door open.

"Come on, boy, come on."

Sidekick arches his head at me and whines. His eyes glint in the dark.

"Sidekick." I fight to keep panic out of my voice. *"Now!"*

Sidekick comes, galumphing through the door. His growling quiets once he hits the threshold. The howling outside continues without pause, without song.

I slam the door and slide the deadbolt into place. I tug aside the faded blue curtain and check outside.

Nothing. Certainly no ship. Nothing but a cloud floating across the pale moon. The dogs' racket ends, just like that.

I settle down on the too-soft cushions of our ancient beige couch. *What a night.* Being surrounded by home is some small comfort. The easy chair covered by the red slipcover I made from an old blanket, the ancient floor-model TV with a grainy picture quality, and, above that, the grinning photo of Mom playing tourist beside the mast of the *Elizabeth II* at Festival Park. Sidekick pants with his usual mellow-dog grin.

"Honey?" a voice calls from up the hall. "Is that you?"

So Dad's home after all. He stumbles up the hall with the clumsy but somehow sure-footed steps of a professional alcoholic and weaves into the room. Sidekick leaps up next to me, collapsing against my side.

"It's me," I say when Dad pauses and squints.

His face is stained a red that means nothing anymore. His skin stays that way. The distinctive snake-shaped birthmark that crawls up his cheek toward his temple is nearly hidden by the permanent flush. He's spent too many years drinking for his angry pores to ever calm down.

"Of course it is, kiddo. I'm headed out . . ." His voice trails off.

I could trace a thought bubble in the air and fill it with the dot-dot-dots as his mind goes blank. It breaks my heart a little, every time it happens.

"Do you need me to give you a ride somewhere?" I don't want to go back out, but I have to offer.

"Nah," he says. "Fine . . . evening for a walk."

I drop my head back against the sofa, closing my eyes only to get a flash of that black ship. I bolt upright to find Dad watching me. He'll be safe out there, won't he? Safe as he ever is?

"Have a nice time," I say. "But call if you need me."

Usually that's Dad's cue to stumble the rest of the way to our small kitchen for his keys, then out the door and to whichever bar in Manteo he's welcome at this week. Tonight he hesitates, wavering on his feet, focusing on me with an expression I don't know.

"You're a good daughter," he says. "You deserved better. I wanted to be stronger for you. I didn't know how."

I ruffle Sidekick's fur, not sure what to say.

Wavering, wavering, wavering, Dad says, "I want you to know that." Then he completes the circuit to the kitchen and the front door, where he fights the deadbolt and wins. He closes the door behind him well enough that I'm able to stay put on the couch. I listen, half waiting for the dogs outside to go crazy again. There is only quiet.

There's nothing for me to do but think about the supreme weirdness of the night.

I have a firm policy of never being the silly girl — the kind who goes to check out what the noise is or who sees things no one else does. The kind who worries that her dad was slightly sadder than usual tonight and whether it means anything. The kind who would call up Polly right now and confess why she ruined the show. The kind who talks to people and trusts them, period.

There's no one for me to talk to, no matter how much I wish for it. I'm best off sticking with the "never be the silly girl" policy.

I plump the waiting pillow and ease onto my side. My eyes drift closed with Sidekick's head on my hip. Dad will wake me when he stumbles back in later.

But this way, sleeping out here, at least I'll know he makes it home okay.

GRANT

I scoot along a wide stone ledge halfway up the outer wall of the four-story building that houses the library and classrooms. Good thing I'm not afraid of heights — though obviously if I was, I wouldn't be doing this. I hum the Bond theme under my breath and press my fingertips into the spaces between the fat red bricks above me. My muscles protest, but flex as I lift myself, leaving the safety of the ledge. No humming during this part.

I fit the rubber tips of my Chucks into the wall, then repeat the whole process again — finger hold, then foot hold — making steady progress toward the window of the library bathroom on the second floor. The one I left open for this very purpose.

I'm cutting it close. They watch the grounds between the dorms and this building like the proverbial hawks after dinner here, so, even if it's on the reckless side, disappearing from the library and scaling the wall both ways made the most sense. The back of the building faces the woods, which makes being spotted unlikely. Most of my classmates will already be checked out for the night, heading to the dorms. I just have to get in — and then out — before Ms. Walter, the librarian, closes up.

I'm not actually worried. I never get caught. Not since I came to Jackson Institute, anyway.

I insert my head through the window to ensure a clear coast and see no one. Jumping through the frame, I land on the tile floor with a satisfying thump.

I grin, imagining the principal's face when he gets out of the academic meet and goes to drive his car home. No way he'll miss the present I left, though it would be even better if he doesn't see it until the morning.

The supplies for making the bumper sticker took me a few months to collect. Adhesive, the right sort of paper, the letters to make the message, all ordered online and sent to the nearby house of a teacher who happens to be on sabbatical for a year. Given the power of delivery confirmation, grabbing them from the mailbox wasn't hard. And after the principal instituted a uniforms-even-on-the-weekend policy six months before, followed with a ban on "personal decorations" — aka posters — in the dorms, the message practically decided itself: *I Heart Fascism.* All I had to do was wait for a night he was here late and sneak off to smooth the sticker onto his SUV.

It took a little longer than planned, though, so I'll have to charm the librarian into helping me with the extra credit assignment I'm supposed to be here doing.

I ease back into the library, and when I hit the checkout desk, Ms. Walter is deep into a thick hardcover book. She holds up a finger as I approach. I wait until she inserts a bookmark and sets down the book. I lean over to read the cover — *The Shining.*

"Don't judge," she says. "It has ghosts, and it's a classic."

"I would never," I say, which is true. People who judge other people's reading are, generally speaking, the worst. But I still won't be checking out that book anytime soon. The last thing I need are *made-up* stories about lingering dead people.

"You're lucky I was reading, Grant," says Ms. Walter. "I planned to close ten minutes ago."

"I lost track of time reading too." *Liar.* "You have any special topics left?"

"A few." She holds up a top hat, the black satin faded from years of use.

I reach in and withdraw a folded slip of paper with a research topic for my life sciences class. I don't need the points, but getting straight *As* and praise from my teachers helps convince my parents they made the right decision by sending me off to boarding school in Kentucky while they're still back on Roanoke Island.

"Seahorses." I look over at the row of communal laptops. The school deems it too risky for budding delinquents like yours truly to have online access in our rooms, so it's those or nothing. "If you're planning to close I guess I don't have time to hit Wikipedia." I give Ms. Walter my most pitiful look. "Any chance you'll let me borrow a textbook? I'll bring it back first thing."

Ms. Walter hesitates. I keep my puppy-dog plea fixed on her.

"Well, if you promise not to tell anyone . . ." Ms. Walter smiles, adding, "I know you'd never really try to cite Wikipedia."

Is she being sarcastic? But, no, this is what being a model student means, the trust of teachers and school officials. I will never get used to being treated like one of the good kids, like someone who causes no trouble for anyone. It wasn't that way back home, that's for sure.

"I'll just get out of your way," I tell her.

I slip back to the science section, grab the right volume, and wave it at Ms. Walter on my way out. I leave her to her ghosts.

*

I toss the borrowed book on the desk in my small, regulation dorm room. No posters or art tacked up — thanks, Principal Fascist — just basic light fixtures bolted to the ceiling and the wall. Again, semi-delinquents can't be trusted with nice things.

Like the computers, the TV room is communal, which means I read even more here than I did back home. Instead of digging into homework, I pick up my novel-in-progress — *The Man in the High Castle*, a rec from Ms. Walter.

I drop onto the bed, settling back, and run my finger along the spine. The book falls open a couple dozen pages from the end, exactly where I left off. The invisible bookmark is a gift I have, way more useful than my other one.

The phone in my pocket vibrates. We *are* allowed to use personal phones, a small freedom, but only at night. And without data plans. My mom is the only person who ever calls me, though, and sure enough, the screen flashes the word *HOME*. I barely feel that way about Roanoke Island — I lasted for all of a year and a half there.

Pretending to miss calls in the mountains is easy because the signals *are* spotty, but I'd better answer. Besides, I already know how the book ends. I always read that first. I don't see the point in risking surprises that can be avoided. Not anymore.

"What if I was asleep?" I say by way of greeting.

"I couldn't make you go to sleep before midnight even when you were three," Mom says.

"Did you have a reason to call or is this just to relive my early years?"

"Just checking in," she says. "Feeling like a bad mother for abandoning my son halfway across the country tonight."

"It's a long day's drive, not halfway across the country," I say, "and you know I'm better off here."

Mom is silent for a moment. "Better off — but are you happy?"

She's never asked that before. The truth is, I'm too isolated to be happy. There's no one here I'll ever be able to tell about being the ultimate freak, no one who'd understand. But I don't like Mom feeling guilty when *I'm* the defective one.

"I'm seventeen — how happy can I be? It wouldn't be natural." She laughs, and I'm relieved. "Is everything okay there?"

"I just miss your face," Mom says. Then she adds an affectionate: "Brat."

"You're still coming up here for Thanksgiving, right?" I ask.

"Of course. But that's months away. And I feel like a bad mother that I can't cook you Thanksgiving dinner at home."

"You're a good mother for coming here instead."

She doesn't respond right away. Finally, after a few long moments, she does. "Okay, you reassured me. I'll let you go back to avoiding whatever homework you're supposed to be doing. I just wanted you to know I was thinking about you. I miss you."

My mom isn't psychic, except in the way all moms are. She has a sixth sense for when I'm feeling a little down, despite being here where at least it's quiet.

"Miss you too. But I'm good here. Better here," I say. "Good night."

"Night."

I hang up, but I don't go back to the book. I'll finish it another time. I wish to be the kind of person who could go home for the holidays, the kind of person who doesn't have to be *here* in the first place. But I'll never be that person. My main "gift" — the reason I left — comes from dad's side of the family, which traces its heritage to the early days of English settlers. Gram always claimed we're descended from little Virginia Dare, who of course disappeared along with the rest of the colonists, so that can't be true.

We never got to talk about it, but I think Gram could sense spirits too. I was thirteen when I first encountered them, the day she died. I don't believe in coincidences that coincidental.

I was outside in our backyard when I heard unfamiliar voices.

She's gone —

But he's here —

Where is my girl?

That's wrong, wrong time.

They chattered away, seemingly coming from gray shadows that glided around me in a chaotic mass — like I saw them through a veil. Around me, the regular grass and trees and sky with these . . . speaking shadows crossing through it.

My mom came outside and put a hand on my shoulder and said, "Dad just called. Your gram passed away a little while ago."

I almost said, *I know.* But I didn't. I didn't know what was happening.

It was like I saw this world, and also shadows moving through some world just beyond ours.

I had no interest in exploring it further. But the spirits didn't take no for an answer. Once I decided I wasn't going crazy — yet — it wasn't that hard to figure out who the speaking shadows were.

The dead.

And they went everywhere on Roanoke Island that I did.

Pressing the voices and the visions away so I could continue to *exist* took constant effort. They were *always* there. A hum, a buzz, a glimpse of movement here, a menacing motion there, and, sometimes, a riot, with me in the middle.

During the worst moments, I developed a theory. Every person who has ever lived and died on the island — and it has been occupied for a very long time — is still there. And I, the only one cursed enough to see them, was left to this pack of spirit bullies, capable of bringing chaos to my mind that I can't even begin to control. I never managed to get Gram, if she was among them, to talk to me, to tell me what to do.

When I confessed to Mom, finally — it got that bad — she made an appointment with a neurologist in Norfolk. As we drove off the island, the shadows and their words faded. Not gone but fainter. A miracle.

That's when I knew I had no choice. I made enough trouble that my parents had to send me away. Dad is the police chief. His reputation couldn't take the hits. I gave the year-round boarding school pamphlet to Mom myself, and she agreed to go along. Leaving was my last hope.

The further from the island we got, the more normal I felt. The shadows quieted, then disappeared altogether.

I've been at Jackson Institute for three and a half years. Roanoke Island is still home, I guess, because that's where my parents are, but me staying here is better for us all.

And so I do crack the science book and learn about seahorses. I can't afford to have Mom worrying about me being here.

I can't risk having to go home.

MIRANDA

I stretch and hit Sidekick with my feet. He's curled up on the other end of the squishy couch. Bright morning light stabs around the sides of the blue curtain, a harsh wake-up call. Dad must not have made it home last night. Or . . .

I get up and open the door to see if he's snoring on the concrete porch. He's not there. Sidekick slips past me into the patchy yard. I leave the door open so he can come back inside when he's ready.

I shuffle down the hall and peek into Dad's room, just in case. Other than a rumpled bed and piles of clothes, the room is empty. I visit the bathroom next. He isn't passed out at the foot of his porcelain master, either, so I brush my teeth and get cleaned up.

I'm not *that* worried. Dad almost always makes it home, but the times he doesn't are because some rookie hauled him to the drunk tank instead of bringing him here like Chief Rawling usually does.

But still, a small measure of worry gnaws at me.

In my room, I dress quickly. I pair a faded red T-shirt with a pair of jeans I patched up using the ancient sewing machine I inherited from Mom. I pause for a longing look at my iPad, a hand-me-down from Polly when she managed to pry out of me that I was upset our cheap DVD player died. She even gave me her Netflix password, like a real friend. Still, I keep my small collection of DVD box sets, grabbed on deep sale, on the shelf in my room, for the inevitable day when the password stops working.

Holing up for a few hours to visit a faraway galaxy, or cheer on hot boys fighting gross creatures and super villains, or even just watch bad Syfy channel movies, would be an ideal way to spend the morning. I've been pretending not to think about last night, but that ship — and my embarrassing outburst — isn't far from my thoughts. My ears burn at thoughts of Jack shaming me in front of everybody. I want to forget about my humiliating drama at the theater, and a marathon streaming session would help.

Instead I'll be making a jail run to find Dad.

This is your life, Miranda Blackwood.

"Outside or in?" I ask Sidekick, still lingering on the front porch by the door. His tail is wagging so hard that it hits the doorframe as he walks through, and I fill his bowl of kibble and lock up behind me.

As I head toward Pineapple, I discover the morning is full of unwanted developments.

Along the driver's side of Pineapple, thick black letters shout the word *FREAK*.

I close my eyes, and colors bloom inside the lids. I wish for something to kick. Like Bone and his friends. Something clever, like maybe *Croatoan*, would've been too much to ask of them. I open my eyes and walk over and test the words with a finger.

Shoe polish instead of spray paint. A small favor.

I consider cleaning it off before retrieving Dad, but I don't want to leave him sweating in a cell any longer than necessary. I'll have to park so he doesn't see it. Otherwise he'll ramble and rage.

My first hint that something is wrong — something bigger than Dad being MIA and Bone being a jerk — comes when I turn onto the main highway toward town. The traffic level screams hurricane evacuation. The flow is way too heavy for this early in the day, even for peak tourist season. Big evacs don't happen without a day or two's warning, and there aren't enough rental cars in the mix. Tourists take off whenever weather threatens, but plenty of locals, including Dad and me, choose to ride out hurricanes the old-fashioned way, with sandbags, boarded-up windows, and peanut butter sandwiches.

By the time I reach the edge of town and Manteo's box of a police station — bizarrely painted bright blue — I'm convinced something is really, *really* wrong. The jail's parking lot is across the street and way bigger than it needs to be, but for the first time I can remember, the lot is *full*.

At least a couple dozen people are milling around outside the jail. Slowing, I watch the woman who owns the town movie theater hug a bearded older man. They're both crying. A local TV van has parked half on the curb, and a cameraman is capturing the pair's worried embrace.

I manage to find a parking spot a street over and hurry back toward the jail. The people spilled onto the sidewalks around the station give off waves of fear and worry as strong as a force field.

I'm about to make my way inside the jail when Chief Rawling emerges from the glass doors of the station.

A sleek-haired blond reporter launches out of the van toward him, snapping her fingers for the cameraman to follow. Her giant blue eyes are like an anime deer's. I've seen her in person before, when she came to the theater to announce the winners of some random, not-so-fabulous prizes. But I can't remember her name. Blondie will do for a mental nickname.

Wait. Scratch that. Blondie and Pat Benatar were tied as Mom's favorite musicians. I won't insult them like that.

I settle on Blue Doe. That's better.

As Blue Doe approaches Chief Rawling, she leans into her left hand to cradle her earpiece and signals for the chief to stop walking using the microphone in her right. The chief looks like he's having a very bad day. He is put together as usual. His black hair is clipped short, face clean-shaven, navy uniform pressed, but deep lines of concern cut into his forehead and around his mouth.

Chief Rawling is always nice to me, one of the few people in town who doesn't treat our family like outcasts. He has a problem child of his own — or at least Grant *was* a problem, before his parents shipped him off to juvenile delinquent school.

I flush just thinking of Grant. My memory of him that day at school stays sharp as a film I can replay at any time. So does the memory of how he looked at me later, like he understood how I felt. It wasn't fair that he could look at me like that after what he'd done.

Someone behind me chokes down a sob, and I put away thoughts of the chief's trouble-making son and shift a few steps closer so I can hear better. The crowd quiets when Blue Doe holds up a finger, signaling that the interview is about to begin.

"Live in three, two . . ." Blue Doe says. As the countdown ends, she puts on an important voice. "Chief Rawling, what can you tell us about the events of this morning? Is this a mass kidnapping? Is it a terrorist action? A hoax?"

I look around, confused. What in the world is Blue Doe talking about?

Chief Rawling rubs his forehead, then lowers his hand, visibly remembering he's on camera. "We're not sure at this point, beyond reports of a large number of missing people."

A large number of missing people.

"How many citizens of Roanoke Island are believed missing at this point?"

"We've had about a hundred missing persons call-ins this morning, but that number is extremely preliminary. Most of those people will probably turn up," Chief Rawling says.

Most of those people will probably turn up.

"Should people leave the island?" Blue Doe presses.

"It's too early to recommend that people leave. What we need now is for people to let us know if a loved one is missing, and to report any unusual activity. I'm sorry, but I also need to ask everyone to please wait at the courthouse. I'll be moving briefings there. We need to keep this building free for police work. I'll give further updates as I have them. Thank you."

The crowd erupts into conversation as Chief Rawling goes back into the building. I can't move. Is Dad *missing*?

My concern must read on my face, because suddenly there's a microphone being thrust into it. "You," the reporter says, "are you looking for someone? Is someone you love among the lost? What can you tell us?"

Her tone holds a hefty dose of false sympathy. I'm reeling, and I make a mistake. I speak. "Leave me the frak alone."

There's a gasp as I stalk off. I need to get inside the station, see if Dad is safe in a cell. I hear unsurprised murmurs from the crowd, and phrases linger in the air: *Behaving like a Blackwood . . . like father, like daughter . . .*

I don't need to hear their whole commentary to fill in the details.

Inside the station, there's a flurry of activity. More than I've ever seen before. Phones are ringing, and everyone is on duty. I go to the desk and find a younger officer manning it. I remember him being on the football team a few years back.

"Hi," I say, and he looks up at me. "Is my dad here? Hank Blackwood."

"Are you here to file a missing persons report?" he asks.

He must be new. "No, I . . . I thought you might have him in lock-up. Drunk tank?"

The officer shakes his head. "No one back there today. Let me take your information. We'll let you know if there are any leads on the disappearances."

"Or if Dad turns up?" I ask.

"Uh, yes, if your dad turns up."

The way he says it makes it sounds unlikely, and it begins to sink in. *Dad might be missing.*

*

At a loss for what else to do besides freak out, I drive Pineapple past Fort Raleigh and the theater to Morrison Grove to check in on the cast and crew. With all these people missing, I might be forgiven for the night before now, no questions asked.

Mostly, I just need to see familiar faces.

This tree-hidden village of multiplex apartments houses the hundred and twenty or so out-of-town cast and crew every summer. It always bustles with action. People who are drawn to the theater live life loudly, and for many players at *The Lost Colony*, this summer of noisy glamour makes up for an off-season of quieter cast calls and failed auditions in New York and Los Angeles.

But when I arrive, uneasiness flutters. The parking lot has only a smattering of cars in it. I park and take the too-quiet forest path, then walk among the Grove's cozy chocolate-brown houses. The entire place is sunk in the deep silence of abandonment, appearing as deserted as it will be come winter. The gentle roar of the sound in the background is the only thing close to normal.

I find Polly's apartment and pull open the scratchy screen door. It squeals under the pressure of my hand. I rap on the door. No one answers.

I turn the knob, and it twists easily. The door releases with a click. Unlocked.

Feeling like a silly girl — both for going inside *and* for being nervous about doing so — I step into the common room. There are kitschy knitting projects and trashy magazines scattered around like normal. A tiny drink umbrella lies discarded on the floor.

"Polly?" I call. No one answers.

I walk around the living room and stop at the dry-erase board on the wall where the girls leave each other snarky messages or notes about errands. But there is nothing there to explain the desertion.

The screen door squeals behind me, and I whirl. Leah from costumes stands just inside it, her face blotchy and eyes shiny. She isn't one of Polly's roommates, but she hangs out with them.

"Where is everyone?" I ask. "Where's Polly?"

Leah comes the rest of the way inside, stopping to pick up the drink umbrella. Her curly black hair is wet, like she just stepped out of the shower. "I . . . I can't find her. She was here. Last night. We were all here. I slept on the couch. Now they're . . . they're missing."

"Polly's missing?"

"Not just her — Kirsten and Gretchen too. Jack just took half my housemates to stay with relatives in Shenandoah for a couple of days until this is sorted out. I was going to stay, but . . . I'm going too. I can't take the quiet."

I don't understand. What she's saying doesn't compute. "How will they get back for the show?"

"The wife of the theater's CEO is missing. He's canceled the show until further notice," Leah says. "The first time ever Jack said, and even he seemed worried. You sure you're okay? Do you want to leave with me?"

I could swear Leah's teeth are chattering. Of course, the idea of the director being worried about anything besides his precious reputation *is* almost as disconcerting as the rest of the morning's events.

"No," I say. I can't leave, but she doesn't know that. "No. I'm going to stay in town. Everyone will be back. It's probably all just some weird coincidence."

But what if it isn't?

Leah starts to giggle, though it doesn't sound like a laugh. "I hope so," she says. She flings her arms around me in a hug before I can dodge. She squeezes me tight. "Hope you're here when I get back."

Leah leaves, but I stay behind in Polly's apartment for a few minutes. I want to look up and see Polly walk through the door.

We'll laugh about all this. How it's all some trick. Dad will be safe at home when I get there.

I've seen *The Lost Colony* performed hundreds of times but never before understood the magnitude of such a loss. I feel trapped in the final moments, when young Virginia Dare tells the audience that the settlers were never heard from again.

How do more than a hundred people disappear without a trace? For it to happen hundreds of years ago is almost unbelievable, but to happen *now*? And for my dad to be one of them?

With a last look, I turn and leave the apartment. It turns out I can't take the quiet either.

GRANT

I pull my favorite vintage-style Clash T-shirt over my head so I can at least have a piece of me hidden beneath my uniform — only to be interrupted by a knock on the door. A man's voice calls, "Grant Rawling?"

That is not the voice of one of my charming Neanderthal fellow students. Too old, and I have a sinking feeling that I recognize it.

Principal Fascist. *Crap.*

"One sec," I call back. I should already be dressed, but I overslept. I let the T-shirt fall, and race to get my standard-issue white button-down over it, leaving the shirt unbuttoned and the tie loose around the neck. I yank on the jacket that goes with it and scrub a hand through my hair.

"Mr. Rawling?"

I tug on my Chucks, then open the door.

Yep, it's him. The principal has a half-moon hairline and a thin mustache. He's tried to figure out my story since the day my parents dropped me off at this semi-reform school. I never considered this guy capable of busting me, but if he's here, I have to assume he's found the bumper sticker and somehow traced it back to me.

Panic ices through me. What if my parents try to make me come home? I can't go back to being tormented by shadows and voices. I won't.

Don't admit guilt, I remind myself. *If he can't prove you did it, it doesn't matter.*

"Yes?" I raise my eyebrows, not volunteering anything. I need to see how bad it is.

The principal gives the T-shirt beneath my uniform a disapproving glance but motions me down the bland beige hall. "Your father's on the phone for you," he says.

What?

I guess I'm not busted after all, but this still can't be good. Dad never calls me. We're just not that close. I had to act out because that was something he could see. He'd never listen to me *or* Mom about my unusual abilities, despite the fact that he grew up as the son of the legendary Witch of Roanoke Island. And I just talked to Mom. They both know students here aren't allowed to use their personal phones during the day, which I guess explains the summons.

Why he's calling now is a mystery that makes my pulse pick up tempo.

"Are you ready?" the principal asks.

I nod.

The kids in the hall are openly curious as I shut the door and follow the principal without a word. I don't hang out with anyone here, and as far as they know, I'm one of the good kids. Not someone who warrants a personal escort from the principal.

I keep quiet on the way down the stairs. When we reach the bottom, Principal Fascist says, "Over here." He leads the way into the dorm's front office, a part of the building I rarely see. The big room has a couple of desks and filing cabinets, along with a counter and a short row of chairs in a waiting area.

The principal points to a small table next to a copier. A light flashes on the phone. "Line two," he says.

I pick up the receiver, finger poised over the button. "Can I have some privacy?"

"Of course." He deflates and scuttles across the room.

I click the line and do my best to hide my nerves. "You rang, Father?"

Dad hates being called Father.

"Grant, finally, *thank God*," Dad says. "It's just . . . there's something . . ." He sounds out of breath.

"What's wrong? Is Mom okay?"

A long pause ensues. Dad breathes heavily into the phone, and I feel no urge whatsoever to make a joke about it. Then he says, "Do you know where they are?"

"Who?"

Dad lets out a sigh, maybe of relief. "Listen, son, I think I need you to come home. Something's happened . . . You might be able to . . ."

I can sense him searching for the right words.

"It's not Mom, is it?" I feel frozen by the thought. "Tell me Mom's okay."

"No, no, your mom is fine. But . . . something bad's happening." The line fuzzes with soft static as Dad pauses. "That's understating it. Maybe I . . . I know you don't want to come home. But I think the island needs you here. I need you here."

That's when I know. Dad asking me to come home is a dead giveaway. If he thinks the island needs me, if he's willing to say that *he* does, then whatever is happening is serious.

In that moment, I long for music, so keenly it hurts. I want to put my earbuds in and crank something loud enough to drown out what Dad just said, to drown out the world. I want to pretend this conversation isn't happening.

"I can't go back, Dad. I can't do anything there. Trust me."

I reach out, and press down the line to hang up the phone. But I keep the receiver at my ear while I figure out my next move. I won't go back. I *can't*. It's so quiet here. My sanctuary.

Decision made, I replace the phone and get up. I catch the principal watching me.

He must think he's finally getting his chance to figure out my past. It's ironic that he's so nosy. He seems to wish he could give us all standard-issue personalities when we enroll, make us into bread slices with the crusts cut off.

The principal walks across the room and lays a hand on my arm. "Your father has asked me to put you on a plane home. I'm to stay with you while you pack and escort you to the airport in Lexington. You are not to leave my sight. Those were his instructions."

Inwardly, I scoff. Of course they were. But outwardly, I just shrug, already beginning to work on possible outs. Maybe I can convince an airline staffer to put me on a flight to somewhere else.

"He told you what's happened, I take it?" the principal asks.

I shake my head. But I have to admit, I'm curious, even if doesn't involve Mom.

The principal says, "You should see this." His tone makes it clear he's playing his trump card. He grips a remote and points it toward the TV mounted in the corner of the office. He turns it on and raises the volume.

Some news network, with the standard breaking news crawl, blares to life. Everything seems to qualify as breaking news these days, but this time it's true. The words *Mass Disappearance in Outer Banks: Colonists Lost Again?* roll across the screen.

The network appears to be broadcasting the Norfolk affiliate's coverage from Roanoke Island. My father steps away and off camera. According to the blond woman holding the microphone, they're just finishing an interview with the chief of police, aka my dad. But hers isn't the face I focus on now — it's the girl standing to one side of the reporter. I drift toward the monitor, and every ounce of attention I possess is locked on the screen.

The reporter turns and shoves her microphone at the girl. After a lead-in, she says, "Are you looking for someone? Is someone you love among the lost? What can you tell us?"

In true Miranda Blackwood style, the girl snaps, "Leave me the frak alone," before striding toward the camera and out of frame.

I feel like someone threw cold water in my face. Miranda Blackwood — I haven't seen her in almost four years. Obviously. But she still has the same too-serious eyes, long black hair curling around her pale, pretty features.

Whatever's happening on the island, she's part of it. I know this the way I know my own name when I wake up in the morning.

"I've seen enough," I say. "Let's go."

If Miranda is involved in whatever's happening there, I have no choice. I owe her.

I should have known I couldn't escape. When I shut my eyes, the memory of the spirits around me is as clear as if I'm already back there.

I shouldn't have gotten so comfortable. The island always wins.

*

A few hours later, I flip up the collar of my jacket and lower my head, the better to fake invisibility. I navigate through the Norfolk airport terminal, skimming past people weighed down with overstuffed carry-ons they're too paranoid to check.

The TV screens I pass are all Roanoke Island, all the time. I catch a glimpse of what looks to be the same footage of Dad from earlier, but I don't stop to watch.

I expected the voices to start chattering as soon as my feet hit the ground, just from being so much closer to home. On the island, listening to music was the only thing that helped. When the plane landed, my phone was ready in my pocket, playlist cued up, earbuds dangling around my neck.

But so far . . . nothing. Not even the vaguest of whispers of ghosts tickle the edges of my awareness. My vision is sharp and clear.

Guilt finally forces me to a stop in front of an arrivals board. The situation on the island will have given Dad extra ammunition for special favors. I'm betting he'll have done his best to get Mom clearance to wait at the actual gate, to make sure I don't pull a runner.

I find the flight number I'm looking for and backtrack, staying close to the wall. Not far, just a couple of gates.

There she is. Mom sits in a chair, waiting for me. Her smooth brown hair is cut shorter than the last time I saw her, framing her face. I notice a few new streaks of gray. She has a tablet in her lap but stares ahead at nothing instead. She looks tired.

I walk to the bank of holdover payphones, out of sight of the gate, and dial her number. Remembering that Dad also has access to GPS tracking, I turn *my* phone off.

"Mom?" I say when she answers.

"Yes, sweetheart?"

She isn't too happy when I confess that I lied when I called her before I boarded in Lexington and told her I'd been switched to a slightly later flight on a different airline — the one she sits waiting for now, not the one I was actually on. She's even less happy when I tell her that I'll see her at home later.

"Grant, how will you get there? Do you know what will happen when you're back on the island? It's been almost four years."

She's always worried about me. I wish she didn't have to worry so much. I wish for a lot of things.

"There's something I've got to do. I'm sorry," I say.

I don't mention seeing Miranda on the news. I can still hardly believe that. I know how hard it is to get her to react, to shatter her protective shell. I did my worst, didn't I? And she just stood there, soaking it in.

I've never been able to forget that day, to forget her. The spirits had overwhelmed me. I wasn't strong enough to protect *her* from them either. This time will be different. I need to see Miranda, and there isn't time to make Mom understand why.

But when I hang up the phone, I realize Mom's right. *How am I going to get there?*

I do the obvious thing.

Mom always parks on the third level in the thirteenth row in the parking garage. That way she never forgets where the car is. I find her faithful maroon chariot and locate the spare keys, which she always keeps in a little magnetic box behind the rear right wheel.

Then I steal the family car.

*

I've never been a good driver — judging by the horn blows of skittish drivers on I-64, my skills have not magically improved. I don't even have a license, thanks in part to when I took Dad's car during my reign of bad behavior and got apprehended by one of the island's stalwart officers. Dad sure regretted teaching me about the gas and brake and steering on a country road when I was a kid.

The long bridge that cuts across the Croatan Sound is dead ahead. Instead of going across at Manns Harbor, I decided to take the new bridge, since it bypasses downtown Manteo for the convenience of people headed to other islands. If Mom has already reported that I took the car, Dad and the rest of the police force will be on the lookout.

I hope Mom will understand why I ditched her once I explain — *if* that's even possible. Truth is, Miranda's face — then, now — transformed the flickering uncertainty inside me into a strong, sure flame. I'm certain she's in danger. Which means I have a chance at redeeming myself. A chance to help keep her safe.

If only you had a clue why you're so sure she's not safe.

I only have an inkling, thanks to how the spirits surged and the things they said about her back then. Like she was important, and I had to not only know, but tell her. The problem is, they made it sound like the *bad* kind of important.

I suck in a deep breath, maybe my last peaceful one. Once I cross the bridge, there's no going back. I'll be home. I have no idea what's going to happen.

Three and a half years of quiet. They were nice.

The bridge rises up in front of me, a green sign with white letters telling me exactly where it will take me. No turning back.

I steer toward the bridge and floor the gas. The car surges forward and whips across the asphalt at dangerous speed. The other side of the highway crawls with cars inching forward like slow-moving bugs, but my side is nearly empty. The lanes go on for so long I don't know how I'll stand the suspense. I suffer for five miles of wide road over the choppy blue sound.

The highway finally levels out onto land, tires separated from the earth by pavement alone. The familiar forest, thick treetops like green bubbles, comes into view, lining the highway. An idyllic glimpse of home. A lie.

The backed-up traffic on the other side of the bridge continues onto the island. Honking tourist rentals and retirees' fancy cars mix with a few older vehicles that probably belong to residents, all creeping toward the bridge. The mass disappearance is real — real enough to empty out a good portion of the Outer Banks at the end of tourist season.

I brace for the spirits to sense my presence.

No whispers. No screeching. No shadows.

Other than horns and road noise and the traffic, I don't see or hear anything. *Huh?*

I pull off to the side of the road as soon as I find a wide spot and roll down the window. An insistent breeze sweeps through the car. It ruffles my hair and T-shirt, but it carries nothing else to me.

I wait, just in case the sudden rush of spirits makes me unable to drive.

The breeze tugs at me, but the only sounds it brings are natural ones. Finally, I shift the car back into gear and onto the road. I'm cautious in case the spirits show without warning. There was never any warning.

Welcome to Roanoke Island, says the sign I drive past. No matter that it feels like someplace else. I'm back. Have I changed or has the island?

The question is pushed aside by a more pressing one. If I'm not going to be sidelined by the dead, then I have an itinerary to keep.

Where does Miranda Blackwood live?

MIRANDA

Once I make it home, I sink onto the sofa. My hands form a tight ball in my lap. Sidekick sits on the floor beside me, big brown eyes full of worry, an echo of what I feel inside.

I wouldn't have believed Dad could *leave*, let alone disappear. Everyone else thinks we're cursed with bad luck, but our family legend is more specific — Blackwoods are doomed to Roanoke Island. That knowledge lives deep in my bones. None of us have ever lived anywhere else. I've never even *been* anywhere else. "Blackwoods are bound to walk this patch of Earth." That's what my dad has always said, ever since I was kid, underlining it with spooky stories about what happened to Blackwoods who dared try setting foot off the island.

But if all those other people have disappeared, if my Dad has, who's to say I won't be next? Even if I'm doomed to spend my life in a place that doesn't want me, that doesn't mean I'm ready to vanish. And *where* have the missing people vanished to, exactly? I can't imagine it's anyplace good.

When I was younger I might have hoped differently, but now I know the truth. There are no waiting fantasylands, no sudden entries to worlds where wizards and unicorns frolic under glittering waterfalls and everything magically becomes perfect.

Wherever all those missing people are, I bet they aren't any safer than I am. Which doesn't feel safe at all.

Maybe I can do something about that. I remember the closet in my dad's room, which he stuffed full of boxes the day we moved in. He caught me going through it soon after, and pulled me aside, shaking my twelve-year-old shoulders. "Don't *ever* go in there," he told me. "There's a gun in there."

When I got older, I thought about going through the closet when he was out and getting rid of the gun. I worried about it, cold and metal and *there*, about Dad and his bad days. I never liked the idea of it, some firearm of unknown shape and size and origin, just waiting to be fired. But Dad told me not to touch it, and I didn't.

Now I walk up the hall and into Dad's room, careful not to look too closely at the messy bed and discarded clothes. The stale smell of boozy sweat makes it feel like he's home. Not missing. Not gone.

Holding the closet's contents with one hand to prevent an avalanche, I slowly open the door wider. I reach up and pull the string that lights the bare bulb, then begin to carefully rummage. I move out a box crammed with the button-down shirts Dad used to wear when he held a straight job, and another that proves empty. Three more boxes follow, filled with dust, old newspapers, and forgotten neckties.

I empty about half the closet's contents, enough so that I can lean inside and look around. Stretching to see behind the remaining cardboard boxes, I spot a thin wooden box about the size of a briefcase, crammed in sideways behind the rest. I make a fist and rap the edge. A hollow echo of the rap replies . . . almost like I knocked on a door.

Behind me, Sidekick whines.

"I'll be careful," I tell him. "Shh."

I wedge myself into the closet, perching on the unstable stack of boxes, and reach over to pull the wooden box up and out.

The case is made of dark wood and has a brass catch. I've never seen it before. At my touch, the clasp springs open easily, and I lift the lid. It takes me a moment to identify the object inside as a weapon.

The dull gleam of hammered metal, the surface as long as my forearm, wavy with the memory of the strikes that created it. A thick base gives way to a thicker barrel, like a small cannon. Jewels encrust the handle, and even I can tell they are the real, glittering thing.

I puzzle over the heavy object in my hand as I shut the closet. This has to be some sort of antique. The bizarre weapon must be worth a small fortune. I can't fathom the fact my dad never pawned it for a bottle. Can this really be what he meant when he told me there was a gun in the closet?

Then I spot the strange symbol nestled between the gems, an engraved sort of stick figure with a circular head, curved legs and straight arms, and an open half moon on top.

I freeze. I've seen that symbol before. The same one was stitched at the center of those three black sails, whipping in wind that didn't exist, flying above the decks of a black ship that didn't exist either.

I shiver with recognition.

Just then a knock sounds at the door, and I go stiff. But then I wonder, could it be Dad?

I creep out of the room and quietly up the hall. I'm almost to the door, the strange gun still in my hand, when I realize it can't be Dad — he would never go with a simple knock if he couldn't get in — and we never have visitors. When I'm not working, I sometimes hang at the Grove with Polly and the crew, but wouldn't dream of inviting anyone over. I prefer to keep what little privacy I have intact.

I have no idea who's out there.

I wait to see if the person goes away. Instead, another knock sounds. I grip the metal of the antique gun. Any weapon is better than nothing. I can use it as a threat or to hit someone with or . . .

A muffled male voice speaks, interrupting my train of thought. "Mr. Blackwood? Or Miranda? Miranda Blackwood?"

There's something familiar about the voice, but I can't place it. The familiarity makes my fingers tighten around the gun. Whoever is out there, my instincts say they're somehow a danger. To me.

Could it be Bone or those idiots he hangs out with? I've never considered any of them dangerous, but I've never been all alone like this either.

Sidekick's body brushes the side of my knee where he stands beside me. His tail thumps a steady rhythm against the coffee table.

Breathe, I tell myself. *You have a weapon. Sort of. Just point the gun with the right amount of menace.*

I open the door in one quick motion, stepping back and raising the weapon. I do my best to imitate a movie stance, to show confidence. My hands tremble, giving me away.

"What do you want?" I ask.

"Miranda?"

Suddenly — *click* — I place the voice, match it against the tall boy standing in my doorway. It's early evening and not anywhere near dark outside yet, but his face is in shadow. Still, I know him. I take in his messy black hair, the glint of eyes that would be more black than brown if I could see them. I never expected to see him again.

"Grant Rawling?" I blink in disbelief, but he doesn't vanish. My fingers loosen, and the gun clatters to the ground between us.

Grant lunges forward, bending over the antique weapon.

"Careful," I say.

"You be careful. You're the one acting like a CIA assassin." He *would* say something like that.

Grant doesn't even look at me, instead leaning forward to check out the gun. "Anyway, I'm safe — at least I think I am." He pauses. "Is that a matchlock? Awfully ornate. And it has a trigger. Hmm . . ." He shifts the gun with the toe of his shoe for a better look.

"What's a matchlock?" I ask, mostly to say something. Anything.

I can't figure out what he's doing here. At my house. Or on the island, for that matter. He got away from here. He's supposed to be off at some reform school. And even if he *has* come home on purpose, that doesn't explain what he's doing on my doorstep.

Grant glances up at me, then looks immediately back to the gun. "Matchlocks were the precursors to modern guns, more or less. Ones like this — although not exactly like this, because this one is weird — were developed during the Elizabethan period, and they're not easy to use. You have to light the barrel, essentially."

The Elizabethan period? That's when the original colonists were here. I might not know about matchlocks, but I know that much. Our family legend has always claimed some connection to the original settlers — is that why Dad has this gun? I can't make sense of it. I also can't help being impressed at Grant's recitation of facts.

"How do you know all that?"

He straightens, and finally looks at me. There isn't much distance between us, just the space of the threshold I haven't invited him over yet. There's just enough light to see that the years that he's been gone have been kind . . . to his face, anyway.

I resist the urge to smooth my hair. I am *so* not interested in Grant Rawling. We couldn't be more different. He has a great family, and he still left.

He's back, though.

Grant shrugs, finally. "My dad's really into antique firearms, and I grew up around the Outer Banks. I'm surprised you don't know. Don't you still work at *The Lost Colony?*"

"I'm an intern, not the prop master," I say, on more solid ground. "Wait. How do you know where I work?" I put a hand up to stop him from answering. A couple more inches, and I'd have touched him. "And, um, why are you here?"

"Why are you answering your door wielding a valuable historical artifact?"

The gun *is* worth money, then. I stoop to pick it up, dangling it by the barrel. "I just found it looking for . . . never mind. Answer my question."

He doesn't. "Can I come in?"

"Why?" I plant myself in the doorway.

"I need to talk to you."

"That can't be true — we don't even know each other." I watch his reaction.

"It won't take long," he says. "But I'm not going to leave until you talk to me."

I almost say no. I don't like being pushed. But he looks so serious that I believe him. I gesture with my gun hand, and swing the metal in a semi-welcoming fashion. "I guess so, then. I definitely don't want you hanging around."

"Thanks," he says.

So much for my ability to land an insult. I shut the door behind Grant, watching as Sidekick noses his fingers. Some guard dog. He slumps onto the floor, tail thumping.

"Is your dad —" Grant starts.

"No, he's not here. Which is good for you. He doesn't care too much for you."

At least, not if he remembers who you are.

"Understood," Grant says, and then, "Listen."

Which I do, but he doesn't say anything else. I move the heavy gun again to indicate the couch. We sit down on opposite ends of it. Unlike at the door, I am careful to create as much distance between us as possible.

Nervously, I fiddle with the gun that lies flat on my lap. Never in a million years would I have expected Grant Rawling to be on our couch. I've never been alone with a boy before — period. What is he doing here? Why would he need to talk to me?

"So," I say, "just get back?"

Grant nods. "Yeah. A couple of hours ago."

I pause, waiting for him to say more. When he doesn't, I say, "So . . ."

He shifts to face me, erasing a fraction of the distance. "Yes?"

I may as well ask. "What's this about? Why are you here?"

"Look, I'm sorry. I know it's weird to drop in here out of nowhere and . . . surprise you. I'm sorry about that. But I had to see you."

I still can't make any sense of what he's saying. I let the gun slide onto the couch between us.

"Please put that thing on the table or something," Grant says.

"What did you call it again?" I ask, keeping it in my hand.

"A matchlock — where did you get it?"

"I —" I stop. "No, I don't think so. Not until we talk about why you just *had* to see me, after all this time."

Grant doesn't rush to say anything.

Wait. I have a sudden suspicion.

"Have you heard about the missing people?"

Even as I say it, I realize why he's come. Injury, insult, the whole enchilada. He thinks it's *my* fault. The realization hurts like a sting. I was too distracted by the surprise of him showing up to see the obvious. "You think I have something to do with this, don't you? Because I'm a Blackwood. Because of . . . everything. Are you going to call me a snake again? We can probably get it on CNN this time."

Grant doesn't say anything, only looks at me. It isn't that different than the look he gave me all those years ago, the one I've never been able to forget. I want to be wrong about why he's here.

Let me be wrong, I plead.

"You're sort of right," he says. "I *am* worried that you might be involved. Is your dad one of the missing?"

I'm not wrong. Anger spikes. Today has been too much already, and now *this*. I pick the supposedly useless gun up and point it at him. "Get out."

He holds out his hands. "Wait. Let me explain."

My phone rings, its high-pitched spaceship sound like a slap. Startled, I squeeze the gun's trigger without meaning to.

Grant cringes even though there's no noise. At least not at first. The *whoosh* comes a heartbeat later as a curtain of black powder sprays from the end of the barrel. It coats him as completely as a shower. A faint burning scent fills the air.

I struggle to breathe. "Are you okay?"

Grant uses a finger to sample the powdery film coating his skin, sniffs, and tastes it. "Just coated in . . . sulfur and, maybe, charcoal?"

"I didn't mean to . . ." *Shoot you.* I can't say the words.

"I know," he says, like what happened is nothing. "No big deal. I'm fine."

The wail of my phone — still ringing — makes it through my shock. "I should get that." I take my phone from my pocket. Manteo Police. My stomach clenches. "Hello?"

"Miranda? This is Chief Rawling," he says.

"Uh, hi," I say. *I just shot your son with an antique gun.* Probably best not to open with that. Instead I go with, "What's up?"

"We, ah, found your father. Can you come over to the courthouse?"

"Be right there," I say, clicking the phone off.

I want to feel relief. Dad was probably passed out somewhere. They found him. Mystery solved. So why do I still feel so uneasy?

When I look up, Grant is attempting to get the worst of the dust off his eyelashes. Having sprayed him with the powder should feel satisfying. He deserves the payback. Especially since he came here to accuse me of — well, I still don't know what, precisely.

GWENDA BOND

"Who was that?" Grant asks. His curiosity seems to transcend the thick powder clinging to his skin.

I consider lying but go with the truth. "Your dad."

Grant jolts to his feet. Black dust flies in the air around him. "What? Why?"

"He needs me to come to the courthouse. They found mine."

"Found your what?"

"Dad," I say. "They found my dad."

Reality crashes down around me, settling into place like the walls of our ramshackle house. Ramshackle, but inescapable.

I place the gun on the table, being more careful. I frown. "I thought you said this thing couldn't fire without being lit by a match."

Grant looks like he's wearing Halloween makeup gone wrong. Sidekick tests his fingers with a lick, then shudders.

"It couldn't," he says. "Or it shouldn't. But this is gunpowder. I can smell the sulfur. So it has a trigger mechanism, even though it shouldn't. Where did you find it?"

The box I unearthed from the closet is a few feet away, and I'm taken aback by how much I want to show it to him and see what theory he has on it. But I have no reason to trust him, not after eighth grade, not after he rushed here to say I'm *involved* with the disappearances. An answer will only provide more ammunition — so to speak.

"You better get cleaned up. I have to go get Dad at the courthouse."

GRANT

I finish washing off my face in the Blackwoods' small, tidy bathroom with its floor of curling linoleum. The worst of the powdery mess that came from the gun Miranda accidentally shot me with is gone. But the scent of fire and charcoal is still in my nose, tinged with the egg-like smell of sulfur.

I stare into the mirror and shake my head.

Great job, Grant. You couldn't have screwed that up any worse.

Somehow I managed to offend the girl I came here to help. She won't listen to me now. And I don't even know what to say. All I have is a feeling. For once, I almost wish for the spirits and their voices. They talked to me about Miranda once; maybe they would again.

I shake my head. No, I don't mean that. That's the last thing I need.

"You done?" Miranda calls from right outside the door. "I need to get going."

I emerge and study her for a moment. Up close, I'm able to see the changes the years have made in her. She's taller, and her curly hair is wilder. I can tell that she's still the same girl, with too much weight on her shoulders, still trapped by the island and what her family name means here. I can relate.

"Will you let me drive you to the courthouse?" I ask.

She frowns in a *what's wrong with you?* way. "I have a car."

"Oh, okay." I don't want to leave her, not yet. But I don't guess I have a choice. "Miranda, I want you to know . . . I didn't come here to embarrass you again. To hurt you. I came to help. I'll be here if you need me."

She's quiet for a moment, and I almost think I'm making progress. Then she says, "I don't need your help."

Which, fair enough. I don't seem to be very good at offering it anyway.

Miranda motions to the door, her car keys in her hand with the teeth sticking out of her fist. I have no choice but to follow her. I hope she's not planning to punch me.

Once we're outside, she goes over to an old yellow car of indiscriminate make parked at the curb across the street. The passenger side is facing me. She doesn't so much as glance in my direction as she walks around the car and gets in.

I climb into Mom's sedan, turn the key in the ignition, and then wait. I have to decide where I'm going next. Home? The courthouse? I could follow her there and see Dad to begin my atonement for abandoning Mom. But that begs the question — why is Dad having her come to the courthouse instead of the jail, anyway?

There's a rap on the window, and I'm startled to see it's Miranda. I roll down the window. "What is it?"

Her cheeks are scarlet. Whatever she's about to ask, she'd rather do anything else. "My car won't start. I could probably get it to, but it'll take too long. Can you give me a ride?"

"Of course," I say, and even I hear that it's too eager.

She gets in on the passenger side, and silence descends. I know better than to try talking right now, not if she doesn't want to.

I drive us out of her neighborhood and into town. I need to find a way to make things right. I'm even more worried about Miranda after the appearance of the weird old gun. But not being able to explain *why* I'm worried — even to myself — is a handicap.

But I'm certain that Miranda Blackwood isn't safe.

Also . . . where are the spirits? I'm not willing to risk trying to call them. Not yet. I summoned the voices intentionally just once, and the response left me muttering in bed for two days, struggling to mute the overwhelming chaos chorus.

Still, the silence is perplexing. I can't help wondering if I left for nearly four years for no reason. The presence of the spirits seemed undeniably real. That they started the day Gram died and then stopped when I left seemed to confirm they were — that they *are* — tied to the island. Maybe not, though. Maybe I have some brain disorder, and the timing *was* a coincidence.

The courthouse comes into view, a grand white building with two-story columns and a wide front landing. The square has a green, and a fountain and gazebo. There isn't a parking spot anywhere in sight. There may not be that many permanent residents in town, but every single one has apparently converged on downtown. Cars cram all the spots that the media's satellite trucks don't occupy. Every major network is represented, along with the local cable station's van.

"Stop," Miranda says when we're almost in front of the courthouse. Her tone is a command.

I put on the brakes, thinking there's a serious reason.

"I can get out here," she says. "Thanks."

The passenger door opens, and she's gone.

She's not getting rid of me that easily.

I start searching the side streets for a gap, and finally find a spot in front of the Pioneer Theatre. The box office is dark, even though the movie theater prides itself on always being open. It's a disconcerting sight.

I need to get back to Miranda. She won't have a way to take her dad home, not without her car. So I'm staying, even though she didn't ask me to.

I keep my head down as I wade through the lunatic fringe clogging the courthouse square. I hope no one recognizes me. The reputation I earned in order to leave makes me memorable.

Thankfully I manage to pass uninterrupted through the crowd and come to a stop near the bottom of the broad set of steps that lead to the courthouse entrance. I hesitate, not eager to face Dad.

But then I see someone I recognize, someone I wouldn't mind talking to, at the top of the steps. Dr. Whitson is doing an interview with the blond reporter I saw Miranda talking to on TV this morning. The doc has a professorial air, though he's an MD, not an academic. And he doesn't seem to have changed a tweed fiber since I left. Despite the hot weather, he's sporting the same fussy suit as always and even has a familiar leather binder clasped under his arm.

For as long as I've known him, Dr. Whitson has been obsessed with the story of the lost colonists. He's a well-known local who's written, oh, about a jillion articles examining different theories about what happened to the colonists — up to and including alien abduction — for magazines with names like *Unexplained Phenomena* and *Hidden America*.

But in addition to his extracurricular obsession, the good doctor is also a shrink. I saw him for a while on my parents' orders. He spent most of our time together talking history and ephemera while I poked through his fascinating personal library. He thought I seemed rational enough, and blamed my acting out on boredom. Then again, I never told him about seeing and hearing the dead. Mom didn't make me, and I didn't want to end up in an institution. Our unconventional doctor-patient relationship ended when I left the island.

I bound up the steps and stop where I can listen. The interview appears to be wrapping up.

"So, where do *you* believe the missing citizens of Roanoke Island are, Dr. Whitson?" the reporter asks.

Dr. Whitson doesn't hesitate. "I don't think this can be that easily explained. All I know is that it happened once before."

"You believe the original disappearance is linked to this one?" The reporter feeds him the line.

"At this point, I think we'd be wise to remember our history. And hope we're not destined to repeat it."

"Thank you. Chilling words from our local history expert," the reporter says. "We'll be right back. In the meantime, share your thoughts using #FindTheMissing."

Dr. Whitson unclips his mic and hands it back to her camera guy. Then he spots me. "Grant?" he asks.

I smile. "Doc."

"Now I know I'm officially going mad," he says. "What are you doing back?"

I ignore his question and gesture back down the stairs at the mob scene. "What do you think about all this, really?"

"What I said on camera." Whitson leans in, growing serious. "This isn't going to be resolved easily. Something big is going to come of this."

That's the opposite of what I want to hear. A lot of people on the island dismiss the doc and his theories — just another local character with crazy ideas — but given the depth of his knowledge, that's not so easy to do. Whitson knows a lot of things regular history buffs ignore.

"I have to go," I say. "There's a girl I have to . . ." I swallow, unsure how to finish. "Is it okay if I drop by later? Talk over some explanations that aren't easy?"

Dr. Whitson nods. "You're always welcome. And good luck."

"Good luck with . . . ?"

"Your girl." With that, he waves and starts down the stairs. Almost immediately he's swarmed by locals eager for his theories. Now that we have our own mass disappearance, apparently everyone wants his opinion.

I watch him be swallowed by the sea of townspeople and then walk the rest of the way to the door. Inside, I nod to the beefy cop on security, one of Dad's deputies. He busted me once for some elaborate graffiti and recognizes me instantly.

"Your dad's been wondering when you'd turn up. And your mom's pissed."

Perfect. I try to decide how best to handle Dad. I'm out of practice at being in trouble.

Despite the sweep of the building's exterior, the interior is no grand vista. The lobby's scuffed marble floor is filled with a crowd of people who aren't usually here. A few tables have been set up, outfitted with phones for a call bank — Dad stands next to one of the tables. He has an office on the first floor here, up one of the hallways branching off the lobby. He prefers not to work in the jail when he can avoid it.

I spot Miranda hovering off to one side of the lobby and hang back for a second, watching her watch my dad. She must be waiting for him to notice her, and all the buzzing activity means that hasn't happened yet.

I'm still unclear why Dad summoned Miranda *here*. It bothers me. There's no reason for him to call her personally with the mayhem going on.

Leaving the phone bank, Dad stops to chat with a state trooper and a pasty-looking guy in a black suit. He looks even more tired than in the glimpse I got of him on TV in the airport. Dark circles hang under his eyes like he's gone weeks, rather than twenty-four hours, without sleep. Dad responds to something the guy in the suit says, and I recognize his body language as dismissive. His mouth falls open mid-dismissive response, though, as he stares at Miranda.

Make that *past* Miranda. At me.

I wave.

Miranda turns her head and frowns when she spots me. "Grant? Thanks for the ride. But you didn't have to come in."

"I wanted to. And you'll need a ride back too, right?" I shrug in Dad's direction. I can tell from the scowl he shoots across the lobby that he hasn't even noticed Miranda yet. I talk fast as he crosses the space toward us. "I'm sorry about before. I don't think any of this is your fault. I'm just worried for you. I did a crap job of explaining before, but you can trust me. I promise."

"I should . . ." Miranda hesitates, tilting her head to give me a closer inspection.

"Grant," Dad says, reaching us.

Miranda steps between my dad and me. "Hey, Chief Rawling. You called me?"

I don't know why she decided to delay my moment of reckoning, but I'm grateful anyway.

Dad looks from Miranda to me and back again, finally seeing her. "Yes, I did. You'd better step into my office." He motions for her to follow him before he speaks to me. "*You* wait here." Then he adds, "Until I come back."

Miranda's frown is back, only now she's puzzled. "Where's my dad? Is he in your office?"

Dad says, "You'd better come with me." He touches her arm with one hand and extends his other to indicate which direction for her to go.

Miranda deals me another surprise when she hesitates and says, "If it's okay, can Grant come with us?"

Dad's forehead wrinkles slightly in confusion, but he says, "I guess."

I follow Miranda across the lobby and along the hallway into Dad's office. The space hasn't changed much. Dad closes the blinds on the tall, narrow windows to the outside, turning the room into a cave. He peers at me from the other side of his desk. "How are you holding up? Any . . . problems?"

"Good, actually," I say. "Fine."

"When we finish here, call your mother. You can drive the car home to her. She'll bring you back here."

"I'm just here to give Miranda and her dad a ride home," I say. "Besides, what am I supposed to do here?"

Dad cringes at the first part, but he only speaks to the second. He lowers his voice. "You know. What you do."

"There's nothing," I say. I do not want to talk about this with Miranda in the room. I may have mentioned the spirits to her way back when, but that's a little different from discussing the extent of my gift in front of her. Especially given that it's currently MIA. "Not since I got back."

Dad frowns. That isn't what he wants to hear.

Miranda coughs to interrupt. "Where is he?" she asks, the question small in the high-ceilinged room.

I don't fully understand why I want to protect Miranda, but I do. Dad is taking too much time on this. It can't just be about releasing her father on a drunk and disorderly or a public intoxication charge.

"You might want to . . ." Dad gestures to the chairs in front of his desk and sits down in his own. Miranda and I slide into the vacant ones. I attempt to catch Miranda's eye, but she's staring straight ahead.

"I have some bad news," Dad goes on.

"Where's my dad?" Miranda asks.

Dad laces his fingers together on the desk. His expression settles into one I've seen before. "I understand this will be hard to hear," he starts.

"What . . . what's hard to hear?" Miranda asks. "You found him, right? He wasn't missing."

There's a strained hope in her voice. I reach out and touch her arm. She flinches.

"We did find him," Dad says. "But —"

"So where is he?" she interrupts. "I want to see him. Is he okay?"

Unfortunately, by now I can guess what's coming. It's all in the grim set of Dad's face, easy to decode for someone like me who knows how to read it.

"Miranda," I say as gently as I can, "let him tell you what he needs to."

Miranda gulps in air, and then says, "No, you don't understand. I promised Mom I'd take care of him."

Dad and I exchange a glance. So Miranda suspects what's coming too.

"Well," Dad says, "I know this won't be easy. I'm glad that my son is here with you." He pauses, probably wondering why the two of us came together. "You've had a tough time of it, Miranda. You've been such a devoted daughter, and I didn't want to tell you alone, but there's no one else to call . . . our social worker is among the missing, and I know you wouldn't want that, anyway. You've been running your household for a while now, and you deserve to know, especially with everything going on. But there's no easy way to say this . . ."

Miranda remains motionless. I'm not even sure she keeps breathing.

"Your father was murdered."

I anticipated dead, or maybe seriously injured, but not . . . "Murdered?" I ask.

"His body was discovered in an alley downtown this afternoon. He's the only one of the missing we've recovered so far. But he brings the reported number down to one hundred and fourteen."

Miranda puts her head down, her hair falling forward to hide her face. I want to *do* something, anything, to comfort her. But I don't know how. Instead I sit, useless and in shock, fixated on the number of missing — 114. The same number John White left behind in 1587.

That can't be a coincidence. Dr. Whitson implied there's a connection between the two events, but what could it be?

Miranda speaks, head still down, her voice muffled by her hair. "What happened? Do you know who did it?"

"The coroner is having some difficulty determining what happened to him, but it's not anything that could be considered accidental or self-inflicted," Dad says. "We've ordered an autopsy, and we'll know more once that's finished. We don't know who's responsible for his death yet." He squints sympathetically at the crown of her head. "If you want to see the body, we can arrange that. I'm so sorry, Miranda."

"I'm sorry too," I say, the only words I can find for her. I have questions for Dad, but they'll wait.

Miranda lifts her head. "I understand," she says, her voice as steady as a flat line on a hospital monitor.

I've heard Dad talk to Mom about notifications before. How most people fall apart before you even get through the facts about how the person died. He always says that the ones who don't are the ones who usually end up taking it hardest.

Miranda rises from the chair, then seems to think better of it and drops back into it. "Do you need me to sign anything?"

Yeah, she's not going to take this well at all.

MIRANDA

While Grant drives me home, I stare out the car window, feeling lost. As lost as the missing people, maybe. Chief Rawling agreed to let Grant leave with me, but he's supposed to end up back at the courthouse. Grant told his dad again there's nothing he can do to help there, making me wonder what the chief even thinks he *could* do, though I have my suspicions.

For some reason, Grant seems reluctant to leave me. I'm grateful for the company now, though I wasn't earlier. Silly as that is. But then I didn't know that soon I'd be alone for good.

The way the chief described Dad's death was so strange, but that only occurs to me now. At the time, all I could think was, *Dad is gone. I failed him. Worse, I failed Mom. All she wanted was for the two of us to be okay, for me to look out for him. And I didn't.*

But now I wonder how the state of his body could clearly indicate murder, but the coroner not know how he died? I can't process the concept that someone murdered *my* dad. Who? And why? Dad was a drunk, but a harmless one. And he was so nice to me last night, telling me I'm a good daughter, that he wanted to be better. Did he know something was up?

The distraction of all these questions keeps me from losing it. They're the only thing.

Grant hasn't said much. He keeps his eyes on the road, his knuckles tight in a death grip on the steering wheel.

"What your dad was asking you before . . . you hear voices still?" I ask.

He doesn't as much as glance over. "You remember."

That's the understatement of the century. Of course I remember. The voices talked to him about *me*. I was in eighth grade, thirteen years old. It happened on the first day of school, not long after the Rawlings moved in from Nags Head. They took possession of the house belonging to the chief's mother — aka the Witch of Roanoke Island — after she died of cancer. Back then Grant possessed the glow of celebrity all new kids have in a town this small.

I was standing against the section of lobby wall that belonged to loner misfits. Grant walked toward me like he was in a trance. The other kids laughed as he reached out a hand and touched my hair. He said things to me, about me. Things that didn't make any sense but that scared me. He called me a bad thing. He called me a liar. A traitor. A snake.

The other kids loved that — a snake. They thought he was being funny. The funny new kid, picking on the Blackwood girl, something most of them had wanted to do for a long time.

Eventually the principal stepped in to pull Grant away and called my dad to pick me up. But the damage had been done. What people whispered about our family had only gotten worse since my mom died. Her death confirmed our bad luck curse. And then this.

Dad ripped through a half-case of beer when we got home, getting angrier with each can. Then he loaded me into the car and drove to the Rawlings' house.

Chief Rawling tolerated Dad yelling and taking a swing at him, though he didn't let it connect. Grant must have heard the commotion, because he came downstairs and stood at the screen door. When he saw me, he ran outside.

"I hear the spirits talking," he whispered. "They talk to me all the time. They said those things about you. They were too loud. But they're *just spirits*, and I hate them."

Then he gave me that look. I could tell he was sorry. Even then, I didn't believe he had humiliated me in front of everyone on purpose.

Finally Chief Rawling sent Grant back inside and drove Dad and me home in our Oldsmobile. His pretty wife with the black hair followed us in his police cruiser. I was surprised that Grant didn't show up for school the next day. Or the next. Or any of the days that followed. His mother home-schooled him for half the year, rumors of his criminal escapades around the island traveling the halls. Then he left.

Now I study his profile, just inches away. Part of me wants to ask him if the spirits said anything else about me back then. That part wants to know. Maybe.

"Is that why you're helping me?" I ask. "You still feel guilty? It was a long time ago. You were just their excuse. They'd have found a reason to go after me."

"That doesn't make me feel better," he says. "I don't know why I want to help you. I just do. It feels . . . right."

Never in a million years will I understand this boy.

"Do you still hear them?" I ask again. "Can they tell you what happened to my dad?"

"I haven't heard them since I got back." He sounds regretful. "I'm sorry." He gives a half smile that looks nothing like a real one. "They've never told me anything useful. I know it must sound crazy — the whole thing."

"When you come from a family like mine, you don't judge." I stare out the windshield and realize we're fast approaching a place I haven't been in a while. A place I suddenly desperately need to go. I need to apologize to Mom for my broken promise, and since Grant can't do it for me . . .

I point straight ahead. "Do you mind if we stop by there?"

A thick black fence thrusts from the ground like jagged teeth, a forbidding boundary of painted iron. The evening light makes shadow spears that thrust toward the gentle slope of tombstone-dotted ground the fence protects.

"I can't believe I'm about to say this," he says, "but why not?"

He slows and turns up the dirt drive that will take us into the graveyard, dust ghosts trailing the car.

*

I get out of the car first and wander through the chalky white tombstones, some carved with angels or winged skulls. There aren't many recent burials in this part of the cemetery.

Grant doesn't follow me. I don't ask him to. I figure he'll join me if he feels like it.

I walk up the slope, and grass that could use mowing tickles my ankles. I look back, and Grant is still inside the car.

It's sinking in that I'm truly alone now. Alone in the world.

I start down the other side of the small hill, out of sight. Here the markers change to reddish marble and gleaming black.

There are plain gray stones mixed in, but not many of the older, paler kind.

I don't care for modern headstones. When Mom died, we were only able to afford a smallish marble rectangle to mark her grave. I wished for something large and sweeping that captured Mom's spirit. Or at least something small and noble, like those old ones. I'm pretty sure the guy at the Outer Banks Monument Company who sold us our stone cut us a deal. There wasn't any way to ask for more charity.

I reach the not-so-special gray stone. Kneeling, I trace the letters of my mother's name with my fingertips. *Anna-Marie Blackwood.*

The tombstones on either side are close. There'll be no room for Dad's marker to go next to Mom's. Not that we — I — can afford one.

Now that I'm here, I don't bother to ask for Mom's forgiveness, but I crave it all the same. I ease down on the hillside next to the headstone and pull up a yellow dandelion growing on the top of the grave. I hate the idea of my mom down there in the cold, damp dark.

I lean against the stone and say, "I didn't forget my promise to watch out for Dad, but I wasn't able to keep it. Not good enough."

The only response I hear is Grant climbing down the hill to join me. He must be stomping as loud as he can through the grass to give me fair warning to compose myself. He isn't turning out to be anything like I would have expected.

I pat the ground beside me as he arrives. He kicks at the grass, then sits down.

"Grant Rawling, meet Anna-Marie," I say.

Grant doesn't say anything.

"She was great," I tell him. I want him to know that, for some reason.

"I'm sorry."

"You say that a lot."

"Sorry," he says. "Last one, promise."

We stay like this for a few minutes, not talking. Low gray clouds pass overhead. The rolling hills of the cemetery grounds are dotted with purple-flowering bushes and a few trees. This is a peaceful place, even with the highway.

I hope wherever Dad is now is a peaceful place too. He deserves that.

"I can't believe he's gone," I say, my heart heavy in my chest. I feel weary. Can someone who's seventeen feel weary? I do. "Sometimes I still can't believe *she* is."

"What was he like?"

I shrug, not sure what to say. Before Mom got sick, Dad was different. He was quieter, not so much of a crazy talker or drinker. He held a steady job, more or less. Mom could make him smile with such little effort. She used to read me book after book — Narnia and Alice and Spiderwick and Harry Potter — while he drank a beer or two, no more, content to listen to us.

I pluck another dandelion. This one has already transformed to a head of white cotton spokes. "He wasn't able to be himself anymore after she died. . . . Losing someone, sometimes it's too much. He couldn't shut out the dark. He gave up."

"I'm — I'm *not* going to say I'm sorry."

I blow on the dandelion, scattering the white particles all over Grant's shirt.

"Thanks," he says, brushing them off. "You have a thing for coating me with random substances you want to tell me about?"

I lie back instead of answering, grass brushing my ears, and watch the clouds drift over us. "I don't know what's going to happen to me. I always dream about leaving, but I never really thought about what life beyond taking care of Dad might look like. Never made any plans." I pause. Grant doesn't know the full extent of the legendary curse. "I never figured there was any point making them."

Grant takes a moment to respond. "That part might be a good thing, though. Right?"

Is it? I'm not going to tell him that I'm doomed to Roanoke Island. Spirits or no spirits, he'll think I'm silly for believing in the curse, and — suddenly — I do not want him to think that about me.

He hauls himself up onto his knees and reaches over me. He touches the headstone. "Nice to meet you, Anna-Marie," he says.

I smile up at him, without meaning to. I should be too sad to smile at all. This is a boy who lends himself to wondering about. Especially when he jolts upright, an uneasiness overtaking his whole body.

He gives me a stricken look. "I don't think you should go home . . ." He hesitates.

"Spirits tell you something about me?" I ask, mostly kidding.

"No," he blurts. He doesn't seem to find the question funny in the least. "You . . . you shouldn't be alone. Come to my house? You can meet my mom."

I nod, despite the fact he's wrong. I am alone. I'll be that way for the rest of my life. Eventually, I'll have to go home and mourn Dad. I'll have to come to terms with how badly I failed on my promise.

But there's no reason to rush home and embrace that pain. It'll wait for me.

That much I know.

*

Grant angles the car up the driveway toward the white two-story house that originally belonged to his grandmother. It's the most perfect, normal, comfortable house I can imagine. His mother sits on the front porch swing.

"Like something straight out of house and beach garden, huh? My mom should be cool, but if she's not, I'll just drop my stuff, and then we'll get you home," Grant says.

He's rambling. He must be nervous about seeing his mom. Or maybe about me meeting her.

"I should probably warn you. My mom might be mad at me," Grant continues.

I follow his eyes to where his mother gets up in a smooth motion. She walks to the top of the steps and waits, arms crossed.

"Why?" I ask, because he is obviously right.

"I kind of, well, borrowed this car. Without asking. From the airport parking garage."

I gape. "You stole your mom's car is what you're saying?"

"Um, yes, but now I'm returning it. It'll be fine." With that, he opens the car door and gets out.

He stole his mom's car. I'm familiar with the legends of his exploits around town, but to be confronted with one in real life.

Wow.

We drag lead feet across the lawn toward the porch. I should just go home.

"Grant Rawling," his mother says, when we reach her. "I should kill you right now."

He ducks his head. "You probably should."

"How are you doing?" she asks.

"Good so far," he says. "This is Miranda."

I direct a shy wave to his mom.

Her arms do not uncross in welcome. "And she is?"

"Miranda Blackwood." Grant shifts. "You remember her."

"Of course," his mother says, nodding after she gets a better look at me. She sticks out her hand, but I don't take it. Unbothered by my snub, she takes my arm and squeezes. "I'm Mrs. Rawling. You can call me Sara."

"I know," I say. "Same way you know who I am. Small town."

"Please come in, and pretend not to listen while I yell at my son."

I blink. That's a joke. I'm not used to being treated this normally by people who live here.

"Sounds like fun," I say.

"It will be," Sara says. She steers me across the porch toward the door.

"Don't worry, I'm here for my entertainment value," Grant says, tagging along behind us. "I bet Miranda's starving. I am."

"Oh!" Sara says. "I'm the world's worst hostess." She drags me through the door, then turns to Grant. "Let me fix you guys something. Go clean up, wayward son. Leave us girls to it."

"Is that okay with you?" Grant asks me, hesitating.

"Go," his mom says at the same time I nod.

Grant obediently disappears upstairs.

"That should drive him nuts," Sara says. She leads the way to the kitchen and shoots me a grin as she pulls a loaf of bread down from a shelf. "Turkey okay?"

I nod. "Perfect."

The Rawling family kitchen isn't small, but it is cozy. Evening light streams in through the back door and a picture window over the sink, further warming the honeyed tones everything was designed in.

Sara starts removing items from the fridge. She asks, "How do you guys know each other?"

That didn't take long.

"We don't, really. Grant just" — happened to come by, so I shot him with an ancient gun — "gave me a ride to the court-house."

Sara places several slices of bread on the sparkling clean counter. "I take it he didn't tell you that he took the car without permission and left me abandoned at the Norfolk airport?"

I slowly shake my head. "Not until we got here. No."

"He has a way of leaving out these things. You said the courthouse. Did you guys go by the office?"

"You mean, did Grant see his dad?" I ask.

Sara nods, waiting for the answer.

"What's the deal with those two?" I ask.

"You saw them in action?" Sara slathers some Dijon mustard across a slice of bread. "They think they're polar opposites. Really, though, they're not so different. Neither of them likes doing what they're told."

She hands me the first sandwich, and I take a bite, talking while I chew. Delicate graces aren't my forte. "Who does?" I counter.

Sara considers me, and I squirm, feeling sized up.

"Is your dad one of the missing?" she asks quietly.

"No," I say. "Not anymore."

Sara frowns. She was obviously expecting a different answer. "Why'd you go by there?"

The turkey sandwich congeals in my stomach. I'll have to say the words out loud at some point. The first time might as well be to someone who's being nice to me.

"He's dead," I say. "My dad's dead. That's why we went to the courthouse. The chief wanted to tell me in person."

Sara is instantly at my side, and she rubs a hand across my back. My mom used to do the same thing when I was upset.

I feel a stab of sharp, mean loss in my chest for my mother, for my father. . . . I put down the sandwich.

"Oh, honey." Sara's hand keeps tracing comforting circles between my shoulders.

I swallow over the lump that burns in my throat. "I'll be eighteen in a few months." I need to lighten the moment, keep the tears away. Dad felt too much after Mom died, and look what happened to him. I have to stay strong. No one will put me back together if I fall apart. "The orphan card will get me a lot of sympathy at school. *Hello*, homework extensions," I say.

Sara smooths my hair back, and I know she isn't fooled. "You deserve better than sympathy."

"Well." I don't have anything else to say to that. I pick up the sandwich.

"You'll stay here tonight."

"Oh no, I can't!" I see her giving me a look that means she's not going to lose this fight. "I have to go home. I have a dog."

Sara considers me for a long moment, traces a last circle on my back. "Grant can go get some things for you. The dog's welcome here too."

"I don't want . . . that is, you know . . ." She waits. "The thought of, um, Grant in my room. My dresser."

"Right," she says, getting it. "I'll go with him and pack you some clothes. That good? I'd like to talk to him . . . if you don't

72

mind staying here alone for a little while. I promise we won't leave you alone too long. We'll set you up in the tub and you can have a nice bubble bath while we're gone. Okay?"

I nod, because what else can I do? The matter is clearly settled as far as she's concerned.

Sara leaves my side to finish making Grant's turkey on wheat, apparently getting that I'm not ready to talk in depth about any of this yet. I can't express the gratitude I feel. My eyes feel wet again, and I blink away the tears.

"Grant is special." Sara doesn't look up from her task. "His dad knows that, but he doesn't understand it. Even though he grew up with a mother who was also . . . special. It's why we lived away all those years. I dragged him back here because he missed it, even if he wouldn't admit it. But he doesn't know what to make of things that aren't easily explained. That you just have to take them for what they are sometimes. He doesn't understand what it's like for Grant. He loves him, but he doesn't understand."

I chew the chalky bread, taking that in. "He worries about him, doesn't he? That counts for something."

Sara watches her. "It's hard not to worry about Grant."

"Why?" I ask.

Grant's footsteps clop on the stairs, coming down fast. Sara winks at me and raises her voice, "Just let me get those pictures. He's dressed like a little cowboy. So cute."

I laugh, and it eases the tightness in my chest. I wait for Grant's mock protest. My laugh fades as I realize why this feels so strange.

This must be what normal families are like.

GRANT

I slide into the sedan's passenger seat. I know better than to ask Mom to let me drive. If I hadn't brought Miranda home with me — and if Mom didn't know about Miranda's dad — I'd still be in major trouble. I'm sure she's only letting me come along so she can grill me. Mom put Miranda in the guest room with an old robe and a bunch of bath products and promised her we'd be right back from going to get her stuff and her trusty Sidekick.

I can't imagine what Miranda thinks of our house, probably that it seems like Normalcy HQ. That's one reason I've never felt too comfortable living in Gram's place. The normal white and normal wood and normal shape are way too normal to be connected to me — or to Gram, for that matter.

But, about to get grilled in the third degree from Mom or not, I'm happy to have a few minutes away from Miranda — not that I want to leave her, but it's hard to think with her around. Deciding what to do next is proving difficult enough.

I heard the words the moment after I touched her mother's headstone, the moment I looked down and found Miranda smiling at me with the first genuine approval I've seen cross her face. One glimmer in the air, and a voice to go with it, low and right in my ear:

Curse-bearer. Curse-bearer, she is a curse-born child.

I can't figure out how to tell her.

"Why is she with you?" Mom asks.

I wish I could explain. "I'm . . . helping her . . . with something."

"I'll need more than that." Mom puts the car in gear, but she pauses with a foot on the brake and squeezes my arm. It's affectionate. She's not hurting me. *I* am forgiven for the car thing. "It's good to see you. Are you really doing okay? You seem . . ."

"Quiet," I say, and I think I'm probably lying about more than just the one voice. Where there's one whisper, more will follow. *So much for brain disorders.* I'm vaguely aware there are stories about the Blackwoods being incredibly unlucky, but I don't understand what curse-bearer means yet. I don't want to. I'll have to puzzle it out anyway.

"Did you load Miranda up with embarrassing anecdotes to punish me?"

"Wouldn't you like to know," Mom says, neutrally.

The two of them were laughing when I came back to the kitchen. I can't believe that with everything going on — a hundred and change missing people, most of the spirits missing too, and Miranda's murdered father — I'm actually nervous that their conversation involved baby pictures, embarrassing anecdotes, and cutesy nicknames being spilled. Moms are psychic *and* evil.

She doesn't say anything else until we reach the end of our cul-de-sac. The questions come along with the turn onto the highway, one of the main drags that more or less runs the length of the island.

"So, it's quiet. Now are you going to tell me what's going on? I can't believe all this is happening." She rummages in her purse and takes out a pack of cigarettes, taps it on the top of the steering wheel. She glances over and catches me frowning.

"You kept smoking?" I ask.

"No," she says and sighs. "This would be my first one since we dropped you off in Jackson." With that, she rolls down the window and chucks the white-and-red package out.

It isn't an environmentally sound disposal method, but it's better than her smoking. Besides, no one will ticket the police chief's wife for littering.

"I hope a wild animal doesn't eat those," I say.

"It won't. They're disgusting." She reaches over to brush my shoulder. "It's good to have you home, no matter what the circumstances."

The circumstances.

No matter how hard I try, I can't get the missing people and Miranda's dad's murder to fit together.

"Grant," Mom prompts, "it's not optional. You have to tell me what's going on if you know. And why the sudden interest in Miranda Blackwood?"

"You have a problem with her? You seemed to like her."

"She's delightful, but that doesn't explain why you felt the need to steal my car to go see her. Or why you brought her home with you." She keeps going before I can cut in. "Bringing her was absolutely the right thing. But I want to know what the deal is. It's really quiet in there?"

She means in my head.

"I wouldn't go that far. But no voices, if that's what you mean . . ."

"*Grant.*"

I don't see any reason not to come clean. "Okay, one voice. I heard one voice — we stopped at the cemetery, and we were at Miranda's mom's headstone and . . ."

"And?"

"It said she was the curse-bearer or something."

The one eye I can see of hers widens. "You didn't tell her?"

"Not yet."

"Good. That's the last thing that poor girl needs right now." She drums her fingers on the steering wheel. "Where do you think the missing people are? Do you think it has something to do with the Blackwoods? That's why you went to see her, isn't it?"

I shake my head. "No, not exactly. That's what I need to explain to her. I feel — I can't explain it. She's in danger. Her dad's murder seals it."

"He was *murdered*? Here?"

"I know." Her shock isn't surprising. It's not the type of thing that happens on Roanoke Island. Tourist drownings and drunken accidents, sure. Murder? Not unheard of, but rare, and almost always due to family crap gone wrong.

"I was surprised your dad called you. But this . . . where do you think all the people are?" Mom asks. She's lost whatever measure of calm she still possessed. "Our neighbors are missing. Half my rook club is missing. Where are they?"

The question sends a chill deep into my bones. Mom's rook club is half youngish moms like her and half little old ladies. They swap out partners and yell about trumps to each other, playing cards late into the night at least once a month.

"They're gone, just like the spirits," I say.

"So you think the two are connected?" she asks.

"I don't know."

Out the car window a few lights are visible through the trees along the roadside. I forgot how dark the interior of the island gets at night, away from the town's bright center. The branches are like fingers, reaching into the sky.

Mom slows at the stop sign, signaling to turn onto Miranda's street. "They had to go somewhere. People don't vanish, not all at once. Not unless they're cult members — and my rook club is not full of cult members. People don't vanish," she says again. "They turn up dead or move somewhere else and start over. None of us believe the original colonists went away forever in a blink. And this isn't hundreds of years ago. People have cell phones with GPS — nice work turning yours off, by the way. I should lock you in a —"

I interrupt before she can go further down that path. "What if they did?"

"Did what?"

"Went away forever in a blink. And what if the rest of the spirits are gone too?"

Mom doesn't say anything, but her expression tells me that she longs for the cigarettes she sent flying out the window. At this moment, I can't blame her.

MIRANDA

I stand in the medium-sized guest room Sara showed me
to. The walls are covered by shelves full of books with cracked
spines, and colorful pieces of art that obviously didn't come with
the frames. I'm trying hard not to think, and harder still not to
feel, but being alone is wearing down my defenses.

And it's only been five minutes.

I gave Sara and Grant both the impression I could use a little
time alone. That I was fine with staying here solo. But despite
their best efforts to make me feel like a welcome guest, I got
itchy levels of uncomfortable the second they left.

It isn't the house. Like the kitchen, the rest of it is cozy,
full of nice but worn-in things and lamps that cast warm glows
through pretty shades. But if I stay in this room I won't be able
to hold out. I won't be able to help it — the thinking and feeling
I desperately want to put off — and then I'll break down. I need
to *do* something.

An idea hits me. Well, not so much an idea as a fact — Grant's
room is on this floor, and there's no one else in the house.

It might be a bad idea, but hey, we're talking about someone who stole a car to come pay me a visit. I need to know more about him. Spying it is. So what if Grant hasn't lived here for years? It's a place to start. At the courthouse when he told me I could trust him, I believed him without understanding why. I put myself between him and his dad because of it. Was I right to believe?

I creep out into the hall, walking fast and keeping my footfalls soft, even though no one else is here. The first room I go into houses a nice sewing machine with scraps of fabric strewn around the workstation. A patchwork quilt that appears to be made entirely of old Bruce Springsteen T-shirts lies folded on the floor.

Sara must be a crafty type, like my mom was. Part of me wants to pretend this is my mom's craft room, that it's her who works at this sewing machine, that this is the life Dad and Mom and I have together.

But it's not. None of this coziness belongs to me. I have no family, not anymore. I nearly stop exploring then.

Don't break.

Instead I leave the sewing room and hurry down the hall. The door at the end of it calls out to me, mainly because of the Jolly Roger emblazoned across the center. The skull-and-crossbones sports a tacked-on set of Groucho Marx glasses. This has to be Grant's room.

I take a breath and listen for any noises, all the while reassuring myself they can't return this soon. Then I turn the knob and enter.

Jackpot.

The room even smells like Grant. A peppery clean scent. Wait — since when do I know what Grant Rawling smells like? I refocus on the task before me.

Grant's room is shockingly messy for a room that hasn't been lived in for three and a half years. Books and laundry are discarded across the entire space. A big duffel bag lies across the unmade bed, a vintage Ramones poster hanging over it.

His desk in the corner is covered with books, a wide variety. There's also an old iPod, earbuds still plugged in. Either he left it behind when he went away or he hooked it up as soon as he got up here, because it's even plugged into a charging strip.

I cross my fingers and snag the iPod. It'll give me something to listen to in the bath, something to shut out thoughts and feelings. I should have time to sneak back in here and put it away before he notices it's gone. Besides, Mom taught me that while eyes are important, music is the real window to someone's soul. Grant heard spirits talk about me, after all. I deserve some intel of my own.

I scamper back to the guest room, crossing into the bathroom and starting the tap. Then I change into the robe Sara loaned me, dump in the bath salts, and lean against the sink to wait for the tub to fill.

I thumb through the music on the iPod as the water runs. There are a lot of artists I've never heard of, but several that I like. Hozier, Neko Case, The National. I sort by favorites and stumble upon a playlist called North Carolina Stuff — The Rosebuds, the Bowerbirds, Ryan Adams. Maybe he did have this with him in Kentucky and listening to it was like a connection to home for him.

I pop in the earbuds, hit shuffle mode, and learn something else about Grant — he keeps the volume cranked *way* too loud. Jumping at the blare, I drop the iPod on the vanity.

I bend to retrieve it, and then look up, into the mirror. I'm not even really intending to look at myself. I just do. There's my tired face. My hair's frazzled. Dark circles linger beneath my eyes. In short, everything I expect to see.

Except for one thing.

A thin, strawberry-colored snake crawls along the top of my cheek toward my temple. Unmistakable. A birthmark, but it's not mine. It's Dad's.

I scream.

GRANT

Mom holds the door as I shimmy inside carrying a plastic laundry basket filled with Miranda's things. The house is dark and quiet. Has Miranda gone to bed already? It's getting late, and she has to be exhausted.

A confusing twinge of disappointment spikes through me. I dismiss it. *You're just helping her. You don't need to say good night to her.*

Mom must read my mind — she's way too good at that — because she clucks her tongue and closes the door. "We have to take her things up regardless, so just be quiet."

The thought of seeing Miranda asleep makes me uneasy in a different way, but I follow Mom to the staircase. The sound of running water meets us at the top of the steps. Mom looks over at me. "You wait out here."

"What? Oh." I stand in the hallway outside the guest room, balancing the basket. Waiting.

I hear Mom say, "Oh, honey." The water turns off, and an awful sound — gasping, keening, like death — rises up in its place.

It's Miranda.

I drop the basket and rush through the guest room to the bathroom. The water surges at the lip of the tub, sloshing onto the floor. It's not full enough to completely overflow, so *this* hasn't been going on that long.

This is Miranda in tears. I take one look at her in a fuzzy blue robe big enough to swallow her whole, rocking back and forth on the floor, heaving like waves in the ocean. Mom ineffectually pats her back and tries to lift her face, and I know.

This is heartbreak.

Miranda Blackwood, heartbroken, right in front of me.

I go to my knees in front of her and join Mom's tentative chorus of coos with words. "Miranda? We're here." I put my hand on her shoulder and say her name again, "Miranda?" I don't know how to get her to talk to me. "What can we do to help? You can trust me."

But if Miranda hears a word I say, she gives no sign of it. I've never felt this helpless in my life, and as spirit-magnet boy, that's saying something.

Mom stands. "You stay with her. I'll be right back. I'm going to get a glass of water."

I move to shift my hand to the side of Miranda's face, but my fingers tangle in the cord of earbuds. I blink at the iPod they're connected to. There's a gold-star sticker on the back. It's mine, my backup music source for those times phones aren't allowed at school.

"That's mine. Did you go in my room?" I ask.

Miranda rocks for another moment, then stops and tips her face toward me. Her green eyes are wide and bloodshot, her hair a mess falling forward around her cheeks.

I almost lose my breath, cliché though it is. In the years I've been away, Miranda has become, well, beautiful.

"Are you mad?" she says, through ragged breaths. "I just . . . borrowed them. I'm s-sorry."

I need to keep her talking. "Did you find anything else interesting in my room?"

She scowls.

Look at that backbone. Definitely beautiful.

She says, "Of course not. I was looking for some music. To listen to in the bath . . ."

"And my taste in music made you completely freak out?" I joke.

A flash of pain crosses her features, and for a moment I think I messed up and she's going to start howling again. I need to distract her.

"So, I get most of them," I say. "*Battlestar Galactica*, those old Joss Whedon shows, *Supernatural*, but . . . why do you own the first three seasons of *The Vampire Diaries*?"

Miranda blinks, but I can't tell if my diversion worked until she says, "You snooped in my room?"

I have her.

"I had to help pack your stuff." I wrinkle my nose. "You have a thing for brooding vampire brothers?"

She raises her eyebrows. "You've seen it?"

Keep her talking. I shrug. "The study lounge at my school has a TV. Doppelgangers are hot, and the dorm has a huge Team Damon contingent. I'm not proud."

"It went downhill after Elena left." She sniffs. "The town reminds me of this one. Repressed and . . . full of secrets. Everybody in everybody else's business." Her eyes widen. She's still scared. "Wait, where's Sidekick?"

"He's in the car — I'll go get him." But instead I stay where I am, crouched in front of her. "I brought that antique gun too. I stuck it in Mom's trunk when she wasn't looking. I didn't want to just leave it at your house. It must be valuable."

Miranda nods, and we stay where we are, silently, until I hear Mom's footsteps start up the stairs. She'll be back any second.

"Will you be okay alone while I go get Sidekick?" I ask.

Miranda blinks again and hesitates, and I see the exact moment when she decides to tell me something. What it is, I have no idea.

"This is why I'm freaking out," she says. She finally turns toward me and pushes her hair back, pointing to the top of her cheek.

It isn't that I memorized Miranda's face or anything like that, but I know in an instant that the birthmark doesn't belong. It's the snake I yelled at her about all those years ago. The flurry of the dead's voices was so intense that day I don't really remember what they said and barely what I repeated, but the snake part was loud and clear. The main reason I left school was because I couldn't stand the idea of listening to jerks taunt her with ammunition I gave them.

"Where did that come from?" I ask.

"I think it's my dad's," Miranda says, watching to see if I believe her. With everything that's happened, I do. "I need to see his body."

Just then I hear footsteps outside the bathroom, and Mom calls out, "Here's the water coming right up."

I quickly consider the options. "Say you're sad about your dad and go to bed. I'll come get you later."

"To go where?" Miranda asks, frowning.

"To see the body." I reach out as Mom crosses the threshold and pluck the glass of water from her hand. "Now drink this." I hold it to her lips to make sure she does.

If she needs to see the body, then my next move is decided. I promised to help her. I won't go back on that. So we're going to visit a dead man.

I'll just have to pray the rest of the dead aren't there waiting for me too.

MIRANDA

I'm convinced I'll never be able to get to sleep, not while I expect Grant to come in and wake me. Visions of drooling on my pillow dance in my head. I don't know if I snore or talk in my sleep or anything else embarrassing. No one has ever told me, but then, who would? Dad? Sidekick?

I pat his head where he lies sprawled next to me on top of the covers. Sara was nice enough to let him sleep in here with me, even though the Rawlings don't have any pets. I rub Sidekick's belly, glad to have him with me while I do my best not to obsess over the *thing* on my skin. . . . I feel myself growing drowsier and drowsier. . . .

When Grant shakes my shoulder, I can tell by the reluctance on his face he's been trying to wake me up for a while. "We can do this tomorrow," he says, the whisper apologetic, "if you need the sleep more. I just figured you'd want some privacy. If we go now no one else will be there."

I yawn, which sends Grant to his feet and scrambling a few steps back.

Okay, so I do look scary when I wake up.

I match his whisper. "You're right. I don't want anyone else there. But . . ." I climb out of the bed, already dressed in a T-shirt and jeans. "This means we're breaking in?"

"Don't worry about it," Grant says. "I've got experience."

The more I learn about Grant, the more of a mystery he becomes. "Why'd you start doing all that crime stuff?"

"Later. We'll wake up Mom," he says. "Let's go, sleep talker."

I thank the low light in the room for concealing the way my cheeks flame traitorously. *Don't ask what you said, don't ask what you said . . .*

"What'd I say?"

"Later," Grant repeats.

I slip on my sneakers. "What about Sidekick?" Whispering with Grant like this in the middle of the night is kind of fun, like a secret mission or a conspiracy. Then I remember why we're doing it, and any hint of fun disappears.

Grant asks, "He'll be quiet if he stays here?"

I lean in to pat his head. "Stay," I tell him, half wishing I could crawl back into bed beside him and forget about doing this. But I have to know the truth.

Grant reaches over and touches my cheek. I manage not to flinch, but it's a surprise. And then, for a second, I let him comfort me. "It'll be okay," he says.

"Good lie."

He drops his hand and motions for me to tiptoe out of the room in front of him. Once we're both through, he pulls the door silently closed behind us. He takes the lead on the steps, and I follow his path exactly. Not a creak sounds on our way down and out the front door.

The night is dark and warm as Grant leads me across the yard, then past its borders. I discover he's already moved his mom's car to a spot up the road. The noise of the car starting will be at most a distant cough from the house. Clearly he knows more about sneaking out than I do.

Once we're settled in, Grant cues up a playlist and puts the car in drive. I say, "You're crazy good at this, Double-O Seven. Why?"

He doesn't answer, just taps his fingers along to the song that's playing. The lyrics are something about a guy being hand-cuffed to a fence in Mississippi. Finally, he says, "I wanted to get sent away."

"Oh. Why?"

"Because I couldn't stand it here."

We're passing a spot where the sound becomes visible. The water sparkles in the moonlight. "I get it," I say. "Small town. Everybody always in everybody else's business." *Stop talking.* "I was jealous that you got out of here. Got to go somewhere no one knew you."

"When nobody knows you, you miss out on things," Grant says, though he doesn't sound like he fully believes it. "You miss getting to know who the people around you are. That's a lonely way to live." That he sounds like he believes.

I'm already the definition of loneliness. Alone. Lonely. I reach up and touch the trespassing birthmark on my cheek.

"Well, there are worse things than being alone," I say, though I'm not sure if *I* fully believe that. "Hey, why do you know so much random stuff like matchlocks and music and ahem, *The Vampire Diaries?*"

For a long moment Grant doesn't answer, instead focus-ing on pulling the sedan up to the curb so the weepy hanging branches of a big tree offer us cover. Not that there's anyone else on the street to see us. Then he turns off the car and looks over at me. His eyes are a black gleam in the barely existent light.

"I had too much I didn't want in my head. I thought maybe if I . . ." he stops, obviously searching.

"If you filled it with other stuff it would crowd out the bad," I supply. It makes a strange kind of sense to me. It's not that different from how I fill my downtime with stories about places far away from here. "Did it work?"

He flashes a smile. I pretend not to notice the fluttery way I feel, like a complete silly girl. This is probably how that dumb reporter, Blue Doe, feels all the time, light and airy, like her head's a bubble and might float away in a cloud of fizz.

"I don't know yet," he says. "Let's go."

"Where?"

"Next street over." He hops out and is around the car and at the passenger door, opening it for me before I can move.

When I get out, I plant my feet on the pavement. "That's the funeral home." I'm confused, and I don't want to go there. "I can't afford a funeral. And who would come?"

"I'd come," he says, which is sweet. "But no, they won't have one unless you want it. This isn't New York — we don't have a real morgue here, just the funeral home our county medical examiner runs. They'll be storing the . . . your dad's body will be in the cold room here until they can get it carted off to one of the universities for the autopsy."

"How do you know this?" I shake my head.

"Police chief's son, remember?"

That hardly explains it, but I nod. "Let's go then," I say as my stomach hardens into a small, heavy stone. The funeral home. I stay quiet while we walk there, and Grant doesn't push me to talk, so quiet must be required, even though the houses we pass seem empty, like so many people's lives on the island right now.

The funeral home's front porch comes into view. It's where the men and the smokers hang out during the big town social events that occur whenever someone even moderately well liked or well-known dies. Funeral visitations are like church — a chance to see and be seen — without all the pressure to be godly that comes along with sermons.

A flood of images rushes over me from Mom's funeral, the people who showed up with whispers and fake sympathy for Dad and me. People who did nothing but gossip for years about why that nice Anna-Marie Johnson — even if she was an out-of-towner, with no family of her own to speak of — went and married a Blackwood. And how her girl, that Miranda, would never amount to anything now.

"Miranda?" Grant whispers, turning to see why I stopped. Until then, I didn't know I had. "You okay?"

I draw in a shaky breath, pushing away the memories as best I can, and catch up with him. "How do we get in?" I ask, careful to keep my expression blank.

"Around back," he says, frowning at me in concern.

"I'm fine." *Just take my word for it. Please.*

He does, and we head around to the rear entrance without another word. When we stop again, the wrinkles of that frown are still etched on his forehead. They vanish as he removes a long skinny piece of metal from his pocket.

"Where do you get something like that?" I ask.

"A lock pick? eBay."

I trust him, or I'm starting to anyway, but still. "What if someone's here? Maybe I should just wait until tomorrow."

Grant steps back off the sidewalk and into the parking lot, so the whole back of the funeral home is visible. I go along, curious. He points to the upstairs. "When Marlon is here, the TV in that room is always on. See how dark it is?"

I nod, and he hesitates. "What else?" I prod.

"I checked the obits for the last week online — there's no one in the funeral home for embalming or viewing, just your dad. And Marlon's wife is one of the missing. He's at their house. Not here."

"Okay," I say.

Grant hesitates, watching me. "But we don't have to do this. Not if you don't want to."

If I balk at this point, I'll have to explain the reason — that I'm afraid now that we're here, I'll be right. That I'm afraid of what seeing Dad will be like, of how it will hurt. I'd rather get this over with than explain all that. I touch my cheek. "No, I need to see him."

Grant gets to work with the tool he brought and has the door open within a minute. He pulls a flashlight out of his other pocket and shines it up the hallway in front of them. I see the powder blue walls, worn navy carpet, framed seascapes lining the walls. Another wave of memories threatens to overwhelm me as I walk inside and inhale that too-clean smell, the scent of tragedy being covered up, a smell that pretends this is somewhere besides the house where death lives. That this is somewhere besides a place that means your life is a ruin.

We make our way up the hall and through a small kitchenette where I hear unfortunate scuttling. Grant unlocks another door, and we pass into a hallway, the beam from the flashlight tunneling through absolute darkness. I can't help imagining that we're traveling to the underworld. With each step, the floor creaks. I'm comforted by the fact Grant doesn't know this place well enough to avoid the noisy ones.

At the end of the dark hall, he opens a heavier door and lets me go in first, then joins me and flips on a light. The suddenly bright room is cold and reeks of formaldehyde. The flat black sheen of a body bag dominates the center of a metal table. I approach it like I'm levitating, unable to feel my feet moving, but getting closer just the same.

"It's freezing down here," I say.

"Actually," Grant says, "it's thirty-nine point two degrees. Not freezing."

I stop at the side of the table. "Shouldn't it be freezing?"

"Freezing would be ideal, but this is a funeral home, not CSI. The cold still majorly slows decomposition." Grant swings around to the other side of the table and checks the surfaces nearby for something, then holds up a thin file folder and flips through it.

I stare at the black plastic, preparing myself for what's inside. Like that's possible.

Dad. I'm so sorry. I shouldn't have let you go alone. I should have driven you. I should have . . .

Grant makes a noise of interest, interrupting my silent apology, and says, "You want to know what the preliminary ME report says?"

I manage to look away from the shape of my father's body beneath that plastic and at Grant. The kindness in his face startles me. "What does it say?" I choke out.

"It appears . . ." He pauses, takes a look at me and, when I nod, goes on. "It appears that all the visually observable bones in your father's body were broken at the time of death. But that he had no outward signs of struggle or harm. No

bruising or cuts. And his blood alcohol level was nearly point one-eight."

I dismiss the BAC off the bat. "That's a baseline." What I don't understand are the broken bones. How is that possible?

"The bones must be why Dad said they couldn't determine cause of death," Grant says.

I focus my attention back on the body bag and concentrate on breathing.

"Do you want me to look for you?" Grant asks softly. "I can describe him."

I have to see for myself. "No."

Grant holds out a small pot of something. "You should at least put some of this under your nose."

I ignore him. Instead I reach forward and fumble with the zipper until it begins to slide open. I stop when the metal teeth get hung up at the waist and pull back the sides to reveal my father's head. I forget to try to breathe. The air leaves my body.

Dad looks better dead than he did alive. The broken bones mentioned in the report aren't visible, not even in his face, which is odd given the description. His eyes are closed — a mercy I thank the funeral director for — so all I have to do is lean over and check.

I put my hand up to my mouth, even though I see exactly what I expected to. The skin of my father's upper cheek gleams at me, clear as polished glass, as smooth as stone, as bleached as bone.

The snake that's now on *my* face? Yeah, it's definitely Dad's.

I don't know what to do except run. And so that's what I do.

My feet thump against the floor as I go, back through the door and into the hall, my body hitting the walls as I keep moving, blood roaring in my ears, getting out of there, getting away from the smell and the body and the house where death lives.

I burst through the door, and the warm night air hits my skin like an electric shock.

You have nowhere to run, I think, and it stops me in my tracks. I have nowhere to go.

GRANT

I want to go after Miranda, but first I have to put back the file and seal up the body bag. Marlon James might not be here, but he isn't a sloppy man. He'll notice if things are disturbed, and given how freaked everyone is about the disappearances, even the most harmless change risks being misinterpreted.

I reach over Mr. Blackwood's chest to close the bag, holding my breath against what's surely a god-awful smell. The zipper fights me the same way it did Miranda, and I have to release my breath while I work on it.

I wait for the stench to invade . . . but there isn't any. Only the sickly smell of formaldehyde's chemical perfume. That's strange. This close, I notice something else strange — Mr. Blackwood's body, pale and perfect, despite all those supposed-to-be broken bones and the lack of embalming fluid to keep the skin from bloating and puffing and discoloring.

I take a handkerchief from my pocket — one of my dad's, a handy tool for breaking and entering — and press my hand across the dead man's cheek.

I have never touched a dead body before — have only ever been in the room with three, two of them relatives. I would rather do just about anything else.

The cheekbone is not broken. I check the right collarbone next.

It's perfectly straight and intact. *Huh.*

I consider doing a more thorough exam, but I've lingered down here too long already, and the thought of it makes me shiver and lose my nerve. I take the zipper and begin to reseal the body bag. I pause when I get to the neck, thinking about the reek of beer on him that night he came to our house years ago. That wasn't unusual according to the conversation I overheard between Mom and Dad.

"You should have been better for her," I tell Mr. Blackwood's body and then finish the job.

I toss the white cloth into a step trash can with a biohazard symbol on top and turn out the lights. I hope Miranda hasn't gone far.

Luck is with me. She sits next to the back door, staring out at the parking lot. She's not crying. That's good, at least. I scoot down the wall to join her, and without thinking, place my hand on top of hers, where it rests on her thigh. She doesn't move, so neither do I.

"Miranda, I'm sorry."

"What do you have to be sorry about?" Before I can answer, she says, "Nothing. You've been nothing but nice to me. I mean, except for that one time. And that was a long time ago. It's not your fault I'm cursed."

I hear the echoing words from the cemetery: *Curse-bearer, curse-born child.* "You're *not* cursed," I say to block them out.

Miranda lifts her free hand and brushes her hair back to reveal the angry snake crawling up her cheek. "Then what's this? What else makes a birthmark jump from one body to another?"

"I don't know," I say. What makes spirits to talk to me? "But we'll figure it out. I'm sorry about . . . bringing you here. I didn't even think about your mom. Her funeral was here, wasn't it?"

"That was a long time ago too." Her words slip out. "That's not even the worst part."

"I'm almost afraid to ask."

She turns to face me. She's so close I can see the green of her eyes, even in the dark. "I was supposed to take care of him," she says.

"You keep saying that, but it's not true."

"Yes, it is. My mom wanted me to — it was like I could practically *feel* her over my shoulder in there, disapproving. *I* was the one left to look out for him. And I . . . I didn't do a good enough job. Maybe I deserve this . . . being alone."

"He was supposed to take care of *you*. And" — I beat her protest — "your mother wasn't in there."

Her eyelashes cast shadows on her pale cheeks. "How do you know?"

I close my eyes for a moment, finding it hard to believe I'm about to openly talk about this with someone besides my mom. I know I told Miranda way back when, inadvertently, but that's different. The spirits are my weakness.

And so, apparently, is Miranda Blackwood.

"I would have known," I say. "There aren't any spirits on Roanoke Island right now as far as I can tell. Or they're hidden somehow. Usually, it's impossible for me to *not* hear spirits here. Usually, they're everywhere, saying everything. All the time. And now . . . nothing."

I can't bring myself to tell her about the voice I *did* hear, the one at the cemetery. I'm not putting that on her right now. That's mine to deal with.

I watch Miranda's reaction, wondering if she's going to think I'm crazy.

She gives me a suspicious look and asks the last thing I expect: "How did you know about the funeral home stuff? About Marlon's TV? If spirits didn't tell you?"

"You think that was . . ." I squint at her. "Not a bad guess. But no, the spirits aren't helpful when it comes to aiding and abetting crime as far as I can tell. Don't you remember the Bela prank?"

She shakes her head, looking curious instead of so lost. I release her hand and put mine over my heart as if she mortally wounded me. "You weren't a fan? Not even a little bit?"

"Of what?" A slight smile edges her lips up on one side.

"My criminal masterpieces — the things that got me sent away? During my brief Bauhaus-wannabe goth phase at thirteen, I broke in here and lettered the sign with the viewing times for Bela Lugosi."

"You are the weirdest person I've ever met."

I make a little bow. "Finally, you're beginning to appreciate my genius."

She laughs, but it doesn't take long for the weight to visibly sink down on her again. Her shoulders actually fall with it. I'm done with letting her do that to herself.

"No," I say.

"What?"

I pick up a stray piece of gravel off the sidewalk and toss it toward the parking lot. "This isn't you. This defeatist *oh, I'm so cursed, woe is me* stuff."

"How would you know?" she asks, mouth hanging open.

I don't care if I've gone too far. I'm right. "I just know. The girl I met in eighth grade was stronger than this. She wouldn't let some birthmark break her."

"I'm not broken . . ." But she lets it trail off. She gets up, and I worry she'll run away again.

"You're right," she says, her hands balling into fists. "I'm being one of those silly girls in distress. Frak."

I get up, loving her *Battlestar Galactica* cursing. I looked up the reference while I was waiting to wake her. "So what are you going to do?" I ask.

"I'm going to find out what happened to my dad. And get this stupid snake off my face. It's ruining my looks," she says with acid-tinged humor.

I simply look at her. "No, it's not."

"What?" The rage in her breaks and turns into a grin. The transformation is as unexpected for her as it is for me. I can tell by the wondering tone of the question.

"It's not." I almost take the last step toward her, even though I know this would be an insane time to kiss someone. We barely know each other. I'm supposed to be helping her.

But I want to.

At least until the sound of a siren in the distance interrupts. *Time to go.*

"We'd better get out of here," I say.

"Does that mean you'll help me?" she asks.

"I already am."

*

Back in my yard, I hold Miranda's hand as she stays close to my side.

The shadows thrown by the trees in the security light — thankfully not motion-activated, or I'd have to climb it and take care of that — poke around us like the long fingers of invisible people. The house remains dark and quiet, and I relax a little.

I was concerned about leaving Miranda's dog behind. Even an obedient dog, happy to be somewhere soft and warm, is capable of whining and waking parents.

We climb the steps up onto the porch, and I stop in front of the door to look at her one last time before getting some sleep. It feels earned, a reward for a successful outing.

Miranda whispers, "Did we really make it?"

The question strikes me as belonging to someone who has never tried to get away with much. I'm still thinking about kissing her, but I'm wondering if that's something she wants me to do now or *ever* . . . I don't want to be another problem for her. She's had enough for a lifetime.

"We did." I smile. "I never get caught."

She rolls her eyes, as she should. "You mean you *always* get caught."

"I was trying to back then."

She rolls them again.

I decide to press my luck. "Good night," I say, leaning forward . . .

The porch light flares to life and sends us both stumbling back like vampires at daybreak.

"Oh God," Miranda says, miserable.

"Don't worry, I'll take the blame," I assure her.

"But I like your mom and now —"

"I'll handle it." I put a hand on her arm and open the screen door. "It's not my mom. She doesn't do dramatic."

Her expression makes it clear she's not convinced *which* parent it is makes a difference, but when I hold the door open she walks through it. I want to tell her it'll work out, that things have been worse, but I can't.

Dad looms in the front hallway next to the light switch. The night-black circles that ring his eyes give even me a second's pause.

Miranda's head tilts down in the universal posture of shame, her feet rooted to the floral carpet. Given what she told me earlier about having to look out for her dad, combined with that question outside, I'd bet anything she's never been in serious trouble. Being engaged in a serious life isn't the same thing.

"Miranda, I need to speak with my son," Dad says finally. Better than what he'd say if it was just me.

"It's my fault. I asked —" Miranda starts to say.

"It's okay," I interrupt. "You don't have to take the blame. It was my idea. Go get some sleep."

With a guilty glance at Dad, Miranda flies up the steps. I hear twin clicks as the guestroom door opens and then closes.

"Where were you?" Dad asks.

I shrug. "Out."

"Do we have to do this, son?" His tone is close to exasperation, the dark circles like a lost fight.

I walk closer. We're the same height. That's new. I can't let him see vulnerability. That's not how we communicate. So I ask, "Do you have to be such a drama king? You couldn't have waited five minutes?"

Without a word, Dad goes to the darkened living room, where he sits on the couch. I follow and note the bottle of whiskey and short — empty — glass on the table. Dad's been drinking. That is also new.

103

I ease into a chair opposite him, trying my best for a relaxed air. The only light is filtered through the curtains and comes from the security pole outside. I imagine this as a dingy prison, with Dad playing interrogator. It's a scene both of us know well.

"Have the feds showed yet?" I ask.

Dad's head comes up. "A few hours ago. To assist, not to take over — yet."

I know he must loathe the thought of the FBI taking over an investigation that directly impacts people under his jurisdiction. I can't blame him. He cares about the job. I can't say that, either, though.

"It is a missing person's case," I say.

"Is it? I don't know, Grant." Dad sighs. "Listen, I know I haven't ever wanted to talk about this before, but . . ."

"I know about the birds and the bees, Dad. Also, about sex." I just want him to drop it, let me go to bed. "I've been at boarding school in Kentucky, not a monastery."

"I don't care about that — not right now." Dad pauses. "Except that you not hurt that girl any more than she's already been hurt."

He waits for my response, and I nod. "I don't plan to."

"That's fine, but plans can go sideways. We need to talk about you — your gifts. I know my mother had them too. I tried like hell to pretend she didn't, but it wasn't hard to miss the stream of women who showed up at our back door so she could talk to their dead. I didn't want that for you."

"But you want it now?" Anger rises. He never wanted to talk about this when the spirits were everywhere, assaulting my every sense.

"I want to find these people and get them home. This whole town . . . an emptiness like the one that's here, it will kill us all. It'll kill this island."

Normally I'd tell him to shove it. I don't have any love for the town. Or any hate for it, really — except when it comes to the way too many people here have treated Miranda, and she's in this up to her temple. "There's nothing right now, but I'll work on it tomorrow. I'm going to be helping Miranda" — I hold up my hand to cover Dad's protest — "find some answers. Those answers are the same ones you need. I think."

"So you have some idea of what's going on here?"

"No clue. But I'm going to find out. If I don't, Miranda's the next to go. Or something bad will happen to her. I don't know what, exactly, but something."

Dad leans forward and pours a drink, then downs it in one shot. He has on his cop face, thoughtful. "Her old man didn't vanish, he died. He was killed. A mystery in itself, since he was a sad drunk. Not hurting anybody but himself. Harmless. But he didn't vanish."

Not harmless to Miranda. "I told you I don't know how, but I think it's connected. Get the autopsy done on him as fast as you can."

Dad shakes his head. "The university can't do it until Monday."

"Use the feds, then. They might as well be useful since they're here. Convince them somehow. You need to know what killed him."

I wait to see if Dad will listen to me for once. Trust me. Finally, slowly, he nods.

"There's one more thing. Mom . . . your gram . . . when she died, she left a letter for you. I was supposed to give it to you. But I kept it."

Dad holds something out to me. It's a cream envelope, Gram's stationary with her initials on the front. The envelope is wrinkled, like it's been worried over.

I don't want to take it. It's been so quiet. I need to keep my head clear.

Dad holds it closer to me. "Your mom doesn't know about this, but I guess now I'll have to tell her. I didn't want this for you, but I don't think I have a choice anymore."

I don't have a choice either. I take the letter, halfway expecting a lightning strike. But the earth doesn't move, the voices don't clamor in my ears. There are no sudden shadows. My name is written across the back in Gram's small, neat handwriting. I put the envelope in my pocket.

Dad knows better than to expect me to read it in front of him. He probably doesn't even want me to.

"You'll let me know anything important?" he asks.

"Of course." If I have to.

"Go get some sleep."

I almost leap to my feet. Dad has never talked to me like this, almost like we're equals. Like he doesn't blame me for hearing the spirits of Roanoke Island.

"Don't think I'm not going to tell your mother what you were doing out there," he says. "Don't hurt that girl. I mean it. She's been through enough."

Which, of course, ruins it.

MIRANDA

I bolt back up to the guest room and press the door quietly closed before Grant busts me on his way upstairs. I already knew he thought my family was connected to the disappearances, but hearing him tell his dad is different.

He really does want to help me. And he thinks I'm the next to go. But go where? Where are the vanished people?

I close my eyes. The only place I *want* to go is the one place I can't — off the island. Blackness waits inside my eyelids. The snake crawling toward my temple throbs.

I'm so tired.

I pull off my jeans and slide into bed next to Sidekick. I consider that moment on the porch. I don't know much about this stuff, but I'm pretty sure that Grant was about to kiss me. Until the porch light and his dad . . .

I groan and pull the covers over my head. How will I face Sara? Sara, who invited me to stay in this nice house, who offered me turkey sandwiches and a bubble bath?

When I close my eyes, Dad's too-pale face swims before me. So instead I study the ceiling, which is painted the pale blue of a spring sky. I remember Grant's reassurance that Mom wasn't watching, but the truth is more complicated — I want her watching. Imagining her watching over me has always made everything hard just a little bit easier.

I roll onto my side and close my eyes. I wait until Dad's face fades, and when it's gone, it leaves behind only darkness.

*

Despite the need to get moving and find a way out of the whole being doomed situation, I linger as long as humanly possible in the guest room the next morning.

I let Sidekick out the bedroom door, knowing Sara or someone would give him backyard access. And I finally managed that bath. Afterward, I paced the guest room. When I got sick of pacing, I picked a random book out from a shelf in the corner and started reading.

The book, *The Haunting of Hill House,* unsurprisingly involves an old house that's supposed to be full of angry ghosts. When the sense of dread in the book begins to mix with the one hovering around me like an aura, I toss it aside and check the clock.

Ten a.m.

Sigh. At least the chief is probably long gone by now. I straighten my T-shirt, and leave the room.

I almost miss the single flower waiting on the floor outside the bedroom door. It's a perfectly formed rose made of . . . duct tape. Intricate silver folds shoot up in a spray of triangular points to form the bloom, and tear-shaped leaves drop from the thick stem.

I pick the unreal flower up and twirl it. I'm feeling a lot better about facing Sara's disapproval if Grant isn't going to be a cliché guy and ignore last night's almost kiss. That's what I feared, mainly because the only guys I know are jerks — witness Bone.

I slip the rose stem through a loop on the waistband of my jeans. The motion reminds me of sliding a hammer into place on my tool belt at the theater. Concern spikes through me for the people at the show — even His Royal Majesty and demon Caroline. And, of course, Polly. Missing Polly.

The smell of frying food tempts me the rest of the way down the stairs and into the kitchen. Sara stands at the stove, transferring crisp slices of bacon onto a plate covered with a paper towel. Sidekick stares up at her with love. His tail thuds against the cabinet, and he watches her every move with great hope. A heap of scrambled eggs wait on another plate.

I hesitate in the entry. "Should I set the table?"

Sara's head whips toward me, startled. I can't stop a cringe as I wait to see whether I'm in for cold distance or a heated talking-to. I'm sure she's of the opinion a Blackwood isn't good enough for her son, and she's probably right.

But Sara gives me a non-angry, motherly smile. "Why doesn't my son ever make that offer? That'd be great." She waves her spatula. "Plates are right up there, silverware in that drawer. Just the three of us."

I take out several butter yellow plates and pick out some silverware. They're matching sets. A novelty.

Sara cranes her neck and yells, "Grant, breakfast!" No response, until she adds, "Grant — I know you can hear me. Oh, and Miranda is already down here."

Feet batter the steps in a fast drumbeat, and seconds later Grant swings around the edge of the arch. I finish the last place setting and select a chair. I hold up the rose and give him a nod, then place it awkwardly on the table next to my plate.

Why did I do that? I'm such a moron.

But the weirdest thing happens. I could swear Grant looks slightly embarrassed.

He moves in close enough to the counter to grab a piece of bacon and hands me half as he sits in the chair next to mine.

Never before has bacon seemed romantic. But, right now, it kinda does. I am keenly aware of my utter ridiculousness.

Sara joins us and sets the plates of food in the center of the table. She raises her eyebrows at the fake rose, but doesn't ask about it. Snapping her fingers, she says, "Biscuits," before turning and attending to the oven.

Grant lowers his voice and says to me, "It's a steampunk rose — I didn't make it, bought it from another delinquent at school. I was going to give it to Mom next time she came to visit. But . . . I had it with me, and I thought maybe you'd like it."

I have to say *something*. "Well, um, thanks for giving it to me. It's beautiful. And it'll last forever."

"Yes, it will." He smiles at me, and I wish with everything inside of me that the snake would disappear, and I could live in a normal world with this strange boy who — for some reason — has decided he likes me.

I crunch my bacon and take in the fluffy, golden tops of the biscuits Sara carries to the table. They look like someone who grew up around here made them. I reached over and take one as Sara sets the plate at the table.

"Where'd you learn to make actual biscuits?" I ask.

The question brings a strange stillness over the sunny kitchen, and Sara gives Grant a look before answering. "The recipe is Grant's grandmother's," she finally says. "She taught me before she passed away."

The Witch of Roanoke Island. I'm desperate to ask about her, given what Grant has told me about the spirits and the conversation I overheard with his father last night.

"I never met her," I say instead. After Mom died, I sometimes fantasized about the Witch of Roanoke Island becoming my defender. Giving the jerks at school boils if they taunted me, or passing me a magical potion that made me normal. Broke the Blackwood curse. I reach up and touch my father's birthmark. Sara doesn't seem to notice it, which makes me feel a little better.

If only I could forget it's there.

"She was a strong woman," Sara says, again watching Grant. He doesn't react except to keep chewing his eggs. "She couldn't stand the thought of someone living here who couldn't make her son and grandson the right kind of biscuits. The house has been in the family for generations, but it's always passed down to the daughters before. Biscuits are part of its legacy."

I can't remember if the chief has any sisters or brothers. "Why not this time?"

"She only had a son — there'd always been a girl child in the family line, as far back as anyone remembered. And they'd always lived well into their nineties, active right up to till the end."

Grant stops eating, but he doesn't interrupt.

"Technically," Sara says, "the house belongs to Grant. His grandmother felt strongly it should be his. That this was the place he was meant to be. We don't really know why. We only know the island's not good for him." I realize Sara is fishing. *She wants to know what the letter from his grandmother said.*

Grant says, "Mom," but she goes on.

"He and his father are both tied to this place, in different ways. I don't think I can fully understand. I never had that. My roots moved when I did. My roots are my family."

Grant's hands land on the table on either side of his plate, and he gets up. "We really should get going." He casts a pleading glance at me and adds, "Unless you aren't finished eating?"

My plate is still half full, but I owe him. If he wants me to stave off awkwardness, I'll do it. "Sure, let's go." I grab a biscuit. "Thank you for breakfast." *And for the bits of info.* "Should we take Sidekick? Is he trouble?"

Sidekick gazes at Sara as if she might drop a crumb or a piece of bacon on his head. She scratches behind his ear, and he leans into her fingers with a good-dog groan.

"You guys go on, do your investigating," she says. "We'll make do. But be careful. Grant, we'll talk later."

I don't realize until Grant steers me through the front door with his hand on my back that he hasn't given any hint of where we're headed in such a hurry.

"Where are we going?" I ask. "Your dad's work?"

"Dr. Whitson's place."

The name means nothing to me. "Who?"

"You know, local expert on all theories Lost Colony. Looks like a professor?"

No way. There's only one guy like that in town — Bone's dad — but I've never called him by his real name. In my mind he's always been Dr. Roswell since I assume he probably believes in alien abductions too. After all, he seems to believe in everything else conspiracy theory-like.

I stop on the steps down to the yard. The day is cooler than the one before, a promise of fall dressed in late summer colors, and a strong breeze wraps around me. The breeze isn't unusual — there's always a breeze, whirling in from the outer islands and the ocean, flying across the salt-free sound. But this wind doesn't come from the ocean. It seems to come from somewhere else and now dances around us, the whole island in its cooler embrace.

Of course it comes from the ocean, I scold myself. *Where else would it come from?*

An image flickers in my mind of that enormous black ship on the horizon, moving fast toward the island, sails filled with uncanny billowing speed on a windless day. I shake my head to clear it from my thoughts.

I choose my next words carefully. "I need help, not a kook."

"Dr. Whitson was my shrink. He knows more about the island's history than anyone around, and we're in kooksville here. We need a kook's perspective."

I sigh. I have no real feelings about Roswell one way or the other — other than him being Bone's dad. He's just a local weirdo I mostly avoid.

"Fine," I say. "He'll probably think aliens murdered my dad." Grant takes my hand and tugs, and in that moment, I know I'll go anywhere he suggests. "But do you mind if we swing by and pick up Pineapple? I miss her."

"Pineapple?" Grant asks.

"Oh, my car. I named her." I'll get to see how Grant reacts to the tangible, mean-spirited reminder of my status here when he catches sight of the graffiti on Pineapple's side. Not to mention confirming Bone's the culprit behind *FREAK* when I see his reaction to my car at his house.

Grant hesitates, but not for long. "Sure."

My hand warms in his as we walk to his mom's car. It's as weird a sensation as the rest of this, having someone on my side. But I suspect this day has something in store for us that will wreck the fragile connection between us.

I ache in advance. Because sure as the ghosts in Hill House, that something is coming. The speaking breeze tells me that.

GRANT

When we get to Miranda's house, I park, then follow her over to where her little yellow car sits beside the curb. I figure I'll stand in the grass and wait to see if it starts. It's not until I step over the curb that I see the word *FREAK* scrawled along the driver's side.

Miranda ignores it and gets in. Which I take it means that the word's presence isn't a surprise to her. But . . . who did this?

I frown. Miranda was quiet on the way here, and I let her be. I had plenty to think about. Sure, my last-second gift of the rose went over well — I wanted to do something to let her know that I regretted Dad's interruption the night before. I don't want things to be weird between us. I want them to be good. But there's been some distance post-breakfast. She's not happy about going to Dr. Whitson's, that much is clear. I wonder if coming here to get her car was a test of some sort, to see how I'd deal with the *FREAK*.

The engine sputters on Miranda's first try at starting it. She makes another attempt, and this time the old yellow beast roar-coughs to life. She rolls down her window. "Get in."

I shake my head and walk around to the passenger side. "Who's responsible for the graffiti?" I ask, climbing inside and dropping the keys to Mom's car next to my feet. I'm careful with the question's tone, not wanting to make a bigger deal of it than she is, despite my anger at the word's presence. If this *is* a test, I hope I pass. "Should we hit a car wash?"

"Don't worry about it," she says.

I can't mistake the sudden prickliness of her tone.

She goes on. "Part of the price of being me. There's no a/c, so you might want to put your window down. And give me some directions."

I open my mouth, but then close it again. I crank down my window.

"Where are we going?" Miranda asks, putting the car in drive.

"Wanchese," I say. "That's where Whitson's place is."

At the end of the street she turns out onto the highway, heading for the far side of the island. "Why does he live all the way out there? Do you know?" she asks, cutting me a look.

I'm not watching the scenery, so I catch it. I lean against the door, angled in toward her. The snake is on the other side of her face, hidden for the moment.

"I never asked him. It's probably cheaper out there?" I reach a hand over to brush a hair off her cheek, and she hiccups the wheel. I laugh in an attempt to break the tension in the car. "Am I making you nervous? What's wrong?"

"It's not just you." At least her voice softens a little.

"Good," I say, keeping my tone light. Then, "Not good that you're nervous, good that I'm not why. Whitson's okay, I swear. Is that all you're worried about?"

"If you vouch for him I guess it's fine." But her fingers tighten on the wheel.

Maybe there's more to her dislike of Whitson than I thought. I assume he's harmless, but . . . "Has the doc done something I should know —"

"So did you know your grandmother that well, Mr. Homeowner?" she interrupts.

I have whiplash from the extreme subject change. I can't read her behavior. Should I tell her about Gram's letter? No, that might make things worse. Instead I turn in the passenger seat to look out the window at the green forest.

"Not that well. My dad always made sure we had limited time together. He didn't want her teaching me . . . stuff."

"Did you want her to . . . teach you stuff?"

I exhale. "No, we never had the chance. I was normal until she died. After . . . I only wanted it to go away. To go somewhere so I could be normal."

"That would be nice," she says. "Being normal."

"That's not what I —" I tap my fingers against the door, a repetitive pattern. It's something I do to calm myself sometimes. "You are normal."

"Just what every girl wants to hear."

I want to break into the silence that follows, but I'm afraid I'll say the wrong thing. Again.

Wanchese isn't that long a drive — even the far side of the island isn't actually that far — but it may as well be a world away. Unlike the tourist haven of Manteo, Wanchese possesses a wilder feel. Despite having a couple of bed and breakfasts, a few boat rental places, and a harbor packed with commercial fishing vessels, this isn't where the big money is — it's where the fishing village is. There is no picture-prettified downtown to echo Manteo's, not even a Main Street. Most of the locals here hope to remain lost to the tourist flood by keeping a firm hold on this tip of the island. It's the perfect place to live if you don't want to be bothered.

"Turn here," I prompt Miranda, pointing to a familiar road ahead that shoots through trees. She obeys, and a short way into the woods, we come to a small rise with a nice cottage on top. Whitson's place.

"That it," I say.

Not for the first time, I think the house must have been originally intended for a timeshare. The sandy paint has faded over time, though, and now the place looks more like a home than a getaway. There's a pickup truck occupying the driveway. That's new, and I have a hard time picturing Dr. Whitson behind the wheel.

"I figured," Miranda mutters. She puts Pineapple in park at the side of the road in front of the cottage.

"Huh?" I ask.

"Never mind," she says.

I climb out of the car, only to realize that she's not following. *What is going on with her?* I poke my head back in after a moment's deliberation. "You coming?" I ask.

"Against my better judgment," she mutters. Her car's motor dies with a rattle of agreement.

I get out and walk toward the cottage. A deck at the back stretches into the woods, the edge of the railing just visible. I stop at the front door, and, once again, realize I'm alone. I turn and call, "Miranda?"

She's still waiting beside her car but finally starts in my direction. The door swings open as she reaches my side, before I can ask if she'd rather not do this, and a skinny boy with hollow cheeks opens the door. He's wearing a light blue Tarheels shirt and exhales in surprise when he spots Miranda.

"If you're here to try to get me in trouble, I didn't have anything to do with your car," the boy says. "So forget it."

Wait a second. I shoot Miranda a questioning look. "Did he —"

"Forgotten," she says, not to me but to the boy in the doorway. "I know it was you, but we're here to see your dad." The boy's mouth opens to say something else, and Miranda sighs. "Not about you, Bone. About something else."

Miranda looks over at me, and I shake my head at her. I can't believe this loser did that to her car. She should have told me. I was right about the test.

I turn back to the door. What did she call him? Bone. Right. "You must be the Boner," I say.

"Just Bone," Bone says, gritting his teeth.

I bite back a smile. "Where's your dad?"

"In the library," Bone says, still suspicious.

"You could wash Miranda's car while we're talking to him," I suggest, not making it sound like a suggestion.

Bone snorts and steps out onto the welcome mat. I'm not a brawler, but I'm also not afraid of this jackhole.

"I didn't have anything to do with it," Bone says. "I already told you."

Am I imagining it, or is he actually nervous? We're far out in the woods, but, *come on.* His dad is home.

"Are you scared?" I ask.

Bone straightens. "Scared that bad luck just showed up at my doorstep." He turns to Miranda. "Interrupt any shows lately?" he adds.

Miranda opens her mouth, and though I don't catch Bone's meaning, I can see the sting of his comment on her face. I've officially had enough of him insulting her.

I nudge Miranda around Bone and through the door with my shoulder. I move fast behind her, shooting my hand back to slam the door and lock it. With Bone still standing outside.

"I don't want to be in the same house as the broken Bone," I say. "What a dick." I idly worry that Bone will do something else to Miranda's car, but I know I didn't imagine his fear, and he isn't banging on the door. Good enough.

Miranda tips her head to me and grins in thanks. "Tell me about it," she says.

Guess I passed.

MIRANDA

I'm not used to having someone stick up for me. I . . . like it. Probably more than I should.

Grant steps past me, further into the house. "Dr. Whitson?" he calls. "It's Grant."

I try to figure out where a library might be inside this neat, but smallish house. Clean hardwood floors, modern furniture, and no TV in sight. It could still be a timeshare waiting for the next guests to arrive. I wouldn't have guessed that Bone lived in such tidy digs — or his eccentric dad, for that matter.

Then the floor shifts under my feet, and I stumble into Grant. He catches me, seemingly not bothered by the door opening below us.

The square section of the wood floor that tossed me off balance slowly rises. It's a trapdoor hatch into a level below. Basements are so unheard of on the island that I've never seen one before. Sure, the house is on a little hill, but what about the water table? Is this guy truly insane?

"Down here." A hand — presumably belonging to Dr. Roswell — reaches over the lip of the opening to wave us down. Feet thump on the rungs of a ladder as the hand disappears again.

"It's safe — I promise," Grant says. He releases my elbow and starts down the ladder, which descends into what appears to be a well-lit, if snug, underground space. He pauses, the opening framing his face like a strange photograph. "It's okay," he says, lower, reassuring, before he continues down, the top of his head disappearing.

That leaves the ladder clear for me. As I put my feet on the rungs and start the descent, I tell myself I'll be safer down there than upstairs, where Bone might reappear. I do my best not to think about being trapped under the earth, about worms and dirt and the things I sometimes have nightmares about crawling over Mom's body in the cold, cold ground. I press from my mind the steps down to the coroner's room, where Dad was laid out on the table, the clear skin of his cheek shining up at me.

I reach the last rung.

The library is a little smaller than I expected. Three walls are lined floor to ceiling with books, some in glass-fronted cases. Framed area maps and prints I recognize as John White's drawings cover the fourth wall. Tables hold high stacks of yellowed documents with frayed edges. All of it is probably arranged in some system only Roswell can comprehend. Frankly, the crackpot's library reminds me of *The Lost Colony* gift shop.

"Do you mind getting the door?" Dr. Roswell asks.

Grant must suspect the effort it takes for me to stay down here, because he hurries back up the ladder. The door *thunks* into place, deepening the hard shadows thrown by the lamps in the corners of the library. Tight spaces don't usually bother me, but I'm already off my game. My hand goes to my cheek automatically.

Roswell extends his hand to me. "Dr. Whitson," he says. "I don't believe I've had the pleasure of making your acquaintance."

"Miranda Blackwood." I shake his hand, ducking my head when it seems like his eyes gravitate to my cheek. The birthmark's not *that* noticeable, is it? That his bearded face is familiar doesn't make him any less of a stranger.

"She's a friend," Grant says. "Her father was murdered the night of the disappearance, and we're trying to figure out if there's a connection."

Roswell is interested, his brows lifting, his eyes eager. "How do you think they're connected?"

"I don' t know. But I know you have theories about the lost colonists," Grant says. "I bet you have theories about this disappearance by now too. I want to know what they are."

"Sit, sit," Dr. Roswell says, taking a seat himself.

That leaves one small wooden chair at the nearest table. I choose to take the carpet and let Grant do the talking.

"Where should I start?" Roswell's question isn't for us, since he doesn't wait for an answer. "At the beginning."

I exchange a look with Grant. *This better help.*

"These are my theories, understand, but they are based on years of research. I am not a crackpot."

I study the loops of the carpet beneath me. "Of course not," I say.

"Go on, Doc," Grant says. He's comfortable with this man in a way that I don't get. "Tell us."

Roswell leans forward in his chair. "The first colony was actually a joint project of Sir Walter Raleigh and John Dee.

Everyone here knows Raleigh — and of course the colony's governor, John White — but are you familiar with Dee?"

Grant makes a sort-of sign with his hand while I quickly scan the character list from the play in my mind. I come up empty.

"Dee was a philosopher, a physician, and an alchemist. His power is difficult for us to understand today, so it may help if you also think of him as something else. A sorcerer. A holy man, even."

An involuntary cough escapes my lips.

"Go on," Grant says.

"Believe me, I know how all this can sound to someone who hasn't sifted through the documents in this room. Someone who has grown up believing the local version of events," says Dr. Roswell, peering at me with way more intensity than I'm comfortable with. "But haven't *you* ever thought to yourself that parts of the story about the colonists are awfully vague? Why on earth would they have traveled across the ocean to live in such an inhospitable environment? If you think about it, you'll discover that I'm right. That, in truth, you know little about the colonists themselves, even less about why they came here, and nothing about where they disappeared to."

What he's saying isn't totally cracked. I think about *The Lost Colony*'s script, knowing it stretches the truth anyway, and can find little except the colonists doing the stuff of daily colony life and fearing starvation and attack. Still . . .

"The colonists who survived were probably absorbed into the local tribes, weren't they?" I say. "That's what most people think now."

Dr. Roswell puts a finger against his lips and studies us. "Do they? It's a very convenient theory, I suppose. No one has to die in that configuration. But here's another little known fact about the colonists — not long before John White left for England to summon help and provisions, there was a murder."

The word murder rings in my ears. My father was murdered. He was so helpless. I still can't understand why.

"A colonist was murdered?" Grant asks.

Dr. Roswell switches his focus to Grant. I welcome the chance to listen without his eyes burning into me.

"Yes, one of the local tribes killed a man named George Howe. They undoubtedly had their reasons for doing so, having witnessed what the colonists were doing on the island."

"What were they doing? And what does this have to do with Dee?" Grant asks.

I suddenly don't want to know. I wish we were alone and anywhere else. I wish us being together had nothing to do with the ancient history pouring out of Roswell's mouth.

"I'm sure you've heard some of the legends about witches during the period we're discussing. They were thought to be people who signed a contract with the devil himself, to do his bidding. But," Dr. Roswell pauses, "according to what I've found, in England witches didn't make a deal with the devil. They made a deal with Dr. John Dee. And the word *witch* meant something besides black cats and flying broomsticks."

"I still don't see how the murder of the colonist is connected," Grant says.

"Of course, I'm being obtuse." Dr. Roswell laughs. "I have found not a little support for my pet theory, which seems borne out by recent events."

"The theory, Doc," Grant prompts.

I'm almost afraid to hear it.

"The colonists weren't witches, but alchemists, under the rule of John Dee," Roswell says. "They came here to build him an empire, starting with a New London."

My mouth opens and closes. "The colonists were alchemists? What does that even mean?"

Roswell ignores my tone. "In those times, witch was as likely a term as alchemist in certain quarters. These were people dedicated to unlocking the secrets of nature, of life and death itself. The discoveries alchemists made during that period became the foundation of modern chemistry. And Dee was at the forefront of that. He may not have been known as a kind man, but he *was* known for his power and intellect. He wanted to rule and believed his achievements meant he deserved to. The colony was part of his plan to do just that. Men like him, they wish to live forever. Dee invented some sort of device that would allow him and his followers to do so, when combined with the right sorcery, of course. Or, more accurately, the right manipulation of the natural world."

"Doc —" Grant starts.

But the older man has warmed to his topic. He's treating this like a CNN appearance. He waves Grant silent, grabbing a book from the table and flipping through the pages until he comes to a painting of a man with a thin face and long beard. And black, black eyes.

Below the haunting face is a symbol. My heart feels like it skips several beats. It's identical to the one on the phantom ship's sails, the one repeated on the grip of the gun I found in the closet. The circle, the curved legs and straight arms, the half-moon on top . . .

I sit up taller. "What's that?" I ask, extending my finger to the symbol.

"This was Dee's own mark, the *monas hieroglyphica*, a key to his alchemical power," Roswell says. He puts his finger on the painting. "Dee secured the land rights to our coast, much of what was known of North America at the time. He arranged for Raleigh to be in charge of transporting his colonists here, along with their sacred artifacts. I believe when John White left the colony, it was not to request help, but to fetch Dee back. The great experiment was set to begin. Dee had forged this device, and the colonists awaited his arrival. I haven't been able to identify precisely *what* the device was. But the coded information hidden in the documents left by those involved make it clear that it existed." He pauses for effect. "What I *do* know is that on the shore of Roanoke Island, they planned to use that device to become the first immortals. I believe they came very close."

I don't risk looking at Grant. The man's explanation is crazy — except for the antique gun in the closet, handmade strikes showing in its metal. Grant must be thinking the same thing.

Lucky I didn't immortal him with it.

"What stopped them?" Grant asks.

"I don't believe they were stopped. I believe they were delayed," says Dr. Roswell. He closes the book on that thin, black-eyed face at last.

Grant reaches out across the small table like he means to take the book but instead lays his hand across the surface. "You can tell all this from examining old documents?"

Not at all the question I want to ask. Mine's more along the lines of: *Are you nuts?*

"Yes," Dr. Roswell says. "The code they used is a fairly simple cipher of the time. Finding the documents that contain the concealed information has been the harder part. Some of Governor White's personal papers and drawings, a few of Raleigh's, a handful of Dee's own letters from the period. It's been a painstaking process, and I'm still missing key pieces, but I'm convinced of one thing."

Again with the pausing. I sigh, caught up in the story despite questioning our host's sanity, and ask, "Which is?"

Dr. Roswell's chin tilts down, and he regards me over the top of his glasses. His beard doesn't seem as neat as usual. Stray hairs flick out from his cheeks, as if he's gone a few days without trimming it, and there are dark circles smudged around his eyes.

I bet he's been staying up all night poring over these papers — all these years haven't been enough, not when it finally matters.

"I'm convinced that the messages were meant to be found. To continue the project," he says. "The plan was disrupted, but it's been set in motion again. That's the only explanation for the mass disappearance."

I climb to my feet, and stand beside Grant. "I don't get it," I say.

"It's a pattern. This is what happened last time, everyone gone. Or, rather, a certain number of people gone. I can't say yet what's next in the pattern," the doctor says. "But there is one other thing."

Dr. Roswell has such a flare for the dramatic that I wonder why he's never come down to audition for the show instead of making Bone work on it. He obviously wants to climb back inside history and live there. Discover its secrets.

I wait for his next words, and so does Grant.

"Well, what is it?" Grant finally asks.

"There was a name removed from the colony manifests that have been passed down through history. It belonged to an ancestor of yours, Miranda. At least, that's a logical assumption."

"What?" I ask. The snake pounds like my heart has moved to my cheek. The family legend has always said we went back that far, but history doesn't support it. It's the only thing that ever gave me hope the curse might not be real.

"There was a Blackwood in the party of colonists," Dr. Roswell says, and I nod, somehow unsurprised. "Mary Blackwood, an alchemist."

GRANT

I wish I could read minds instead of hear spirits chatter as I watch Miranda's back disappear up the library steps. She bolted as soon as Whitson said those insane words: *Mary Blackwood, an alchemist.*

"You're sure about that?" I ask him.

"I hope I didn't offend her," he says. "I thought it was an interesting piece of family history. After all, you came here for a reason, I assume?"

I nod, but I don't feel comfortable discussing Miranda with him. Or leaving her to face that jerk Bone by herself.

"Thanks, Doc. I'll talk to you soon."

I rush after her without waiting for him to say goodbye, up the stairs and through the house to the door. It's open, so she's already outside.

I don't know her well enough yet to know how bad this is, if it connects to something else for her. I don't know the right thing to say. And I definitely don't want to make the situation worse.

Turns out Bone has already done that.

Miranda parked her faded yellow car with the driver's side facing the doc's house. Instead of washing off *FREAK* like a decent person, Bone has decided to add to the message so it includes me. It now reads *FREAKS IN LOVE*.

"And tools doing graffiti!" I call out, hoping Bone is near enough to hear. I don't see him anywhere, but the truck's still parked in the drive.

Without slowing her pace, Miranda holds up her hand for me to stop. She levers open the car door and climbs in, the harsh set of her features not promising.

I jog across the lawn, curious if she'll actually leave me behind. Thankfully she waits until I get in before she starts the car. "Miranda," I say, "it's not a big deal — what an idiot. *He's probably in love with you.*"

Miranda shakes off the hand I tentatively attempt to lay on her arm and puts the car in drive. I'm still watching her when she finally looks over — past me, out the window.

I should have expected the loser to put in a final showing. Bone lounges in the open front doorway. His whole head is flushed pink, and by my estimation not from the sun. He raises a hand and salutes us with a tight grin, and I decide that he's absolutely burning some kind of torch for Miranda. Why else would he go to so much trouble to torment her?

Miranda flips Bone off and jams her foot on the gas, throwing up dust and sand as she angles onto the narrow road.

"I know that was a lot to take in . . ." I say. "But I need some help figuring out what's upsetting you the most?"

"Witches," she says, teeth gritted. "Alchemists." She's forced to slow behind a pickup truck hauling a fishing boat called *The Lucky Strike*.

"I know it all sounds crazy, but the gun — it's got to be Dee's missing object, right?" If I can get her talking everything will be okay. "That's his symbol on it. The *monas hieroglyphica*."

Miranda's eyes flick over to me, and then she veers around the fishing boat. "It does sound crazy, that's for sure. Where did you put that thing? Is it still in your mom's trunk? Maybe we should throw it in the sound."

"No," I say, qualifying when that earns a scowl. "What if we need it to . . . save the people? Or you? We don't know enough yet."

"Where is it?" she demands.

"Still in my mom's car. I didn't want her — or especially Dad — to see it. He's an antique firearms nerd, remember?"

Miranda nods. "Right. And it's not just valuable, it's magic. The long-lost alchemists — of which my frakking ancestor was one — could come to retrieve it at any time."

She turns at the next major intersection, heading back toward Manteo, and I make another attempt. "Where are we going next?"

Her mouth opens as if she's about to speak, to answer, but she doesn't say anything. She speeds up. The hula girl on the dash shimmies hard with the force of the pressure.

"Where are we going?" I ask again, getting concerned and trying not to show it.

"I'm going to see," she says, "if I can get off this island."

I'm surprised. I let her drive on in silence for a while before I chance speaking. "We're just going to abandon everyone?"

She laughs, without humor. *You don't really know this girl,* I think. But I know her well enough to know this isn't like her.

"Why shouldn't I? What has anyone here ever done for me?" she asks.

"I can't just go." I didn't want to come back, to get involved. But I can't leave without seeing this through.

Miranda gives that humorless laugh again. "You believe what he said?"

She breezes through town way over the speed limit, and we're now past the turn-off to Fort Raleigh. I want to understand what switch has flipped inside her to send her running. But I don't want to answer her question. Not yet.

I open my mouth to say something innocuous, and she shocks me into keeping quiet with her next words. "Did you know I've *never* been off the island? That's part of the family 'curse.' Our feet 'are bound to walk this patch of earth.'"

She's quoting something but not anything I've ever heard. There are plenty of whispers and rumors about the Blackwoods. I heard a good share of them in my short time on the island, after I went raving psycho on her in the school lobby. Nothing like this though. It was always just the usual — that Blackwoods never amount to much, that they're the unluckiest family on the island since forever, that her dad was a drunk, that her mother had been soft-hearted, that Miranda has bad luck just because she was born a Blackwood.

The stories always struck me as local legend, the kind of reputation earned by families who made the mistake of hanging around Roanoke Island too long. Like the Rawling family *gifts*.

But this . . . is it possible?

I struggle to keep my voice level, to betray none of my skepticism. "You're saying that you've literally never been off the island?"

Miranda's head bobs in a fierce nod, and she looks over at me, engaging with me fully for the first time since we left

Whitson's. "That's exactly what I'm saying. I grew up" — she slows the car a little, the dashboard dancer weaving to a more peaceful melody — "being told by my father that I could never leave. That Blackwoods have been here since the colony and that we are cursed to stay here. Being told stories that gave me nightmares . . . that *were* nightmares. Stories about how my grandmother walked off the island toward the mainland once and lost her mind at exactly the tenth step. She sat in a rocking chair for the rest of her life picking grains of sand off beach glass. That if I ever left, my feet would burst into flames. My body would disappear, and I'd become a ghost."

What kind of lunatic was her Dad? I wonder. "This island is eight miles long. About two miles across. How have you never left it?"

"I tried to test the stories when I was a kid. I waded out to my waist in the Sound and nothing happened, so I started to swim further out and then . . . I've never been so sick. I only got better when I swam back."

"Maybe it was psychosomatic? Maybe you freaked yourself out. You said your dad told you that you couldn't leave."

"He told me those stories, and I don't know if I believed them. I told myself I didn't. But I guess I believed them enough to not risk leaving for real. Not after that one time. No matter how much I wanted it." She shakes her head, black curls jostling. "You must think I'm crazy."

"I see and hear dead people," I remind her. Briefly I wonder if I've ever heard the voice of her grandmother. Not that I'm able to distinguish individual voices and forms. I picture the cream envelope that holds Gram's letter — I haven't been brave enough to open it yet. I planned on asking Miranda to read it with me later.

The Manns Harbor Bridge and the waters of the sound are coming up fast in the distance. Perfect rows of tall trees flank the highway, the sign that bids visitors farewell just ahead. It's a postcard view.

Miranda pulls the car off to the shoulder before we reach the bridge and steers into a parking lot bordered by sand. There are some rocks, a bench, and a tree prettily arranged beside the patch of beach, and then the bridge itself stretching over the greenish blue water. A cluster of purple birds on the beach flies away at our arrival, rising from the sand in a shuddering wave of colorful wings.

"What are you planning to do?" I ask.

"Stay here," she says, getting out of the car. "I don't want you to get hurt."

I jump out to follow and catch up to her on the sand. The wind tosses Miranda's hair in a storm as I grab her shoulder and spin her to face me.

She isn't crazy. She's just acting crazy. I understand the things in your own mind that can make you push the world away, flailing.

"If it's this important to you then I support your crazy plan," I say. "I think you should try to leave."

Her eyes narrow. "You do?"

"We need to know exactly what we're dealing with. Whitson," I say, "he helped — at least I think he did — but he admitted he doesn't know everything yet. It'll be an experiment. And if you can leave, then you'll feel better, right? Having an escape route?"

She's still wary, still waiting for me to disappoint her, I think. But she nods.

"We should just take the car across the bridge," I say. "Together."

"No, I'm not risking you getting hurt. I'm going on foot."

Miranda whirls and crosses the small slice of beach that remains, continuing without pause over the grassy patch next to the bridge. I stay right behind her.

She doesn't hesitate so much as brace herself when she reaches the white line at the edge of the actual highway. Her shoulders rise and fall on a deep breath, and then she steps onto the road. One deliberate step, followed by another . . .

I check her progress over the side. The next steps are the ones that will take her off the mainland, over the water of the Sound. How precise are curses anyway?

A sob rips from her throat.

I hurry to her side. "What's wrong?"

"Oh God . . ." Fear etches her features, but she moves forward. A baby step. She trembles in the wind blowing across the bridge.

Seven steps, eight, nine . . .

What if the story about her grandmother is true?

"Grant, it hurts. It *hurts*," she says. Misery and pain fill her voice. Then, she howls. The scream is like knives are stabbing her.

Miranda stumbles, lifts her foot . . .

Before she can complete the tenth step, I grab her and haul her back to the edge of the bridge. She barely fights.

Miranda is breathing so hard I'm afraid her lungs will burst. What if the curse can do anything it decides to?

"Miranda, talk to me. Please."

"It stopped when you put me back here." She wails. "I can't leave."

I'm desperate to do something to help her. A yellow SUV drives by with its horn blaring and I flip it off, which makes me feel marginally better. I guide Miranda over the barrier, afraid she'll dash back onto the bridge if we stay near the highway.

"I can't leave," she says again. She tears herself loose from my hold and kicks the sand. "I can't fucking leave this place."

Fuck instead of frak. This is bad. "Miranda, I'm so sorry . . ." I reach out to her.

"You're sorry," she says, laughing that crazy laugh from the car. But she shuffles closer to me. I catch her, hands on her shoulders, steadying her.

She goes on, "Do you believe Roswell? Witchcraft plans, immortality, my family cursed since the start of the colony?"

"I wasn't sure before, but . . . yes. Now I believe it. We have to do something — and leaving is apparently off the list."

She pushes against my chest, leaving her palms flat against it. There are noises in the background: a few cars, birds flapping and calling overhead, trees rustling in echo of the water. I barely hear them. The sadness in her face is too much.

"I can't leave," she says. "But you can. You made it off. Why would you ever come back here? What if Mary Blackwood was evil, and I am too? Maybe that's why I'm cursed. What if our family deserves everything we got?"

"No." I slide my hands down her arms and back up again. I'm desperate to stop the pain, to bring her back to being Miranda. I tug her closer by her shirtsleeves, meaning to kiss her.

She lets me bring her in close.

For a moment, I'm winning her, bringing her back. Until she shoves me away.

I fall to my knees, hitting the sand hard. A keening sound emerges from my throat that I can't stop.

Then I realize that Miranda isn't the reason I'm falling. What pushed me down and down and down is far worse.

The spirits return with hurricane force, and the screaming shadows rip my sense apart.

MIRANDA

I can't believe what I just did.

Grant stays with me while I'm acting balls-out crazy, and I pay him back by *shoving him to the ground*. Full-on rejection when I don't want to reject him. When he is, in fact, the only person I have on my side.

My flare into anger in Roswell's library, the way I drove here, the — oh God — true stories I confessed about not being able to leave the island, insisting on walking out onto the bridge . . . I came this close to telling him about seeking fantasy escape routes after Mom died. All that pales next to what flooded from my mouth after the childhood stories were proved right. It's nothing next to pushing him away.

One thing I know, in this moment, none of those actions or words belonged to me. Or maybe they poured from some small part of me, but it was a part I'd never willingly let take control.

Sand swallows my feet, and I pull them free to kneel before him. It's only once I'm close that I see Grant is in pain.

Oh no.

His head slumps into his chest. I gently shake his shoulder. His face lifts a fraction, enough to show that his eyes are squeezed shut. The wrinkles at their edges are like wounds slashed into his face. He cries out with pure anguish.

"Grant?" I do what I can to tamp down my panic.

He tips forward and rolls onto his side, forming an untidy ball on the sand. His eyes stay closed as he rocks into the grainy embrace of the ground beneath him. His hands lift to shield his ears from sounds I can't hear.

"The spirits," I realize. "They came back, didn't they?"

What do I do about it? is the real question. This is the kind of thing I should have brought up in polite conversation with Sara earlier. *Hey, what do I do if your son suddenly turns into a spirit tuning fork again?*

I pet his shoulder with a tentative hand, and he grabs it. I detect a slight tug, or think I do, and — despite how strange it feels — I lie down beside him, pressing my body against his in the sand. The hand gripping mine moves to re-cover his ear, and his body trembles against mine. I hold on, afraid that if I let go, he'll be gone forever.

"Home," he says after a while.

Reluctantly, I let go. I get up to help him off the sand. I stumble, then freeze as I look out over the water.

The tall black ship sails toward us. Three black sails of varying sizes swell in the wind. The ornate symbols stitched on them in gray clearly bear John Dee's mark. The immense shadow the ship throws across the water nearly tricks me into thinking it's real. Real in the way I'm real, the sand is real, Grant is real.

The shadow shifts and billows like the black sails. We need to get out of here, stat.

Turning away from the phantom ship's menacing glide, I bend and pull at Grant's arms until I get one of them over my shoulder. "We have to get up now," I say.

He manages to climb to his feet and leans heavily on me. A low moan escapes his lips. "Home," he breathes.

I rotate us in a slow circle, not comfortable leaving the black ship and its shadow unobserved. "Do you see it?" I ask, searching the horizon.

But there's nothing to see. A bridge, calm waters, a brilliant blue sky.

No wonder old John White always seems so cranky by the end of the play, looking for something and finding nothing.

It takes an age to cross the ten feet to Pineapple with our clumsy tandem footsteps. "We're never going to be on an Olympic team for anything that requires synchronization," I say. Grant is unresponsive, but I talk at him to ease my nerves, like he's in a coma and the doctor has told me it might help.

"We could be in the freak Olympics," I say as I deposit him against the rear passenger door. "Well, I don't have any actual skills. No, no, that's not what I mean. I have skills, but not like you have skills."

Sand coats us both in a fine, scratchy second skin. It clings to his eyelashes, his eyes still closed. He looks like he's asleep standing up.

"If there *was* a freak Olympics," — I get the door open and slip my arm around his side to help him ease into the seat — "maybe we could get training so we didn't suck so much at this." I clump his feet over the edge so he's in the car.

On impulse, I brush sand from his cheek, then more softly from his eyelashes. They flutter against the pressure, and Grant opens one eye. Bloodshot rings the brown iris.

"Miranda," he says.

"That's me," I agree, glad for the sign he's in there some-where. "I'm taking you home." Careful not to catch some limb of his in it, I shut the door and scurry around to my own side and into the driver's seat. "Not that you're going to change the subject that easily. We really need more practice if we're going to medal."

"Music." The word is a moan.

"I see how it is," I say, "trying to shut me up."

I turn on the used CD player I installed in Pineapple's dash — one of my prouder moments — and crank the volume. Neko Case croons about red bells. Deep red bells.

I drive, grateful to stop talking. I have to think.

What Roswell shared with us was on the crazy side, but I can't deny how much being on the bridge hurt. I counted my steps until the pain forced the numbers out of my head. My feet burned like I was walking into a furnace — like I was a girl forced to dance in hot iron shoes, a mermaid forced to split her tail and walk on land. Fairy-tale level is the only description that captures it.

Which means magic isn't so crazy. Not when you factor in the leaping birthmark and our family legend, the missing peo-ple, and John Dee's symbol.

How Dad died is important. Grant said so, and maybe his dad has learned more. Roswell's theory might explain some things, but it doesn't explain everything. We know more than he does now.

I look over at Grant. His neck is crooked back, eyes shut, mouth moving in silent accord with the lyrics or the voices he hears. The intensity of the pain has faded from his expression, at least.

He's in no shape to help you, though.
"My turn," I say.

*

When we reach Grant's driveway, the first thing I notice is the unfamiliar vehicle parked beside Chief Rawling's cruiser. The hulking black SUV gleams like someone polishes it constantly to remove any speck of sand or dust. I watch too much TV not to guess what it means — there are federal agents inside the house.

Maybe they already know who murdered Dad, maybe that's why they're here. The rush autopsy might be complete. I turn off the car, the swell of Neko's voice dying so abruptly that the silence makes Grant moan.

"You stay here," I say, making a split-second decision. I won't subject him to the prying eyes of strangers when he's like this.

Smoothing my hair and T-shirt, I walk to the front door. Sure, I want to know if the missing pieces of the puzzle are found, but first I need Grant's mom to help get him inside. The door opens before my second knock.

Chief Rawling looks around and, without asking for Grant, says, "Come inside, Miranda."

"Chief, I . . . is Sara . . ." I try to banish the memory of the chief interrupting Grant and me the night before.

"She's in here," he says.

He leaves me no choice except to follow him across the creaking planks of the floor. The footfalls of his heavy-soled work shoes echo. Sara sits on the floral couch in the living room, an unusual primness in her posture.

Across from Sara, on the love seat, are the expected agents. A man and a woman in nearly identical dark suits — he's young but already bald; her graying hair is slicked back into a knot at her neck. The tight quarters of the love seat force them to sit close together, and their spines are stick-straight to compensate for the lack of room.

Based on these two, I assume that most TV shows get FBI agents half right. They *are* serious and intimidating, but neither one is attractive enough to inspire decent fan-fic anytime soon.

"Um, hello . . ." I linger in the doorway as Chief Rawling pulls out a spare wooden chair near the wall for me to sit on, then returns to the sofa beside his wife. The feds watch me with interest. Too much interest.

"Sara, could I talk to you alone for a minute?" I ask. Sidekick chooses that precise moment to come bounding in from the kitchen, crashing into me with oblivious happiness.

"You'd better sit down first," Sara says.

The warning in her flat tone is subtle enough to be unde-tectable to anyone who hasn't been around her before. I think of Grant waiting outside in the car, but I have no choice. I can't bring him into this. I sink onto the chair, ruffling Sidekick's fur in reassurance that I didn't abandon him.

"This is Agent Malone and Agent Walker from the FBI," says Chief Rawling. "They're the new heads of this case until it's resolved. We're cooperating fully. This is Miranda Blackwood, the murder victim's daughter."

The woman smiles at me coolly. "I'm Agent Malone," she says. A tiny piece of lint clings to the lapel of her black jacket, and I focus on that.

"Okay," I say. "Hi."

I can't stop worrying about Grant. What if he tries to make it inside on his own? But Chief Rawling and Sara's tense expres-sions keep me pinned to the chair.

"I'm sorry about your father," Agent Malone says. She waits as if planning to take notes on my reaction.

"Thank you?" I offer.

"Do you know anyone who would have *wanted* to kill your father?" Agent Malone asks. The light streaming through the pale curtains on the window behind her creates a halo that doesn't match her business suit.

I catch the chief laying his hand over Sara's. What am I missing here?

"Honestly, no," I say. "You probably already know he wasn't the citizen of the year, but no . . . I can't imagine why anyone would have killed him. No one in town would have loaned him money, so he didn't owe any, except to me. He didn't have a job. His disability check covered his bar tab and most of our bills. He almost never got in fights. He was harmless. I'm sure the chief has already told you all of this."

A glance at the chief tells me I've said way more than I should.

Agent Malone leans back. The other agent — Agent Walker — shifts forward. Bad cop time.

"What are you doing here now?" Agent Walker asks. "At the Rawlings' house?"

I go still. I don't what game this is, but honesty suddenly seems like the wrong tactic. "I came to get Sidekick. Sara was nice enough to babysit him while I did some things today. She let me stay here last night."

"Is that because you're dating her son?" Agent Walker lets one side of his mouth tick up. "Young love, it can make you do the strangest things."

"I don't know what you mean," I say with a frown.

The chief opens his mouth to protest, then closes it. "Wise decision," Agent Walker says to him, "since that fact came from you."

"This will all be cleared up," Chief Rawling says. "You're making the wrong leaps."

"You see, Miss Blackwood," Agent Walker says, eyes not leaving the chief, "it's interesting to us that you and Grant Rawling are so close, since he's been away for the last few years."

I stare at him. "What is this?"

"We've gotten a warrant to search his belongings, his computer — we have agents up at his school. If you're colluding on this, we will find the evidence."

"Colluding on what?" I don't think this is a game anymore.

"On your father's murder," Agent Malone says. "Which you don't seem too upset about."

Chief Rawling stands up. "That's enough," he says, turning to me. "Miranda, you don't have to say anything. You can ask for a lawyer. You should know, though, your father's body . . . it's missing."

"What do you mean, missing? Like the people?"

"When Marlon got to the funeral home this morning to meet the federal expert for the autopsy, he was gone." Chief Rawling shakes his head. "They think Grant had something to do with taking the body."

My chair clatters as I leap to my feet. Sidekick dances out of my way.

"That's insane," I protest. "He wasn't even *here* when the murder happened. He's the one who told the chief to get the autopsy done. Last night. Chief, tell them."

Chief Rawling frowns at me. Oh, right, I was eavesdropping. That hardly matters now.

"He already has," Agent Walker says, "but Grant Rawling *was* in the body storage room. We found his prints on a handkerchief discarded in the biohazard receptacle. He almost got away with taking your father's body, Miss Blackwood."

My head is shaking and so are my hands. *No.* "No, that's not what you think."

"Where is the boy now?" Agent Malone says, standing up, which prompts her partner to do the same. "We know you left together this morning."

She walks around the living room table and puts a hand on my arm. I want to shrink from her touch. How can I stop this purposeless witch-hunt? Witch-hunt, haha, very funny. Maybe the spirits will warn Grant to bolt. Maybe . . .

Agent Malone's tone softens to silk. "Miranda, I understand your dad may have deserved whatever he got. If you're just honest with us, we can make this a lot easier on everyone. We know you couldn't have gotten rid of one hundred and fourteen people. We're mainly interested in crossing your father's murder off the list of leads."

And the Emmy for most transparent attempt at manipulation goes to . . .

"Do you think I'm that stupid? Don't you guys watch TV anymore? I'm not falling for —"

The sound of the front door opening interrupts my vow to get an attorney. Not that I can afford one or know of one who would represent me for free. A heavy thump and breaking glass come next — the family portrait on the wall next to the door, I'm guessing — and then the noise of a body sliding to the floor.

I'm not the first one out of the room. I'm the last.

When I turn the corner, I see that they have Grant. Sara bends beside him, fingers lifting his eyelids to check his pupils, shattered glass surrounding them on the floor. Agent Malone lets handcuffs dangle from long fingers and glances over her shoulder at me with something that looks an awful lot like pity.

They have Grant.

I have to find a way to fix this situation, to help *him*, and I can't do that in FBI custody. I've got to get out of here.

GRANT

Coming coming —
No, they are here —
They have always been here —
Under the bed —
Stealing us —
The spirits swarm around me — so many, so loud. I'm swimming in them, *drowning* in them.

It's never been this bad, not even the one time I summoned them on purpose as a test and then spent days in bed when they surrounded me.

I barely know where I am. Back then, interacting with the real world was a challenge. I was able to do it, though. I slowly explained to Mom that the spirits had descended with such fury and fierce babble, and I couldn't make them leave. I had to wait a day for the clamor to fade, for some to leave. But . . . I knew who I was.

I still know who I am.

I cling to that. Clear thought is impossible when the world of shadows is as present as the real world. I fight for some snatches of clarity, attempt to see beyond the clamor, but it's exhausting. It's not at my command. Nothing is at my command.

The shapes and shadows of the spirits, the hiss and howl of their voices, is all that I can swear exists. Dark fingers reaching for me, bringing darker words . . .

We want to live —

Liar liars —

The red streaks will be blood, will run like —

Coming back for you —

Water running over us all —

Death is here —

You won't know them —

You'll be too late —

She's the cause of it —

The ship —

They'll use her —

Listen to me, my boy, listen —

Bluebell, blue sea, blue waves, I'm going mad —

You saw the snake —

We're all mad —

Coming, coming, they're coming —

"Grant?"

The voice is my mom's, I think, and I'm shaking. Or is someone shaking me? I can't manage to answer. I wonder where Miranda is . . . I don't think she's with me anymore.

I dimly remember my weight against her, a ghost of a memory. I tried to reach her when I fell. I asked her to bring me here. Home.

I must be home.
You have to listen —
No, listen —
We're here for a reason —
Don't fight —
I'm not. I don't have the strength to. Someone lifts me to my feet, something cool slides against on my wrists.

I laugh, but I don't know why or at what.
Listen —
I am. What else can I do?

MIRANDA

Grant's parents and the agents are distracted. Sara is warning Agent Malone away from her son while Agent Walker argues with Chief Rawling. Grant's cheek presses into his mother's hand, his eyelids fluttering like he's having a bad dream. The agents won't understand what's wrong with him. They'll want to ask me more questions. And I have too many questions of my own that still need answers.

Where can Dad's body be? Who would take it? Why can Grant suddenly hear the spirits again?

Hard as it is to run out on Grant, it's the smartest thing to do. I know it's what he'd tell me to do.

Sidekick pads toward the cluster of people, no doubt to gift Grant with a reviving face lick. The snap of my fingers is so quiet I almost expect Sidekick to miss it. But he comes to my side, the best boy in the world, and lets me lead him through the kitchen by his collar. I hold my breath as I press the screen door open just enough for my dog to slip through, then me.

Thank you. I silently direct gratitude to Grant for being the kind of rule-breaker who tightens and oils hinges, who wouldn't risk being in a house with random squeaks. He probably checked every door and every step of our route out the night before, just in case.

The backyard has sandy dirt and clumps of brown-fingered grass mixed with its short ragged blades. The grass is damp from the efforts of a green garden hose nearby, and brightly colored flowerpots are arrayed alongside the house. Sara must have watered not long before.

Heading around the side of the house to Pineapple, I realize there's no way to take my car and make a getaway. Pineapple doesn't start quietly at the best of times, and given my legendarily terrible luck, the car will sputter and be stubborn. Instead I simply ease the passenger door open, crouching, holding Sidekick's collar so he won't jump in for a ride.

The keys to Grant's mom's sedan aren't in the passenger side floorboard, where I thought he'd left them after we switched cars at my house. *Crap.*

Someone at the back door calls my name. "Miranda!"

The chief, I decide.

His call is followed by the non-dulcet tones of Agent Walker: "Miss Blackwood, you're making this worse for everyone!"

Okay, I'll deal with not having the keys later. I'll get the strange gun from the trunk of Grant's mom's car where he stashed it . . . somehow. At least I know where it is. That's something.

I release Sidekick's collar and bolt toward the woods just past the Rawlings' driveway, making it to the tree line just as the front door opens. The tree I selected isn't overly wide, so I stand sideways to maximize its cover. Then I remember Sidekick. He shifts on uncertain feet beside me, unconcealed. I crouch and then lower myself onto my belly, pulling him down with me. His tail wags, and I reach back to stop it.

Proof that he's the best dog in the world? He doesn't even whine.

Sara and Agent Malone step out on the front porch. Chief Rawling and Agent Walker join them, body language revealing how much the two men are hating each other. Grant is still inside, probably still suffering too.

I wait without much patience during their examination of my car and what appears to be a clipped conversation. I can guess that Grant is their greater priority, and they'll worry about picking me up later. They need to get back to the station, see if they can get him lucid enough for an interview, check in on the status of the missing people *and* my father's body.

These aren't agents from the Fringe Division, not secret carriers of X-Files or paranormal investigators. They are *not* looking for supernatural causes. Aliens haven't abducted the people of Roanoke, perpetrators have. Or maybe this is a cult thing or a tourism stunt gone wrong. Something understandable. That is the kind of explanation they want.

Oh, and the police chief's son murdered his girlfriend's father, which might be connected.

I should know better than to expect outsiders to decode the island's mysteries. They're just here to get in our way.

"Secret alchemists," I whisper after the agents go back inside the house, presumably to collect Grant. "There's your lead."

I get to my feet and set out at a fast clip. My house is a couple of miles' walk, if I cut through the woods and along less-visible roadways than the main drag. As I go, I say a silent prayer to beat any searchers there. I pray for the spirits to talk to me and tell me how to jimmy open a locked trunk.

I pray that Grant will be okay.

Once the prayers are over, I get this uncanny queasy feeling that speeds me up. I tear through the woods like a chupacabra is chasing me.

I know the dead don't walk . . . I know it the same way I know witches and alchemists don't exist. So I feel silly for worrying that Dad is traipsing around, zombielike, on the island . . . that he'll come after me . . . that even now he's in the forest with me, watching as I run.

I don't feel silly enough to stop running, though.

Getting home takes longer than I expect. Once Sidekick and I reach our neighborhood, we have to navigate through an obstacle course of backyards. We make our way around zigzagging borders filled with broken down lawnmowers and refrigerators, toys, and chained dogs with anger management issues. They hate Sidekick on sight, of course. Finally, the back edge of our unfenced, not recently mown yard appears, then the back door of our house.

My house now, I correct myself. I close my eyes against a sudden image of Dad sitting at our sticky kitchen table. His pale, birthmark-free face grins at me over a cup of stale coffee, his eyes and mouth as black as open graves.

No.

There isn't time to be weak. If those federal agents catch up to me, they'll be more convinced than ever Grant and I were in league to do something to Dad, more inclined than they were before to lock me up. No one would save me either.

I insert my key into the flimsy back door lock, then the sturdier dead bolt above it. I force my feet over the threshold.

Your father is dead, I tell myself, *not sitting at the kitchen table.*

"Right," I say, walking into the kitchen — no zombie father, thank you — and stick a quarter-full sack of dog kibble in my messenger bag. "Sorry," I answer Sidekick's mournful silent plea. "No time for chow." Sara would have fed him a few hours ago, anyway.

I head to my room for the smaller toolbox I keep stashed at home. I've locked myself out of Pineapple a couple of times before. The same principles I used to break in then should work on the trunk lock of Sara's sedan.

I find my room lightly picked over by Grant and Sara. My *Vampire Diaries* boxed sets sit on top of my pillow — Elena's reclining body upside-down and come hither.

It puts a smile on my face, even now.

Grant is a funny boy.

I retrieve the small toolbox and carry it outside. Up the street, Mrs. Powell is on her front porch with her nose in a paperback, her hair forming an astronaut-suit bubble around her head. Her long-range vision is shot, so I know she won't see me. She can barely see the book, as evidenced by the way she cups it an inch from her face.

Popping my toolbox open at the back of Sara's car, I rummage through it and select a specialty screwdriver. I take a length of steel wire and put it into an opening below the head. The tool is perfect for dislodging stray sequins or costume beading in cracks on set — and for this kind of job, which is why I keep one at home.

I slide the metal into the trunk's lock and work it around, searching for the release. No immediate luck, so I shift my leg to change the angle of approach.

There's nothing for me to trip over, but I do anyway. I have to abandon the tool to keep from falling. I stand and pull on it. When it doesn't come free, I wriggle it harder.

The wire is lodged in the lock. And the release doesn't give a millimeter.

"Frak," I say, in case Mom's listening. Sure, Grant said she isn't, but that was before his spirits came back.

I kick the ground, then a tire on my way around the side of the car. There's nothing that could cause me to trip. Except . . .

I touch my face, just below my temple. *Of course. The snake.*

"Frak."

I think of Dad and how he was always . . . unsteady. Not always, though. He wasn't always that way. At first, he stumbled into things more. I can see his hand gripping the frame around the photo of Mom in the living room to keep it from falling after he touched the glass too hard. Then, the drinking became a problem, bringing more stumbling with it, making him fight his own limbs.

I can see how his behavior changed over the years, and in an instant, I understand the reason why. The snake is mind-controlling me somehow. Not all the time, but like a radio frequency that tunes in and out. When I was so pissy to Grant on the drive to Roswell's . . . and when I just tripped . . .

I eye the sedan and purposefully think like myself. Not like Grant, not like whatever rogue impulse randomly invaded my body earlier. Not like whatever caused me to trip over nothing. Like myself.

There has to be another way into the trunk, an emergency method to open it. Or a way aimed at convenience.

Mrs. Powell isn't deaf, but I take the chance. Selecting a hammer from the toolbox, I go around to the other side of the car — checking the street one last time for anyone else — and smash in the smaller of the rear windows.

Mrs. Powell lifts her head, but she can't see anything this far away. She goes back to reading.

I reach inside to pull up the lock, then open the door and feel around the top of the back seat until I locate the plastic release lever. I yank down on it. The back seat falls into my hand, flattening to provide trunk access.

The box that holds what is apparently Dr. John Dee's greatest invention sits inside, waiting like it was in Dad's closet all those years.

"Frak," I say, pleased. And also absolutely terrified.

GRANT

The snake inside —
The things they'll do —
Can't be stopped any longer —
I'm not at home anymore. That's one of the few things I know.

I'm not sure where I am. I try to keep my eyes closed to shut out the shadows, but the spirits' voices chatter incessantly anyway.

Strangers took me away from Mom's cool hand on my forehead, from her voice attempting to get through to me. There were unfamiliar voices, breaking glass. I didn't manage to say a single word to Mom before they brought me here. Wherever *here* is.

The past and present are a syrup I swim through, heavy against my limbs. They weigh me down. Down. Down.

He's had so much time —
All the time he needs —
They're coming, you'll know —

My cheek rests on cool wood grain. The desire to see my surroundings develops slowly. The will to open my eyes builds. Finally, I manage it.

The black bars of a cell greet me, visible through a kaleidoscope of shadow gray forms, lips moving where I can make out shapes. On the other side of them stands Dr. Whitson. He's shaking his head. Then the bars are opening, and Dad is behind the doctor, and there are strangers in suits and . . .

Stolen life —

COMING, COMING, COMING —

My eyes close again as hands force my mouth open and deposit a few pills inside. The gel casings gum on my tongue, and I sputter as water pours down my throat. But I manage to swallow, even though I know better than to think the drugs will do a thing to dam up the flood.

The voices roar.

No delays —

What's past the end —

Is there anything, can we wake —

COMING —

The racket wakes me from the fitful, sweaty sleep I didn't realize the pills had thrown me into. I hear the dead's every twisted syllable. I rock against the hard wood bench until I achieve the momentum to sit up, then press my head back against cool cinderblock. All the physical sensations are muted, as if they're happening to someone else — someone far, far away, on a movie screen, or in the past. Someone barely real.

Not me.

The voices of the dead overlap in chaotic fragments, but then they sync, melding into a single word, as loud and clear as shattering glass. The chorus repeats again and again and again:

COMING, COMING, COMING, COMING, COMING, COMING, COMING, COMING, COMING —

I fall onto my knees on concrete, squeezing my eyes shut, holding onto an image of Miranda in my mind.

Miranda on the beach, thinking she pushed me down . . .

Thinking that I don't understand . . .

Then . . .

Silence. There is a single moment of perfect silence.

I'm alone again.

Until I'm not.

MIRANDA

I'm not sure what to do after I retrieve the box, but staying at home seems like a spectacularly bad idea. It can only be a matter of time before the FBI or cops show up here. I can't go back to Grant's house — Sara being there doesn't change the chief's obligation to cooperate with the FBI.

Morrison Grove will still be deserted, what with Polly and others missing and everyone else having blown town. So, my friend's apartment it is.

I set out on foot again, since it's the only choice available. Pineapple is still at Grant's house, and the keys to Sara's car are still MIA. After I spot a couple of tank-style SUVs — clearly belonging to the feds — in the distance, I steer Sidekick off the roadside. We'll hike through less visible terrain.

My messenger bag is heavy with the gun box and dog food inside, and I'm at war with my legs. They protest every plodding, uneven step. Poor Sidekick trudges alongside me, no longer bothering to gallop ahead like he did on our earlier trek.

Adrenaline vs. Exhaustion: Which will be the ultimate victor?

"This is the only time you will ever hear me say it's a good thing we live on an island this small, dog," I mutter. If Roanoke was any bigger, not having a car would have sunk me.

I focus on putting one sneakered foot in front of the other, but what I know — and the larger shadows of what I still don't — threatens to drag me down. None of it seems random. John Dee's hieroglyph — on the gun, on the phantom ship's sails, in Roswell's book — is too much of a coincidence to be a coincidence.

Deep in thought, I don't notice the enormous shadow that descends over me. Not until I stumble over a rock cloaked in the sudden darkness it casts. Sidekick growls at whatever is behind us.

I don't want to turn and see what it is. But I do anyway.

The ship sails across the land as if nothing inhabits it. The sails stretch a hundred feet in the air, the elaborate gray symbols pulling taut in gusts of phantom wind, the gleaming hull below polished black. People stand on the deck. I can't make them out in detail, not through the shadow. They are a line of still silhouettes, a wall of stone statues staring out over the island.

Logically I know shadows don't fall forward at this time of day, with this position of the sun, and that they never fall this far in front of an object. But that hardly matters. The ship's appearance nearly breaks the rational part of my mind anyway.

Morrison Grove isn't far now. The tree line and roofs of the first buildings are visible ahead. I pick up my pace, but Sidekick barks his head off behind me. He isn't following.

"Sidekick!"

I can't leave him, even if it means the shadow eats me whole. I double back and pull at his collar.

The ship glides slowly, steadily forward. Real or not, I don't want to be overtaken by it. We need to get out of its path.

Every dog within earshot strikes up a chorus of barks to match Sidekick's. His body thrashes against the pressure of my hand.

Just like the night Dad died.

I have never leashed Sidekick before, but there's nothing else to do. I drop my messenger bag and remove the strap. He growls as I click one end onto his collar. I pick up the other end and heft the bag with my free arm. Then I put all my weight into heaving him forward. I won't leave him.

"Come on!" I plead.

He fights me, desperate to face the threat, but I refuse to give in. I move forward as quickly as possible with the bag clutched awkwardly against me. I drag Sidekick along. I don't stop to look back until we are at Polly's door.

The ship is only a dozen feet away. It's going to sail right over us.

I give one last jerk to get Sidekick inside, then slam the door and sling the bag aside. The box inside it clunks against the floor, the kibble rattles.

I wait for the impact of the black ship against the house. I suddenly wonder if this is what happened to Dad. I wait to feel all my bones break as the phantom ship crushes me whole.

The impact never comes.

When I open the door, the shadow has vanished. The ship too.

Oh, it's still out there, sailing through the air. I feel certain of that. The line of dark shadows stands on its deck, watching and waiting for an arrival point. Something is coming.

I need to get back to Grant, to get through to him that we don't have much time left — that with the big black ship sailing toward me, maybe *I* don't have much time.

But the thought of going back out defeats me, finally. Adrenaline never had a chance. Exhaustion wins.

*

I thrash in my sleep. Sidekick's periodic low whining makes for a restless night. Despite that, I'm tired enough to get some shut-eye, but not soundly. Instead I watch my dreams, nightmares really, play like movies I haven't bought tickets for.

At first, the images are of the sinister black ship, sailing ever forward. But this dream takes place in a beachside clearing that I recognize as the settlement the theater set mimics. There is no ship, but there are people.

The dream settlers stand in rows facing the sound, packed sand beneath their feet. They wear clothes resembling costumes from the show — with one change. Long gray cloaks hang from their shoulders like so many pairs of broken wings. A storm has soaked the beach, and thick thunderheads above threaten its return.

The settlers chant words I can't make out. As they raise their arms, their cloaks float in the air, broken wings straining to fly, and always, always, the settlers pass between them some object hidden from me by their bodies.

I wake as the last of them is about to turn, the secret about to be revealed.

Polly sits on the edge of the bed, looking at me.

Her expression is oddly serious, but other than that she appears normal. Prematurely gray hair, T-shirt with paint spatters, familiar brown eyes. A copy of a John White nature sketch hangs on the wall behind her like a floral crown.

Am I still asleep? Why hasn't she said anything? I reach out and touch Polly's arm.

No. She's really here.

I scramble from beneath the covers. "You're back," I say. "How? Thank God. I'm sorry, I know it's weird that I'm here, I didn't know . . ."

"Your face is a welcome sight," Polly says.

"When . . . where . . . what happened to you?" I force out.

Sidekick edges closer to lay his head flat on top of my feet. He isn't growling or whining, but his furry eyebrows twitch up and down.

Polly gives me a strange look. "I'm not sure I can explain that to you."

"You're okay, though?" I can't believe she's *here.*

Polly inclines her chin. "Why are you in this house?"

I search for a place to start. My father's death, a cute boy swooping in from the past, Roswell's revelation about my ancestor . . .

"I'm sorry about taking your bed. It's a long story. We didn't know if you'd be back or when —"

"We?"

Grant. I hope he isn't still being eaten alive by wild spirits. But somehow I don't think that would matter to Polly. Polly, whose expression has yet to change. She's as solemn as young Virginia Dare telling the audience the settlers will never return.

It's weird. *She's* being weird.

"Is it just you who's back?" I ask.

"No," Polly says, and her features shift into a frown. "I believe everyone managed to return."

"Return from where?" I ask. Even if it's negative, Polly showing any emotion is a small comfort. What has she been through?

Polly stands, ignoring my question. "The others have breakfast."

166

I glimpse my reflection in a small round mirror on the wall. The snake crawls up my cheek, and I fight the urge to touch it. At least Polly doesn't seem to have noticed its presence. I check the position of my bag against the wall, not fully understanding why the idea of leaving it makes me uncomfortable. Other than the fact it holds the possibly sacred, possibly evil, almost certainly magical gun.

"Come on," Polly says from the doorway. "Breakfast."

I go with her; it's that or make a scene. Sidekick moseys along behind me. In the main room, I find two more familiar faces at the small table in the kitchen — I feel guilty that I never really worried that much about Polly's missing roommates. Kirsten and Gretchen are the type who stay out late and pick up tourist boys on vacation. I don't know them that well. But still.

"Hi," I say uncertainly.

Polly grabs a seat at the table and smiles toward the other girls in a way that doesn't reach her eyes. I take the chair next to Polly, but I don't want to be obvious about observing her. So I watch the others instead. They have the same serious expression as Polly — more disconcerting on them than on her. My memories of them not at work involve giggling and downing fire-red shots at after-parties.

Something's not right.

Kirsten grips a doughnut in one hand. She takes an enormous bite of it, chewing with an energy that says she's either starving or the world's biggest doughnut fan.

Gretchen says, "Good morning . . . Miranda . . ."

The way she trails off leaves me waiting for more, but Gretchen says nothing else.

Polly fills the silence. "Have some doughnuts." She taps the box. "Kirsten would talk of nothing else."

167

Having finished her previous, Kirsten selects an enormous cruller shaped like a curled hand from the box and bites into it. She uses her other hand to shove the box toward me.

"Um, okay," I say.

I choose the smallest doughnut in the box, though I'm more of a chocolate than a glazed girl. The box, soggy with icing, proclaims its origin at the Stop and Gas less than a mile away. "When did you guys get these?"

"I walked for them." Kirsten speaks around a mouthful of cheap pastry. "The man at the gas station showed me a picture of us." Her eyes flick to Gretchen, who tilts her head in curiosity.

"You didn't say before," Gretchen says.

"No, you didn't," says Polly.

Kirsten chews and says, "They were not good pictures." She pauses. "Photocopies. He knew we were missing. The picture said so."

I manage to swallow the one bite I've taken. "Everyone knew you were missing. There were a lot of you."

"We know," Polly says.

"He gave me the doughnuts," Kirsten says.

Maybe they were taken by a cult after all, I think. *Is this what people who've been brainwashed act like? Not like themselves, but not entirely different.*

"That was nice," I say carefully. "So, what happened to you guys?"

Kirsten hasn't lowered the doughnut, and the three of them gaze openly at one another, having a private conference without speaking. "We can't tell you," she says.

"Yet," Polly adds. "We are not ready to tell you yet." She attempts to soften the words which a smile, which makes me even more uneasy. I need to talk to Grant.

Unfortunately, he's probably still in police custody.

"Have you checked in with the police?" I ask. "They've been looking for you guys. You should probably go over there."

"I called," Polly says, "and after breakfast, we will go to the courthouse. That is where they want us to go."

Relief nearly sends me falling off my chair. I'll take my chances at being caught if it means getting out of this house, away from these stiff, doughnut-scarfing girls who don't seem remotely the same as before they disappeared.

"Great," I say. "I can drive you in your car if you want" — Polly frowns at me, so I come up with a reason — "you know, if you don't feel up to operating heavy machinery."

"Heavy machinery," Polly echoes. "That sounds like a good idea."

GRANT

Morning comes and I lie on the bench, listening to the first clues that something big has taken place overnight. The staccato din of ringing phones, shouted queries, and fast footsteps reach my cell.

Shadows flicker at the edges of my vision, and low voices buzz around me, but it's nothing like the screaming horde that smashed into me yesterday and took over my consciousness. This is what I'm used to — or *used* to be used to. It's the rain without the storm, the never-alone sensation I associate with the island. Only now it's dialed up a notch because the spirits' voices have a disturbed edge, sharper than usual.

The voices are upset.

They're not the only ones.

I must have freaked everyone out in the most major of ways — including Miranda. Trapped Miranda, who truly can't leave.

I stand up and confirm that I'm still in my jeans and T-shirt instead of a terrible prison jumpsuit. At least they left me in my own clothes. That's something. Now I just have to get out of here. Somehow.

I grip the cell bars in either hand and press my forehead onto the metal. Shouldn't I have a tin cup I can drag back and forth over the bars until someone comes to shout at me? The one time I broke out of jail, I still had the police force's amused graces on my side and talked my way out. Now that everyone knows my reputation, that won't work.

Not to mention . . . why am I even in here? All I remember are my parents and Whitson and . . . frowning strangers in dark suits, barking questions I wasn't able to respond to. Who are they?

Just then Mom rounds the corner and pads down the hallway, a Styrofoam cup of coffee in one hand. The dark smudges around her eyes nearly match the depressing gray cement wall behind her and the ghostly shadows of the spirits I see her through. She almost drops the steaming cup when she catches sight of me, clearly surprised to see me upright.

"Mom," I say, "good morning."

She straightens. "Is it?"

I try to ignore the buzz and hum raining through my head. "Better than yesterday."

"Anything would be better than yesterday." She can't have slept more than a few hours, if that. She takes a sip from the coffee.

"Why am I in here?" I ask.

Her head snaps up. "You don't remember."

Given the busy noises from the station floor, I doubt anyone is snooping on our conversation. I speak softly anyway. "It wasn't like anything that's ever happened to me before — all of a sudden the spirits and their voices just . . . overpowered me." I pause, attempting to make space away from the buzzing spirits. I focus on Mom. "Is Miranda all right? How freaked out was she?"

Mom shifts so she rests against the bars beside me. She doesn't want us to be overheard either, I realize. "Grant, you're in here because the FBI think you and Miranda worked together to murder her father and then you stole his body."

"What? I wasn't even here when he died! I was a million miles away. Well, several hundred." Their theory is as far off as the moon.

Mom grips her cup with one hand and reaches out with the other to touch mine. "I know, hon. But they don't understand where the body could be."

Something in my memory clicks, and a snatch of the shouted questions directed at me drifts through my mind. *What did you do with the body?* one of them asks, a man. An FBI guy.

"Someone took Miranda's dad's body," I say, not a question.

Mom nods. "And you guys were in the funeral home. Why exactly were you in the funeral home?"

So I'm in trouble with Mom too. "Miranda needed to see him and —"

"And you couldn't just ask your dad to arrange it." She shakes her head. "Grant, what happened to you yesterday? You were gone. Unreachable. Do you know why it was so bad?"

My forehead touches the bars. "I don't understand it either. It has to have something to do with the disappearance."

"The spirits are back, aren't they? The regular ones you hear?"

I nod.

"I knew from your eyes," she says, waving her hand next to her own. "I can tell when you aren't alone. When you're haunted. You *look* haunted."

Mom checks her watch, looks over her shoulder. Is it possible there's more gray in her hair from one night? Or is it a reflection from the shadow that glides in front of her?

"The agents will be coming in soon," she says. "Maybe we should ask them to transfer you to the mainland. I don't want to ever see that happen again."

I frown. Mom is on my side, always. "I'm not leaving. Where's Miranda?"

Mom's eyes land on the wall behind me. "She took off — she's currently evading federal custody. Any idea where she is?"

Miranda Blackwood, federal fugitive. I'm a bad influence. I can't stop a grin.

"I don't know," I say, and the truth of that sinks in. I don't know her well enough to know where she might go, but I know she's stuck here. "She's still on the island. Mom, you have to get me out of here. I'll find her."

There's a renewed force to the clamor in the front room, and someone breaks out in a cheer. It sounds like they're watching basketball out there. They might have, even in the middle of the apocalypse. But this is the wrong season, the wrong time of day.

Mom's coffee cup vibrates. Her hand is shaking.

"Mom, what's going on?"

The question rests between us for a moment.

She sets the coffee cup on the cement floor. Then she rises and put both hands over mine around the bars. "They're back," she says.

"Who? The spirits? I know."

"The missing people. They're back too. Your dad's scheduling a . . . group cattle call at the courthouse, to do a headcount and make sure it's everyone." She lets me process the news but goes on before I can ask anything else. "So why don't I feel like the danger has passed? The danger to you."

The missing have returned to Roanoke Island. I allow the brittle edge of the spirits' voices to bite into me, sure the dead's return is linked. But how?

No longer trapped —

Trapped there —

Trapped here —

"It hasn't. Because this isn't over," I finally say. "But you don't need to worry about me — I need to get to Miranda. *She's* the one in danger."

Mom removes her hands from mine, refusing to meet my eyes. She's never refused to meet my eyes. "Then maybe this is the safest place for you," she says.

"No," I say. "No."

"I'm . . . I'm sorry. I think it is, and I'm your mother."

"You have to trust me."

"This is new territory and . . . I can't let you go wandering around in it. My job is to protect you. This is the only way I have to do that. You can go back to being bad boy genius when this is over."

Mom doesn't bother to pick up her coffee cup. She just turns and walks up the hall, leaving me all alone, except for the spirits.

*

The minutes creep by, and I wish to make them pass more quickly. I drum my fingers on the legs of my jeans, struggling to push away the brittle voices while I wait. To focus.

Mom might be scared, but that leaves me to sort this out on my own. So I wait — and wait — for the noise in the station to die down. From what I can overhear, they're planning to take everyone they can spare to manage the crowd and check the identities of the returned at the courthouse. There will probably be just one or two guys left behind at the jail.

By the time it finally gets quiet, I'm more than ready to put my plan into action.

I stand, take a deep breath, and then launch my body forward, passing through the few shadows still in the cell with me. My knees hit the cement floor near the bars, and I shout in real pain. I bang my fists on the floor, hard enough to bruise my knuckles. I raise my hands and tear at my hair. I dive so deep into the performance that I barely notice when the officer appears outside the cell.

"Are you okay?" he says. "Your father's not here."

I turn my head toward the voice. I don't know this particular officer, some younger guy who can't have been on the force that long. I push away everything in my view that isn't in the bright, solid colors of reality and shout again, my cry fading when I hear the officer curse and start to walk away.

"Wait . . ." I choke out the word. The choking part comes easily, given how little I've had to drink and the fact I really did spend the night moaning in agony. "Meds," I say. "Need Whitson meds. Call doctor."

"I don't know," the officer says. "I can call your father and ask —"

I cut him off with another roar of pain. *"Meds,"* I beg, *"call Whitson."* I double over in what I hope is a realistic imitation of pain. At the corner of my vision, I see the guy nod.

"Hang on," the officer says. He's talking to himself as he walks away, "Sure, Chief, I'm the one who let your son go crazy. Sorry about that. Maybe you should just never promote me in return. . . . Crap!"

I moan some more, settling into a pattern of pitiful cries, and lower onto my back on the bench. I keep the pitiful sounds low enough that if I strain to block out the spirits — they seem less agitated, almost cooperative, at the moment, or am I imagining that? — I can hear the officer's return. It doesn't take nearly as long as I expect.

"Uh, Grant," the officer says, "your father actually had the doctor leave these."

I bet he did.

I moan louder and fight my limbs into an elaborate sit. I jerk to my feet. The officer has a small glass of water and a handful of several pills. This will be the hard part. The part I have to pull off, otherwise I'll be stuck in here while whatever bad thing that's come to town goes after Miranda.

"Thank you, officer." I force out the words like a zombie, my tone loud and broken. I stumble to the bars, then bounce off them and fall down onto the floor. I watch through slitted eyes as the officer realizes he doesn't have a free hand to unlock the cell door with, then maneuvers the Styrofoam cup between two fingers of the hand that holds the pills, and angles the key smoothly with his left hand.

Not a fumbler then.

I wait for him to get close and reach up for the pills and the water. Looking skeptical, the officer guides the cup to my hand. I have a flash of insight. I need to convince this guy. So, I do the last thing the guy will expect based on my reputation. I cooperate.

I open my mouth and extend my tongue. The officer hesitates, then drops the gel-coated pills into my mouth.

I take a sip of water and spill the rest on the floor, making sure it looks like clumsiness. I grab the officer's arm before he can leave. "Can you . . . can you . . ." The officer has to believe it's hard for me to get the words out. "Take me to the bathroom."

The officer's eyes narrow again, and I let my own become flying-saucer huge. Huge pupils are disconcerting, and mine should do the trick. I note the last name on the guy's tag — Warren — without recognition. I don't remember any Warrens, so maybe this guy's family moved here after I was sent away. Maybe he hasn't gotten the full dossier.

The officer shakes his head. "The chief said to keep an eye on you, but leave you put."

"Please." I tremble. "The meds. They knock me out cold. Haven't been to . . ."

"There's a toilet in the cell." Officer Warren points at the corner. I know almost no one is ever made to use that thing. In a town this size, that's tantamount to treason against a fellow citizen. Tourists, on the other hand . . .

"Not the tourist toilet." I grab his arm again, struggling to my feet. "Please, I don't have long. The meds. Take me."

Officer Warren's attention flicks back and forth between the cell toilet and me. "Crap. All right. But don't tell your dad, okay?"

I close my eyes and flick them back and forth behind closed lids with a moan. Then I pop them open. "I'll tell him you helped me."

A satisfied smile transforms the officer back to high school age. *God, he looks younger than me. In all the ways that count, he might be younger than me.*

I give a moment's regret to the trouble this guy will be in when Dad comes back. *Maybe they'll bond over it — I've tricked my dad enough times.*

First, I have to get out of here, though. I bend as I stand, enough to dump the pills in my hand with a casual tired swipe across my mouth. Then I lean my weight heavily against the officer. My timing has to be perfect.

We walk — the officer normally, me half-stumbling — up the hall and into the station. The key's back on his belt, and I happen to know he'll only need it to reopen my cell. The bathrooms are on the far side of the large open room, on the other side of the break area.

Officer Warren isn't the only one left after all. A vaguely familiar man in a black suit that screams FBI sits at the big coffee table in the break area. His head is tipped back to watch the muted ceiling-mounted TV.

The man's presence complicates things. I trace the consequences — of both success and failure. Once I take the next step in this plan, I'll be in the kind of trouble I've always avoided. The kind that isn't so easy to get away from. At seventeen, dosing a federal agent will probably get me in non-juvenile-record trouble.

The decision is mine to make.

In that moment, wrecking my future doesn't seem to matter so much. Only today matters. Only tomorrow matters. Only Miranda matters.

I feel certain I have a part to play, and it's not in this jail.

The FBI guy is drinking coffee. Another cup rests in front of the vacant chair next to him. So he and the officer have been watching the coverage together, drinking coffee. I banked on both. After all, who wants to miss the action? That guaranteed the TV would be on. And I'm betting all the officers have been working round the clock since the disappearances were reported, which meant the need for even more caffeine than normal.

On the TV, the brittle blond reporter, the one I watched Miranda dismiss so perfectly, beams. The scene behind her shows the crowded chaos in the courthouse square.

I raise my hand toward the screen. "Oh my God," I say.

The weight of my extended hand carries me forward, the FBI agent spinning with a moment's surprise.

"What is the kid doing out here?" The agent gets up, agitated.

Shadows dance around the agent, and so I turn my focus back to the small square of TV, my hands shaking like some arthritic old man's. Officer Warren grabs my other elbow to steady me, and says, "He's the chief's son, and he's having a hard time of it."

I really will have to put in a good word for Officer Warren. This guy wants to stay local. He isn't courting the fed's favor a bit. He's loyal to Dad.

The FBI guy must reach the same conclusion. "That's not your call — that boy may have murdered an innocent man just because his girlfriend wanted him to. And your chief promised we could question him after the head count. Take him back."

"You know none of us think that's what happened." The officer's shoulders square. "I'm not taking him back yet."

The fed takes a couple of steps toward us. The time has come. I either act fast or go back and wait for John Dee's main event, per Whitson's theory. At this point, given that Dee's symbol is all over everything and the gun is a good candidate for his immortality device, I have to assume Whitson is right.

The spirits' voices kick up a notch in volume:

You can't let it —

Act now —

Can't, no —

They want me to act.

I ignore the fed and blink like I'm dazed by the images on the screen. I power forward, breaking free from the distracted officer's grip. In an instant, I slip my hand into my pocket and then back out as I crash into the table. I hit hard enough to rattle the cups, but not hard enough to upend them.

"Oh God, so sorry — can't control . . ." I say.

"Grab him," the FBI guy says.

I reach out quickly, innocently, to slide the cups back into place. My hands float over the tops before I release them, trailing the powder from the sedative capsules I crushed in my palms into the coffee cups.

The FBI guy moves forward to shoulder me away from the table. I turn and gratefully grab the officer's hand.

"You think this kid's trying something, Agent Walker?" Officer Warren says, disgust in his tone, as he leads me toward the bathroom. "He's suffering. And I seriously doubt he's the murderer, since he has an airtight alibi. Down here, we require you to back up accusations with facts."

"Small town nonsense." The fed stalks to the chair, yanks it out, and swings back into place. My teeth press into the flesh below my bottom lip to stave off a grin as the fed picks up the cup and drinks from it.

Like a horse to water.

I cross my fingers that the pills don't taste too strong or work so quickly that Officer Warren catches on before the plan works. After all, he has to suck down some coffee too.

I make it to the bathroom with a smoother step, indulging in a few deep breaths, as if the meds are kicking in. "The pills are working," I say, keeping my voice weak. I go inside, count off an eternity of fifteen seconds, then flush and open the door.

The officer nods. "Back to the cell."

He isn't half bad at his job. I check on the FBI agent as we pass, afraid he'll already be slumped over and the officer will bust me. But Agent Walker is upright, freshening his coffee cup from the half-full pot and eyeing the screen. He refuses to look at us.

We reach the hallway with the two cells the jail possesses. I have to move quickly now. The drugs put me out in only a few minutes, but I was in much worse shape. Still, not much time.

The officer removes his keys and opens the cell, hooking them back onto his belt. I make my hand fake-spasm as I grab a bar. I give Officer Warren an embarrassed look. "I hate this," I say. "Being weak."

The officer says, "Just lie down and wait for your father to come back. He'll get you out of this."

No one can get me out of this. I grab the man in a clumsy hug. "Thank you," I say, meaning it.

Officer Warren frowns. "Well, not a pleasure, but . . . I hope you're better. And you'll tell your dad like you said?"

"Bet on it." I go inside and ease back onto my bench. "You better go check on Agent Moron."

The officer's face splits in a quarterback grin, despite himself. "Babysitting detail," he says. "Not sure who I'm supposed to watch more — you or him."

He rolls his eyes and leaves, the cell door clicking into place. I echo the gesture, rolling my eyes and laying my head against the cinderblock wall to wait. All part of my plan. The key I took from him warms in my palm, and I slide it into my jeans pocket.

You just dosed an FBI agent. And, soon enough, that nice cop.

But I could swear that the spirits seem upbeat. The chattering has taken on an energy that feels like approval.

Good job, our boy —
There you go —
The devil is here —
Already here —

I've never noticed the spirits reacting to anything I do or anything going on around me before. They have only talked *at* me.

Maybe, just maybe, the spirits will keep behaving while Dr. Whitson's medicine does its trick.

MIRANDA

We pile into Polly's Toyota — well, I pile. There's a stiff quality to the others' movements, like they're relearning how to walk. They climb in slowly.

Hanging out with Polly and her friends is nothing like it was just a few days earlier. Polly has always been chatty and warm, with a serious undertone that makes her competent and good at her job. Now the serious has overtaken the warmth. The other girls aren't much for the BFF giggles anymore either.

I never thought I'd miss their endless inside jokes. But I do.

I casually place my messenger bag on the console beside me, the strange concealed weapon inside. No way am I leaving it behind again.

After the others are in, I hesitate instead of starting Polly's car. "Are you sure Sidekick will be all right here?"

Polly's riding shotgun, and she doesn't answer.

Kirsten insisted on bringing the few remaining doughnuts along with us, and the sagging box is propped on her knees in the backseat. Polly's head whips around at the sound of the doughnut box opening. She frowns at Kirsten. "Get control of yourself."

Gretchen reaches out to grab another doughnut for herself, frowning too. Like she doesn't know what she's doing. She complained in the house that the sugar in the doughnuts made her stomach hurt. I had to explain that's because she usually refuses to eat carbs or refined sugar. Gretchen's expression then mimics what her face looks like now, disapproval tinged with confusion.

I felt the urge to explain what carbs and refined sugar even are. Which is ridiculous. She's obsessed with them. The day the overly skinny and diet-obsessed Gretchen Wolcott doesn't know the definition of these things — along with descriptions of every diet popular in the past five years — is the day that my ancestors turn out to be witches, people who sold their souls to some weirdo with an Elizabethan mad science lab.

Oh. Well.

"Let me just go get him," I say. I should keep Sidekick with me, in case these girls forget that dogs aren't something they eat when the doughnuts run out. Okay, that's not fair. They're acting strangely, but surely they wouldn't . . .

I glance in the rearview. Kirsten's cheeks puff out with her fifth doughnut.

Actually they might. And I'm leaving here with no intention of being the one who brings them home.

"Gretch is frightened of dogs," Polly says. "Best leave him here."

Gretchen offers no agreement or denial.

I reluctantly nod. I'll come back for Sidekick later. Before these girls make it home, as soon as I manage to ditch them. Sidekick won't know to worry, anyway; he's probably snoozing or nosing through the trash for wadded up napkins with doughnut residue.

I start the car and drive toward town as fast as I dare, meaning the speed limit. The feds will no doubt still be looking for me.

My hands clench for a moment on the steering wheel as I think about their crazy theory . . . and my dad. The snake on my face makes me feel closer to him than I have since before Mom died. He bore this curse too, and I'm beginning to understand what that means. It isn't just a birthmark. It's something that snakes its way inside too. Dad wasn't strong enough to fight it. The curse beat him.

What if I'm not strong enough either?

I shake my head. I have to be.

Polly barks a choppy laugh that barely sounds like her. "Having a conversation with yourself, Miranda?" she asks.

"Just an earworm." I slow the car as it enters a line of vehicles heading into downtown. I refuse to glance over at my friend . . . my friend who is being *extremely* weird. I want out of this car. "We might as well park back here and walk it, don't you think?" I ask.

"Fine," Polly says.

I pull up to the curb and turn the car off. Walking with the others to the courthouse square is risky, but a crowd will be the easiest place to lose them. At least the agents only met me once, and I don't fool myself that my face is capable of launching a thousand ships *or* lodging in someone's memory. They are trained to remember, though. I'm not fooling myself about that either.

Polly grabs my arm before I can get out. "It is good to see your face."

Whatever fate I'm fleeing, these guys may have already faced. I wanted Polly to come back, and I certainly hadn't wished for the other missing people to be gone forever either. That they've returned should be a good thing.

"You too," I say.

I slip the strap of my bag over my head, and we leave the safety of the car. We join a horde of townsfolk swarming toward the square.

The air smells of sunscreen and sweat, of summer's end. I realize there's every possibility the town rumor mill already knows I'm suspected in Dad's death. Not that they ever cared about him before. Then again, the chief will try to keep it quiet for Grant's sake, and there's the return of the missing to fill the ever-present need for something — or someone — to dissect with the scalpels of gossip. Maybe no one knows yet.

Based on the size of the crowd in front of the courthouse, everyone left in Manteo has turned out. The news trucks squat in the same locations they claimed before. Near one, Blue Doe has a microphone gripped in her hand and a wild gleam in her enormous eyes. The courthouse itself is cordoned off by police tape, setting a perimeter about fifteen feet past the columns and broad porch. A lesser mass of people wait inside the cordon, standing with such patience it's clear they're waiting.

The local police have help from state troopers on keeping gawkers away from the tape, while one of the older officers on the porch uses a bullhorn to repeat: "Only the missing are requested past the cordon. If you're one of the missing, come up to the courthouse."

Gretchen and Kirsten move toward the tape immediately, a state trooper shooting them a nod and smile as they go under the cordon.

When Polly doesn't follow, I pat her shoulder. "You should go with them now," I say. My voice shakes a little, and I hope she doesn't hear it.

"You will wait for me?" Polly asks.

I'm a terrible person. "Of course," I say. "Now, go. Your parents are probably worried sick." If I remember correctly, I think they live somewhere in upstate New York.

Polly's lashes flutter, and she says, "I forgot about them . . . my parents."

Where were Polly and the others for the days they were missing? Where would make her forget about her parents?

"They'll never know that," I say instead of asking. "Go on."

Polly blinks at me, then finally walks toward the trooper and under the yellow tape. I turn away quickly when he shifts in the direction Polly came from. Going into a crowd full of law enforcement is not among my smartest decisions ever. If this were one of my favorite shows, I'd scream, *'Get out of there!'* at the screen.

I thread my way back through the crowd, intending to do just that.

"Is that everyone?" officer bullhorn says.

The crowd continues to talk. They're busy speculating about how much tourism will pick up after this, how it must've been an arranged stunt, who was in on it and who wasn't. I can't blame them for spinning theories to make sense of the mystifying event now that the missing people are herded before them, no longer missing.

"Silence, please!" the officer roars into the bullhorn. "Now, do we have everyone?"

The crowd stops talking, necks craning to see inside the cordon. I stop too. I'm afraid to keep moving when no one else is.

"Last call for members of the missing to join us behind the tape," the officer says.

I turn and watch Chief Rawling come through the front door of the courthouse and stride over to take the bullhorn. "Welcome back, everybody," he says. "We knew the town would want to see you, to know that everyone is okay. That's why we're doing things this way. If you could just stay here, we'll be coming through to take your names and then escort you inside for your statements. We'll get you back to your families as quickly as possible."

Being in the crowd has felt like being under a spotlight the whole time, but suddenly the snake pulses on my cheek. I scan the mass of people and, all the way on the other side of the square, Bone is pointing at me. I read his lips: "There she is!"

He's with his friends, but his father is standing behind them, and he cuffs Bone's ear. Dr. Roswell focuses on my location. The crowd has begun a low buzz of conversation after the chief's announcement, and that saves me. I have to get out of here.

I take one last look at the courthouse, at the missing. They're arranged in a familiar formation. Some are higher, standing on the landing between the columns, and some lower, down the stairs, on the sidewalk and lawn. In tidy rows, each of them turns to the other in sequence. They aren't wearing the gray cloaks from my dream, but their arms wind through the air in the same fashion.

The crowd hushes again, and I have trouble breathing. This is no dream. I force myself to look away from the movements of the no-longer missing and discover Roswell cutting through the crowd toward me. He drags Bone along by his arm.

I shove my way past people murmuring about the bizarre arm-waving actions of their returned friends and family members. Grant trusts Roswell, but I barely know him. And I definitely don't trust Bone.

I get to the crowd's thinner edge, ready to head for Polly's car, but I can't resist checking behind me one last time, to confirm what I saw. The missing people remain clearly visible on the raised landing and just below it in their rows. But they stand normally now, arms relaxed, making me wonder if I imagined their actions.

No. The crowd — other people reacted. This isn't like at the theater with the ship. Everyone else saw their movements too.

About to take off, I almost miss him. He walks under the police tape and enters the rows of the returned people. He stops and looks, unmistakably, at me. I wouldn't recognize him if I hadn't seen photos from their wedding day. That suit was from the Salvation Army, but this one is nicer. Better cut. He could be a businessman.

Instead, he's my father.

I can't breathe.

He's dead. I saw his body.

But now his hair has been trimmed into a tidy cut, and no stubble shadows his cheeks. His complexion is pale instead of ruddy, his eyes clear. I never knew Dad could clean up so well.

He tilts his head down, as if to greet me.

I want to go to him, as if compelled by some magnetic force. I take a step toward him without meaning to.

"Come to me." The whisper seems to come from beside my ear. I stumble.

"Miranda Blackwood!" Dr. Roswell calls out, and a few people nearby notice me.

"Poor girl. Her father got murdered — that family truly is cursed," someone says to the person next to them, and Roswell calls "Miranda!" again.

I snap out of my blind-need haze. No one else recognizes Dad. And why should they, when I barely do? They might gossip about him, but I doubt anyone has ever bothered to look too closely. To them, this man is a clean-cut stranger in a suit. They probably think he's a disappeared tourist.

The man who *has* to be Dad — but who doesn't feel like him, somehow — curves his lips in the slowest smile I've ever seen. The expression is as foreign as his made-over appearance. I'm certain the voice next to my ear was his, even though his lips didn't move, except to offer that slow smile. Even though I didn't recognize the voice as Dad's.

A couple of rows away from him, Chief Rawling holds a clipboard and talks to one of the returned. He pauses to scan the crowd, which probably means he heard the good doctor's shouts. The woman the chief was talking to swiveled. It's Polly. The sun falls directly on her features, her face pinched as she follows the chief's lead and scrutinizes the surge and press on the other side of the rope line.

I shrink behind a large man in the crowd, hiding. *My father is dead.* I call up the memory of him on the shiny table in the funeral home, the cold air and antiseptic smell of the room returning like a sudden sweat.

"Miranda!" The shout sounds nearer. "I just want to talk. It's about Grant!"

Nice try. That crackpot is going to get me caught.

I make sure the keys are ready as I head toward Polly's car. There's no looking back this time, no Sidekick to get distracted by the evil phantom ship, no one but me. And then I'm behind the wheel, tossing my bag into the back, and turning the key in the ignition, jerking the car into drive and out of the spot.

I execute a three-point turn in the middle of the wide street. I'm not willing to do a drive-by of the scene or risk getting caught on a throng-blocked street. Just this once, I don't miss Pineapple; Polly's is a far more reliable getaway car.

In the rearview mirror, I spot Dr. Roswell standing on the street behind me. His hands are propped on his hips, and his face is as pink as Bone's when an insult lands. Too bad if I hurt his feelings. Grant can apologize for me later. I don't have time to worry about him.

My only worry is for my father — or is that the man wearing my father's body? Dead men don't hit the salon and go out for a stroll, not even on Roanoke Island. Or do they?

I have no idea where I'm going. I just drive.

GRANT

I wait as long as I can stand. I compose a symphony with the drumming I inflict on my legs. It helps me ignore the spirits. But I can't sit tight any longer. Either the drugs have worked their sleepy magic or my plan has tanked and I'll be headed directly back to this jail cell. There's one way to see whether my fate is door number one or . . .

"Opening door number two," I murmur.

I stick my hand through the bars and fit the pilfered key into the lock. I clamp on to the door with my other hand and avoid a clank by holding the metal in place when the tumbler releases. Slowly, I crack the door open and move into the hallway. The spirits are faint, only a few shadows, their voices quiet enough to shut out. It's almost like they're worried about giving me away.

So far, so good. No angry young officers or federal agents in sight. I hurry up the hall, stepping softly, glad for my sneakers. I hit the end of the hallway, the front door of the station in sight, and judge it an acceptable risk.

The cough startles me.

In the waiting area, Officer Warren slumps in a chair. He looks like he's fighting hard to stay conscious. I check the station floor and spot the FBI agent. He lies forward on the coffee table, his head on his arms like a kindergartener at naptime. If kindergarteners were bald and wore black suits.

Officer Warren's next sound is a massive yawn mixed with a frustrated moan. He manages to get out, "Don't . . . be . . . stupid."

I note the gun loosely gripped in the cop's left hand. "I'm not," I say. "That's always been one of my biggest problems."

That and the dead.

The officer clearly puts forth a massive amount of energy to get his next sentence out. "You'll go to jail. For real."

I nod. "Probably."

"I hope whatever you're leaving for is worth . . . that."

She is, I think without a pause.

I go for the door. "I'm not leaving, I'm staying," I say, shocked to discover it's true. Under my breath, I add, "For once."

I press the glass door, then crook my head back. The officer may or may not be asleep, but I say, "You'll both be fine once the drugs wear off. I'm not that stupid."

As I hit the parking lot, I consider my options. They aren't great — none of the things I need to do mesh, and I have no idea where to find Miranda. I scan to make sure the area is deserted and stop dead.

Across the street in the police station parking lot, the driver's side door of an unfamiliar blue Toyota swings open. Before I can take off, someone steps out of the strange car, someone who isn't a stranger. Her hand grips the top of the door.

Miranda.

I blink, wondering if she's an apparition, but, no. She shines like a star compared to the shadows that flicker in the air between us. What's she doing here?

We both stand where are, looking at each other in disbelief.

I move first, jogging over to the car, and she walks forward to meet me. I stop, and she does too, half an arm's length separating us.

Miranda puts her hands in her pockets.

I grin at her.

"I'm sorry," she blurts. "For pushing you down."

Wait . . . what? When did she push me down? I remember being in sand, but I thought I fell into it when the spirits came back with such strength.

A few whisper, but I press them away. I focus on Miranda.

"We have big problems," she says, talking fast. "Huge, really."

"Well, yeah. You're a federal fugitive," I offer. "For one."

"Oh," she says, "I didn't mean that."

"I am too," I say. "A fugitive, I mean."

She angles her head in the direction of the station house, "You didn't?"

I duck my head. "I did."

"You escaped *from jail?*" She says it like it's the craziest thing ever, which it sounds like when she puts it that way.

"Guilty," I say. I fidget a little, embarrassed.

Miranda's hand comes out of her pocket, and she pushes the top of my right shoulder with her palm. She shakes her head. "Get in the car, Houdini."

I get in without a word and so does she. She shakes her head at me again and puts the car in drive.

I pat the dash. "Whose is this?"

"Polly — the stage manager at the show. A friend," she says. "Or she used to be."

"How are you?" I ask. "Last time we were together, you were . . . freaked. Understandably freaked."

"I'm more freaked." She bites her lip, foot on the brake as she turns to face me. "But about yesterday . . ."

I don't want her to apologize again for whatever it is she believes she did wrong. Has no one ever just forgiven her? Given her the benefit of the doubt? Made her understand that being yourself is enough to make things very, very hard sometimes?

Before she can say anything else, I touch her cheek, below the evil birthmark, the one that shouldn't be on her skin. I stroke my hand over the curve of her cheek, reassuring her without words that I'm here. That I'm not going anywhere.

She looks at me, eyes big and wondering, not protesting, and I think about kissing her. That'll be how we get busted. *Well, judge, they were apprehended lingering outside the jail while making out in a stolen car.*

I would stay inside this moment, right where we are, regardless of if the cuffs are coming. But she doesn't need that from me right now. She needs something else.

"You don't need to apologize to me for anything. Ever," I say.

She relaxes a slight fraction. "If you say so."

I drop my hand and catch sight of something in the back seat. "Your last doughnut spoken for?"

She laughs, a real laugh, almost in hysterics, as she faces forward and begins to drive. "That creepy doughnut is all yours. I'm surprised they left one. And, for the record, I'm never eating doughnuts again."

"Tell me what I missed," I say, snagging the doughnut, which appears not creepy so far as I can see. I take a bite.

"Well," Miranda says, swallowing, all seriousness again. She stops the car before she turns out onto the road and looks at me. "I just saw my dad downtown."

Doughnut flies from my mouth. "What?" I sputter. I can't believe what I'm hearing.

She nods. "Walking around all cleaned up, hanging out around the returned people. But it didn't feel like him."

"What do you mean?" I ask.

"I'm not sure. Just when he looked at me, it didn't feel like it was him. It felt like someone else."

"Who?" I ask.

She shakes her head. Neither of us has an answer.

*

As we begin our slow approach to my house through the woods, on foot now, I'm still absorbing the bulk of what Miranda told me. I still can't believe her dad is up and walking around town like nothing happened. The spirits thankfully stay backed off for now, shadows and gray flickers, a note of confusion in their words.

We won't be able to keep her friend Polly's car for long, but our options are limited. I press a low-hanging branch aside so Miranda can pass in front of me. "I promise after we do this, we'll go get Sidekick," I say. "And return the car so they won't say it's been stolen. Sound okay?"

Miranda turns to me, the green branches turning her into a haunted creature from some other realm, the kind who lures men into the forest to their deaths. She's taken her black hair down and it hangs wild with tangles. She fiddles with the strap of her messenger bag, which has John Dee's weapon in it. She didn't want to answer *how* she retrieved the gun out of the trunk of Mom's car, and so I dropped it.

"You're sure we can't do this later?" she asks. She wanted to go get Sidekick right away, but she hasn't insisted.

"It's just going to get riskier to come back here. People will be back at the jail soon. I need to get something from my room before they realize I'm gone." The letter. I'm hoping that it'll provide some guidance, tell me what to do with my gift. Finally.

"Maybe we can still beat Polly and the others back to the Grove." Miranda doesn't sound sure of that.

What she told me about how strangely her friends were acting doesn't make any immediate sense to me. I decide to focus on making another plan — isolating the steps we need to take to figure out the endgame in all this. I hope whatever I come up with will work as well as the escape plan I'll eventually land in jail for.

On the other hand, there is at least one good thing about Miranda's father being back. I should be off the hook for any supposed murder.

Except he was dead — undeniably, indisputably dead — in Marlon's cold room. How his body got out of there, got up and around, is a looming question. One I don't have the answer for.

We travel through another stretch of woods. Birds and insects chirp around us, as if it's any normal day. Miranda stops near the tree line, my yard just steps away. A quick scurry across, and I can climb the tree outside my room and get the letter. Simple.

"After the Grove, we'll head to Whitson's —" I start, but Miranda tosses me an *I'd rather not* look over her shoulder. "We need to question him more about your family history, right?"

197

Miranda says, "I guess. But I told you — I ran away from him at the square."

"You should have, I wasn't with you." I puff my chest out and put my fists on my hips in parody of a superhero, an attempt to make her laugh.

I'm gratified by her teeth biting into her lower lip. "Captain Ego!" she says.

"I prefer to go by . . ." I search for a better name.

"The X-Prisoner?" she offers. "You know, like the X-Men."

"I got it." We don't have time for this, but I drop my mouth open in false outrage. "But a pun? How could you?"

"Mischief Man?" she tries again, smiling now.

I tilt my chin down and shoot her a look full of acid disapproval.

"Okay, okay. That one sucks." She bites her lip again, thinking this time, and then thrusts a finger into the air. "I've got it. Random Fact Boy!"

I consider. "Not bad. Except facts aren't random, you know —"

Just then the front door opens. I move to Miranda's side and pull her hand down. We crouch, wordlessly, letting the dense ground cover conceal us.

Mom steps out onto the front porch. She scrutinizes the yard and trees where we're hiding, but she doesn't come any closer. When she goes back inside and closes the door, I'm pretty sure she hasn't spotted us.

"Damn," Miranda says. "She's home."

I frown, more at Miranda's *damn* than at the news Mom's home. I expected her to be.

"I like your mom," she says. "Don't get me wrong."

"Not that. Why didn't you say frak?"

Her cheeks flush. "You noticed I do that?"

I've missed hearing her say it more than I'm comfortable with. It's a Miranda-thing. Part of what makes her who she is. "I like it."

She flushes again. "I know it's goofy, but Mom never liked it when Dad cursed. So I just . . . don't. Like she's watching or something. But you said she wasn't, so . . ."

So it's even more a part of what makes her who she is. I came here to help her because I felt moved to protect her, to make amends for the past — but now I want to know her. I want to know all there is to know.

"But the spirits are back, so . . . maybe she is?" I say. She sits up with a hopeful look.

I have to shake my head with regret. "I can't tell the difference between them. They're just *there*. Talking. I don't know."

"Oh."

We fall silent, and the noise of the woods seems to surge around us, a wall that melds with the whispering, chattering spirits that meander through the woods. This girl could steal me into the wild, and I wouldn't entirely mind.

"Anyway, I like your mom," Miranda says, bringing me back to the present.

"Me too, but she's not on my side right now. Not how we need her to be."

"Because she cares about you," Miranda says.

"Why doesn't matter right now. So you'll wait here and —"

"No," she says. The levity of the past few minutes disappears, the darkness around her eyes like an aura. "My father. He . . . I can't . . ."

She's scared to stay here alone, I realize. Bringing her along will make getting out dicey if anything goes wrong, but I don't want

199

her to wait and suffer either. We just need to storm the castle fast, make it in and out before Mom has a chance to catch us.

My kingdom for a couple more sedatives and a cloak of invisibility, just in case.

"I get it," I say. "You'll come too."

MIRANDA

Grant insists on climbing the tree outside his window instead of sneaking in the front or back doors. I can tell he's surprised I don't argue — and that I'm proving to be an ace tree climber.

This is something Mom and I did together back when I was a kid — one of my few good memories. Mom calling me a monkey and laughing, even though she was just as good at finding holds for her feet at the right angle to avoid ankle twists, at gripping the bark without scratching her palms, at looking up and going there. Maybe we had an advantage in that a fair number of island trees tended to grow strangely, with dips and curves, or with trunks split by hurricanes and storms. Bent, deformed, cursed trees. No wonder I always liked them so much.

Grant reaches the thick limb that extends almost to his window, and I raise myself up behind him, staying near the trunk. He scoots toward the window. The limb thins near its end, and I'm not sure it will survive his weight.

"You don't have to stay back there. It'll hold us both," he says. He maneuvers into a crouch, just where the thin end begins to bow.

"Wait," I protest, "that looks —"

But Grant just hops across the space between the limb and the window, landing in an upright crouch on the ledge. As if he's done this a million times.

"— dangerous," I finish.

He grins at me. "It is, I guess."

"That's not what I want to hear," I say, stalling. What if the curse decides to manifest? This would not be a good time to randomly trip like I did before. "How do you know it could hold us both? Entertain a lot of girls when you were thirteen?"

"Of course," he says, "because most thirteen-year-old girls would have no problem with what you're about to do."

I trace my palms over the scarred bark. He means come across.

"What is it?" he asks. "You climb like a . . ."

"Don't say monkey."

"Leopard," he finishes.

The limb sways in a breeze.

"Maybe I should stay here and wait." After all, what are the odds that the dead man who looks like my dad can climb trees?

"What's wrong?" he asks.

I have to tell him. "Breaking into your mom's car, I tripped when there wasn't anything there. I'm not usually klutzy. I think it's the birthmark or something."

"Oh." Grant touches his cheek. Then he holds out his hand to me. "Give me your hand. No matter if it's a snake moment, I'll catch you."

He'll catch me. All right, then.

I pull my messenger bag's strap as tight as it goes, then shimmy a few inches further until the branch bends with my weight. I grab Grant's hand and climb unsteadily to my feet. He takes my other hand, and, rather than get across in any graceful way, I count to three and jump across to him. I squeeze my eyes shut, only opening them once I land.

Grant catches me as promised, but we sway on the ledge with the force of my jump. He grabs at the windowpane with the curled fingertips of one hand, and I brace against the brick wall that forms the ledge. There's barely room for us both.

Finally the swaying stops.

Grant is so close I could tilt my head and bite his nose. Which is a ridiculous thought. He holds my elbow to keep me steady.

"Not *so* klutzy," he says, "but a little."

He turns to the window, and I suck in a dismayed breath at the sight of the windowsill. "Nailed shut?"

He maneuvers a fingernail under the edge of one flat metal circle and pops out the nail. He does the same with the other. "It was a problem the first time, but after that . . ."

The window glides open under his hands, and I accept his help climbing through it. Having solid floor under my feet again is the height of luxury, like maid service or a hot water heater that never gives out.

Luxurious until I remember we are in Grant's room.

Together.

Alone.

When he touched my cheek at the station and told me I never had to apologize . . . that was the moment I started to trust him. It feels impossible that I have someone to count on in so short a time, but I feel certain that I do. And when I saw him outside the police station, I realized I'd missed him. A day and I missed him.

Complete silly girl, and I don't feel like there's anything I can do to stop it. I don't really want to.

So it's a *good* thing we don't have time to do anything but retrieve this mystery item. I'm guessing it's the letter from his grandmother, but I don't want to pry.

Grant's giant duffel bag has been transferred from the bed to the floor, and said bed is as rumpled as the shirt he's wearing — make that the shirt he whips over his head. He tosses it toward a corner, standing frozen and shirtless. He has a nice torso. I can't stop looking at it.

The moment has an intensity that makes me want to laugh, except the air is too thick with tension. I cross to his duffel and pick out a black T-shirt.

Grant stays exactly where he is, and I walk to him. I lay the shirt flat against his chest, its fabric between my hand and his skin. His hand lifts to cover mine . . .

And then I do laugh. I'm too nervous not to. I lower my voice, so his mom won't hear and come running. "Now you put it on," I say.

"Right."

He takes the T-shirt and pulls it over his head. A gray-silhouetted ninja races across the front.

"And get what you came for," I say.

"Right."

Grant moves past me and kneels before the bag, carefully going through the contents until he finds a certain shirt and unfolds it to reveal a small cream envelope, tattered with time. His name is written on the back.

I feel drawn to touch the envelope, much like I felt drawn to the gun. The gun in my bag. The gun I blasted Grant with. *Black dust only. It didn't hurt him.*

Both of us flinch at the sudden sound of the front door opening, then slamming shut. Grant presses his finger to his lips, and we wait. I'm not sure for what. Then, faint but unmistakable, a car engine cough and turns over.

"Mom left," he says, seeming confused about why. "She must have taken Dad's old car. Hardly ever leaves the garage."

I don't want to mention that the likely reason is Grant's jailbreak.

He fills the silence. "Means we have a little breathing room here now."

"So, what's that?" I ask, curious if he'll tell me. My fingers still itch to touch the paper.

"It's a letter from my grandmother. To me. She gave it to my dad before she died, and he just decided to turn it over. Because of . . ."

"Everything. I know," I say. I have to be honest with him. "The other night I listened in on your conversation."

Grant blinks at me. "From the top of the stairs. Exactly what I would have done." He seems pleased about it.

"What's it say?" I ask.

He shrugs helplessly. "I don't know. I meant for us to read it together and then everything went haywire."

He meant for us to read it *together.* I'm afraid for him, afraid what's in the letter will end up hurting him. Afraid I will. But still. He meant for us to read it *together.* Like we're a team.

"Do you want me to read it to you?" When he doesn't answer right away, I add, "I understand if you don't. This is private."

He looks at the envelope. "It's a little scary. I don't think I told you . . . when Gram died, that night was the first time I saw the spirits, heard them speaking."

"I don't blame you for being a little scared," I say. "Are there any here now?"

He shakes his head. "No, they're keeping their distance for the moment. I don't know why."

"You loved your grandmother?" I ask. The answer might not be so simple. I never knew either set of my grandparents.

"I did."

"And she loved you?"

His lips soften with his nod.

"It'll be okay then," I say. "Let me read it to you."

He hands it to me. The envelope opens with a whisper of old paper against itself. I pull out a single sheet folded into thirds. Tidy, slanted handwriting in blue ink bleeds through the back of the page.

"'Dear Grant,'" I start, pausing to give him time to change his mind.

He waits without speaking. I shift closer to the light of the window, and read on.

"'I'm sorry about the gift I know will now fall onto your shoulders . . .'" When I stop to gauge his reaction to the beginning, he gestures for me to keep going. "'. . . but the most important fact about our family is our lineage. I know you believe my stories are just those of a silly old woman. But it is what makes us who we are, the keepers and protectors of this island, a ground with as many names as our gifted have borne over the years. You will not find their names written or their actions detailed, but know that our family line has a long history of service to this place. It would not have been safe to document that history. And so it has been a tale told by one bearer of the burden to the next.'"

I clear my throat, dry as if dust bunnies from under the bed had migrated there. These secrets were never meant for me to hear. I know that much.

"Go on," Grant says.

"'In the past, the gift has passed down through the women in our family, fate's way of ensuring its preservation in our line. When I was able to bear only one child, a boy, your father, I thought that meant that I would be the one to finish our task. That either we would end or the island would. Your father never developed the gift, never understood it. But you, Grant, you are different. I see now that you will be the last of us. We must have been very close to the edge when your father was born — maybe I was to be the final protector. But events were turned from their course. I don't know how long you have, and I know you were not properly trained. I have failed you on that score, afraid your father would never allow it, and for that I am sorry.'"

"I removed myself," Grant says.

I continue. "'Our line stretches all the way back to the first appearance of the devil on these shores. A child was left behind on the beach when the devil's cohort was forced to abandon its plan. I know you have never believed this, but your ancestor — and mine — was taken in and protected by the Secotans. Virginia Dare was a child well hidden before that bastard John White ever returned, searching for his master's weapon. That child was freed from her parents' sins, left on the island's rough ground because she was too young to promise herself and follow his acolytes into the other world. The tribe knew that decision tied her to this land. Just as the traitor Mary Blackwood's decision tied her. Her line was to be marked with the serpent as agents of betrayal.'"

I choke out my own last name, barely stopping to wonder that it's stayed the same all these years later. Being chained to a cursed name is a curse of its own.

"Is that the end?" Grant asks.

I flip the page to finish: "'The devil and his cohort are bound to return, my boy, and it will be your task to prevent them from staying, to prevent *him* from bringing a black night over this world. He will claim his acts are of nature, but they are not. He is clever and powerful, and he will not be alone. But know, Grant, that you are not alone either. Let your gift guide you. Use all the strength available to you, and protect this land as we are sworn.'"

I stop and look up. "It ends there. She didn't even sign it."

Grant runs a hand through his already-messy hair. "So John Dee's the devil."

"And I'm a traitor."

GRANT

This is difficult ground to navigate. Land mine, trapdoor, quicksand ground.

The late afternoon light traces shadows under Miranda's eyes, hollows out her cheeks. I wish for more light on her face, enough light to see inside her head. Gram's letter, which she'd probably be horrified to discover anyone besides me has read — not even getting into the Blackwood thing — is clutched in Miranda's hand.

"You are not a traitor," I tell her. "The letter did *not* say that."

Miranda holds her hand next to her face, flourishing like a showroom model. "Because the serpent is equal to light and sunshine, and agents of betrayal are all the rage." She lowers her fingers, the gesture tired. Not defeated, *tired*. "That's exactly what it said. Grant . . . maybe you shouldn't be helping me. You have a job in all this, on the side of the angels" — her lips quirk to one side — "literally, I guess. And I have the exact opposite."

I come close enough to lift the letter from between her fingers. I'm careful not to snatch it away. A surge of shadows appears and looms around us, *talking, talking, talking.*

This is the key —
All we have to rely on —
She knows it —
The devil, the devil is here HERE —

I do my best to shut them out. This is between Miranda and me. I look at her so hard I can't see another thing.

"I'm supposed to protect the island, right?" I say. "How can I do that without protecting you? Your dad . . ."

"He's the devil in this now, isn't he?" Miranda says. She used that same flat tone when she found out about his death. "He has to be," she continues. "He was dead. We saw his body."

I wave the letter. Her eyes follow it like the single piece of paper has made solid everything she suspected about what her family curse means. I fold the page quickly — better to put it away, out of sight — and shove it inside my pocket.

"Gram never met a situation she couldn't add drama to. She and my dad had that in common. But that's *not* your father. You told me it didn't feel like him when he looked at you. Your father's gone."

"Like the people from town were gone?"

She's too smart for me to manipulate. And I don't want to. The beginnings of a theory about the disappearance and the return hangs unspoken between us. What if the people who came back aren't the ones who left, but rather ones meant to be long dead?

"If the Blackwoods are betrayers and traitors, then maybe it *is* my dad," Miranda adds when I don't reply.

"Even if it is, or some part of him, or an ancestor . . ." I reach for her hand, but she skitters away. "He isn't you. *You* aren't your family."

"No. *We* are our families. Both of us. That's why we're in this. We are the historical baggage twins. That much, I get." She blows out a breath. "If I do turn out to be the bad guy, you have to promise me something."

I already don't want to do whatever it is. "What?"

"This town has never treated me like anything except its trash. These people — most of them, anyway — have never done anything for me, except call me a freak. Except make me feel like one. And that's okay. That's what people do. They whispered about my mother after she died. She wasn't one of us. She deserved better."

I want to tell her she never has to do anything for the people she's talking about, that they don't deserve her consideration. Gram's words prevent me, though. My family is sworn to protect the island, and I'm guessing that includes the people who live on it. My mother and father are among that number.

I've been the first to run from my responsibilities, but no more.

Miranda isn't done. "They couldn't help themselves. All that was part of my being a snake, a Blackwood. But if I'm the bad guy, you have to promise not to let me win. I've resented all this, all these people, for so long. But I can't be responsible for whatever Dee, my father, whoever, has planned. I won't prove them all right."

Her shoulder trembles. I don't dare touch her, but I say, "I promise not to let you be the bad guy."

"Thank you."

"But what does he have planned? You have the weapon, which seems to be the key to everything." I stop when I detect a hint of sirens in the distance. Did they just start or did I not notice them before? I answer Miranda's questioning look with, "Sirens. You hear them?"

They're coming —

Go, boy, go —

You have your marching orders —

I press the spirits' voices away, as much as possible.

Miranda pivots toward the sound of the sirens. We're both facing the doorway when Mom steps into my room.

A shadow glides in front of her.

Listen — God — go — go —

"I'm sorry," Mom says, "but what was I supposed to do?"

She has on gardening clogs instead of real shoes. I'll bet anything she didn't go much beyond the driveway.

I underestimated her. My mistake.

Miranda's alarm is clear, which means I need to stay calm, even if the sirens are getting closer. "You faked leaving?" I ask.

"I've learned a few things from you over the years," Mom says. "And you know how I hate borrowing your father's car. I drive a stick like somebody your age, not mine."

"Were you listening the whole time?"

"Your dad shouldn't have given that to you," she says, looking at the letter in my hand. "I wouldn't have let him. And I won't have you sacrificing yourself for this island. Not for anyone on it. I love you too much."

"So you called Dad."

Mom drops her false calm. "You drugged a police officer and an FBI agent?"

She's pissed. I understand.

"You did *what?*" Miranda clamps her mouth shut as soon as the question's out.

"It's not good for Miranda to be mixed up in this either," Mom says, appealing to both of us. "Your father can protect her."

I wish.

"Mom." I sigh the word. "I know you're worried and feeling all maternal, but you *have* to let us go. If they take me in now, no college, no nothing. Jail. If we stop without finishing this then . . ."

"The devil?" Mom prompts. "The devil will come back and what?"

The devil is already here — go — get out —

I realize then that she waited to come in until the sirens were on the way. She's trying to delay us. She didn't want us to leave before the squad cars rolled in. "Why didn't you warn them not to put on the sirens?" I ask.

"The feds were a little too upset to go the quiet route."

Maybe I can use her worry to convince her to let us go. "If we stop what's happening, then it won't matter so much what I did today. Miranda's dad is, um, back."

The tilt of Mom's head means she's listening, but the sirens are getting closer. "How is that possible?" she asks. Then she shakes her head. "It doesn't matter. There's no other way for me to protect you from getting in even worse trouble."

GO, GO, NOW

Sirens. Voices. All getting louder.

"Yes," I say.

Boy, you have to go —

Even the snake knows —

213

She can't stay here —

I look with longing at the window. If only I had time to plan an escape. The voices pick up in pitch, their shadows streaking the room in frenetic motion.

When I look back, Miranda is pointing John Dee's antique gun at my mother.

The sight isn't my favorite. But I'm not worried — even if it does go off, the black powder won't hurt her.

I fight to focus on the two of them.

Mom shakes her head. I don't mistake how angry she is. "That's clearly a museum piece, and the police will be here any minute," she says. "Guys, I'm the adult here. I rarely pull rank, but I'm doing it now. Listen to me."

Miranda ignores her — or pretends to. "Grant, can you help me get over to the tree? You'll go first," she says to me.

I doubt getting out will be that simple, but it's worth a shot.

"Yeah," I say, "I think we can make it."

I cross to the window, and Mom moves to stop me. Miranda blocks her, leveling the enormous jeweled gun. "No," she says.

Mom barely pauses, and I watch as Miranda's finger squeezes the trigger.

I shut my eyes, a reflex against the memory of the powdery burst, a burst that shouldn't have been possible from an unlit matchlock. *It's a magic gun, no fire necessary.*

Only this time, there's the immediate scent of burning. The first sign something is wrong.

The second is the way Mom collapses in a heap on the ground, her head rolled back against my duffel bag. A film of pale dust coats her upper body. Her face is white as a cloud.

The snake —

We keep saying —

Blood, blood, blood —

They're here —

Miranda tosses the gun on the floor, and dives for Mom. "Oh God," she says. "*Oh God. I shot your mom. I didn't mean to.*"

I struggle to blot out the renewed roar of the spirits, the sudden rush of blood in my ears. I'm by Mom's side, my shaking fingers on her throat, feeling through the chalk on her skin to find her pulse. It's steady, if slow. Her breathing is regular too but shallower than normal. I gently smack her cheeks, check her pupils. No response.

They're here and so —

The snake will know —

You get out —

Careful now, son —

The sirens are almost here — at least two cars, maybe more. I fight to think, to breathe. *Mom.* We're in a terrible place. And Mom is out. What's wrong with her?

Before I know what I'm doing, saying, I turn to Miranda. "How could you?"

"I didn't," Miranda says, bringing her hand up to cover her mouth. I see her through a gray movement, a ghost between us. "I didn't mean to. It's the curse."

Whatever the gun did, the cops won't have a clue. We can't leave Mom here. Dr. Whitson might be able to help us figure out how to fix it.

"We have to take her with us," I say, a snap decision. "There's no time."

YES, WE SAID TO —

IT'S LOUD HERE NOW —

The sirens are so close now; they scream louder than the voices of the spirits. I swear I hear gravel flying at the end of the driveway.

I heft Mom into my arms and cradle her against my chest. I can't carry her far like this, certainly not through the woods. Dad's personal car — wherever she parked it — is the only possibility we have for getting away.

"I need you to be ready to help me, just in case, okay?" I say to Miranda. My voice is colder than I mean it to be.

She didn't do it on purpose. It's the snake. Not her.

"Carrying her like that won't work," Miranda says. She scoops up the offending weapon and jams it back into her bag, then motions for me to release Mom's legs so we can each get an arm under one of her shoulders.

"She's not nearly as heavy as my dad was," she says.

Out —

Go —

Now you have to the devil —

Is here losing time —

You are —

The sirens reach the house, followed by the sharp sounds of car doors slamming.

"We have to go now," Miranda says.

The protest and frenetic movements of the spirits are difficult to ignore as we go down the stairs. They urge us on. They're not incapacitating, though. Just like at the station, it's as if the spirits are paying attention to what's going on. Is that even possible?

We hit the first floor. People are talking outside, and the cruiser lights project a colorless pattern against the walls in the daylight shadows.

"Back door," I say.

I put my hand on the doorknob to the sound of the front door exploding open on the other side of the house. And we're out.

MIRANDA

I shoulder the door open. We put on an extra surge of strength to lift Sara over the threshold without speaking, neither of us looking back toward the noise of our pursuers entering the house two rooms away. Twisting his body so he can use the hand not supporting his mom, Grant closes the back door behind us.

I spot his dad coming around the side of the house before he does. Chief Rawling's weapon is unholstered, if not trained on me. Compared to Dee's old pistol, the black handgun gleams like a toy fresh off an assembly line.

Oh, the irony if he *shoots* me.

"Chief," I say, "it's not what it looks like."

Truthfully I'm not sure *what* it looks like. No one would leap to the conclusion that moments before I accidentally shot kind, funny Sara Rawling with an antique magic weapon.

Except it wasn't by accident — not exactly. I no longer harbor any doubt that being a Blackwood brands me a traitor. Not one part of me planned to pull the trigger of John Dee's gun. I removed it from my bag as a phony threat. This wasn't even like when I shot Grant — no phone, no sudden jarring sound. Only the repeat of the sirens and Sara moving toward Grant. Only the snake on my temple crawling with fire and the need to use the weapon.

I was powerless to stop the contraction of my finger on the rickety mechanism. And that blast of white powder and smoke . . . who knew why it shot in a different color this time? Not me.

Grant stiffens at the sight of his dad. "It's really not. Dad, you have to let us go."

Up close, Chief Rawling's face looks like a combat zone. His mouth drops open as he realizes whose body we're supporting. He rushes toward us.

"Sara . . . what's wrong with her?" He doesn't forget himself enough to speak loudly, but his questions tumble out one after another. "Will she be all right? What happened?"

"I don't know yet," Grant says. "I think she's stable, but it's hard to tell."

Chief Rawling touches the pale skin of his wife's cheek, relief clear when chalky powder comes away on his finger. His attention darts between Grant and me, taking in the smears of powder on our shirts and skin, then to a small storage shed at the edge of the yard.

"Over there." He swoops in to lift Sara from our arms, carrying her easily.

We follow him to the scant cover the shed affords. Grant doesn't wait for a better chance to bargain. "Dad, we have to get out of here. I think . . . we need to take her with us."

The chief asks, "What happened? No, there's no time for that. What are you going to do for her that I can't?"

Sara's peaceful face is tucked in to Chief Rawling's chest, like a fairy tale princess sleeping under some witch's enchantment.

A wicked witch, I think. *Or the devil in me.*

"I'm going to take her to Dr. Whitson's," Grant says, "while we figure out how to stop what's going on. All this" — he nods at his mother — "has to do with the missing people. You brought me here because the island needed me. I'm here. And I'm telling you there are things going on that do not follow your laws. Things that can't be explained."

The chief looks down at Sara's face. "I know. I believe you. Your mom parked my car in your usual spot — I won't tell anyone I saw you. But you find a way to get me updates." His fingers rake across his wife's hair, smoothing the powered strands back with a tender care that steals my breath. "I wish my mother were still here. She could fix this."

I remember the conversation I eavesdropped on the other night and what Grant's grandmother wrote in the letter about her son's unwillingness to believe, his inability to understand. Apparently that's changed.

"Dad, what changed your mind?" Grant's surprise is plain.

"I saw the new and improved Hank Blackwood earlier."

I go cold. The man wearing Dad's body isn't bothering to hide his wrongness. And the chief would recognize him even if nobody else did, after all the time he spent as Dad's personal police caretaker.

A woman, not so far away, shouts "Chief Rawling!" and the chief turns to us. "Give me two minutes to get their attention elsewhere, and then get out of here. Grant, I know you'll help her. Do what you can to help us all."

Grant takes his mother from his father's cradle hold. His dad leaves us at a fast clip, disappearing around the side of the gardening shed. I nearly close my eyes at the way Grant is looking at me over his unconscious mother. His sympathy is plain. He must know how terrible I feel about having done this to Sara.

"You didn't mean to," he says. "It was an accident."

I didn't mean to. He's right about that. But there was a terrible moment, right after the gun was fired, when I felt two things in equal measure:

The first feeling was my own, shock at seeing Sara lying on the floor. The second was worse, a gloating sense that I had accomplished a goal. That wasn't mine, but I felt it all the same.

The letter got it right.

I betrayed Grant and Sara. I betrayed myself.

*

I insist on riding in the backseat and cradle Sara's head in my lap while Grant drives. He can barely drive the stick shift, but he manages.

When we reach Roswell's house, the driveway is vacant, and the windows are dark. By all appearances, no one is home. Roswell could be anywhere — in town eating dinner, doing interviews about the townspeople's miraculous return, roaming around Fort Raleigh working on his theory.

"Any change?" Grant turns off the car and shifts to check out how we're doing.

"She's no better." I stare to the left of him, not able to meet his eyes. But I want him to hear me. "I think you should stay here and let me take the car back out to the Grove. You're better off on your own."

Grant doesn't answer other than to get out of the car. I sigh, and then he's opening the door and leaning down beside me. He won't let me get away with telling the back of his head.

"Sidekick will be fine," he says. "We need to help Mom now." He touches his mother's hair.

"You're right. She has to be your priority, and you seem to be forgetting that I shot her. Grant, you were right. What you asked back there . . . how could I do that?"

"It's not going to be that easy," he says.

"What?"

"Getting rid of me." He holds up a hand to stop my objections. "When this is over and both my mom *and* you are safe, *then* you can get rid of me. Okay?"

I say nothing. What can I say?

A sudden gust of wind buffets Grant hard enough that he pitches forward. I raise my hand and it lands on his chest to steady him. A shadow falls over his face.

"Look," he says. The word slips out and his eyes dart around us.

"At what?" I ask. But then I see and hear them. "The birds."

Above us, the sky is filled with a wheeling mass of uneven shapes. The frantic noise of their beating wings and screamed calls surrounds us. Grant stands, gaping, and I slide out from under his mother, placing her head gingerly on the seat.

A few birds swoop lower, and the cries from the mass are like those of warriors in battle. The frenzy of their flight causes some of them to injure others, and a small bird drops from the sky to the ground a few feet away. In death, its dingy brown feathers droop like autumn leaves clinging to a tree limb. Its eye stares at nothing, a tiny unseeing bead on an invisible necklace.

"They're so frightened." And so am I.

"Something's making them panic," Grant says. He shuts the door to leave his mom safe inside the car. "Come on. Let's get the door open and then I'll come back for her."

As I watch, the mass of birds starts heading into the distance, still calling to each other in a panic. One last sad shape falls to earth. I don't want to stay over here alone, so I nod.

No one answers our knock, and Dr. Roswell's security turns out to be a laugh — Grant gets past the front door lock with a debit card and fifteen seconds. "Old style locks like this barely exist anymore," he says.

Inside, the house is dark, empty.

Grant states the obvious: "They're not here."

I call out anyway. "Bone? Doctor?"

No answer. I flinch when Grant brushes a strand of my hair off my cheek. His touch on the snake makes it throb.

"You would never have hurt her on purpose. I know that much." He puts his finger to my lips when I start to protest. "Shhh. We'll figure out how to fix it."

I will pay for what I did, one way or another. But I don't say it out loud.

"But why was it different this time?" Grant continues. "Why the white dust? It didn't smell the same either. No sulfur and charcoal. It looks like chalk and something else, maybe . . ."

"Whatever it was, there was too much of it for the gun to hold, wasn't there?"

He frowns. "Now that you mention it . . . it was emptied once already, and you didn't reload it with anything, right?"

I shake my head no.

He goes on, seeming to think out loud, "And why did it put her into a coma" — I must look like I'm about to have a heart attack because he says — "or a trance or whatever. Even a magic gun should be a little predictable."

I suddenly have a thought. "What's different now than the first time I shot it?" I don't wait for him to answer. "The difference is that they're here. They're back. My dad — or Dee, the devil — he's back."

"That doesn't tell us how to wake up Mom, though."

"Maybe there'll be something in Roswell's papers. I'll get started." I cross the living room and pull up the hatch that leads to the library. "Go get your mom." Then I'm gone, my feet thumping down the ladder. At least I have something to do. A purpose.

A way to atone.

There's a light left on down here, thankfully, next to the table and chair where Roswell sat on our first visit. The book he showed us before lies open on the table, still turned to the page featuring John Dee's portrait. He's a perfect specimen of the kind of an old-fashioned noble. His thin face is framed by a high collar. A flush of color lights his cheeks in the portrait, pinched spots like the waxy skin of cherries. His eyes stare up at me, two black beetles about to crawl off the page.

Maybe not *the* devil, but definitely *a* devil.

The *monas hieroglyphica* mocks me from beneath him. In addition to the name and the fact that it's Dee's personal mark, the text says that the design represents the *unity of the cosmos*, each part standing in for the moon, the sun, or the elements.

I close the book and move on to search Roswell's desk. My neck warms like someone is here, watching me unseen. But the house is deserted, and Grant will be down any second.

Behind the desk, I turn and face the room — empty.

In front of me, the doctor's desk is a mess of stacks and volumes and handwritten notes covering pages and pages, some lined and some not. On the ones that aren't lined, sometimes there are diagrams and drawings, lines with arrows at the end or circles. They make no sense, the content of his research notes as jumbled as the material heaped before me.

You're alone . . . alone with Roswell's fire hazard.

There's one tidy spot at the exact center of the desk. A single oversized journal with a weathered brown leather cover sits directly in front of Roswell's chair. Its brass clasp is similar to the one on the box that housed Dee's gun.

Interesting.

Based on its placement, I'm guessing it must be more important than the rest. I pick it up, then add another couple of legal pads and books to make a pile in my arms, just in case the journal isn't the jackpot I want it to be.

I select a spot and sprawl on the floor, setting the notebooks and research materials in a semicircle around me. My fingers trace the leather book's cover, the surface cool and smooth. The snake on my face itches like a bug bite, and I scratch it.

Then, snapping open the clasp, I flip open Roswell's journal.

I quickly realize something — the man is insane.

Heavy globs of ink form scribbled out sections, bleeding into a sketch of John Dee. And there are notes. Lots and lots of notes. *The key to their return?* bumps up against *The alchemist's promise.* There are names, including my ancestor Mary Blackwood's. It's small and circled, included in a short list of others, entitled *Presumed Dead.* The words SLEEPING POWER are written at the side of the sheet in all caps, circled in a repeated spiral.

I hear movement from above. What will Grant make of this madman's scrapbook? I know he respects Roswell, but this guy seriously needs a new hobby.

I turn the page, noting that Roswell has pasted in some of John White's paintings. Heavy ink highlights some sections of the art, with notes written messily beneath. A sketch of a Native

American hunter from the period apparently concealed a message, which Roswell translated into: *The promised land was to belong to him. Become the New London. The home of the Great Work.*

The next page features the detail of a flower and the legend, *The boundary once crossed permits only one return. All must be in readiness.*

"Only one return too many," I say.

Flicking past a few more pages, I catch photocopied reproductions of letters with words underlined — *weapon, prepare, bloodline* — and then another page with two words connected by an arrow: *Weapon ——> Immortality.*

I advance to the next page and find the one facing it blank. This is the last page Roswell used.

Just then Grant climbs down the ladder. I don't look up until he speaks.

"That took forever . . ." he says. "I don't want you to think I don't work out, but, well, who has the time?"

He's giving me a little smile. I realize he's playing the normal game. It's one I often play in my regular life. The one where I pretend my day was fine, that whatever happened didn't solidify my freak status.

Peering over my shoulder, Grant says, "Whoa."

"Nice surfer impression, dude," I say, playing along. After all, the normal game only works if other people play along. No one ever has for me.

"Is that . . ." Grant's expression darkens.

"Yeah." I wish I could calm down. "That's me."

The sketch gazes up at us, rendered in Roswell's too-heavy hand, my eyes enormous and black, the snake mark circled on the side of my cheek. The birthmark is more detailed than the other features, and for that I'm almost grateful.

Almost.

Being grateful is impossible, given the words at the end of the arrow that extends from the side of my face.

THE CURSE SURVIVES

GRANT

I close the journal on the drawing and slip it from Miranda's hands. "There's no reason to think that's the whole story," I say.

"Really?" she scoffs. "Because I feel like it tells us everything."

"No," I say, sitting down in Whitson's desk chair. "It doesn't. We just need to figure out the context that makes sense of it."

"Good luck with that," Miranda says. She perches on the side of the stiff leather chair beside the table and rummages the jeweled gun out of her bag.

"What are you doing?" I ask.

"Trying to make sense of this," she says, squinting at it.

There's a resolve in her voice that makes me leave it alone. I can't say anything without making it seem like I'm afraid she'll accidentally discharge it again.

I begin to look through the doctor's journal, trying my hardest to decipher the meaning of the scrawls and artwork. There aren't many spirits with us down here, and the ones that are meander, gray shadows circling, whispering. It's not hard to shut them out by focusing on the pages.

I flip through the journal again, the sequence of Whitson's thoughts seeming almost . . . random. These are the questions — and some of the answers — that surfaced in his research. But the notes weren't left for someone else to read. They're the doctor's notes for himself. But I don't know his shorthand.

What I *do* know is that Whitson clearly has a better view of how the pieces of Roanoke Island's weird history fit together than we do.

"No matter how many times you look, it's still crazy," Miranda says. "We should get out of here. Just bring it with us."

"He's not crazy — this is his life's work. An obsession, but he's not crazy. I don't think."

Miranda isn't looking at me but still at the jeweled gun. Her hands turn it over and over again as she examines its mechanisms with steady, competent deliberation. She stares down its barrel, and my heart pounds.

"Miranda, what are you doing again?"

Her focus on the twisted, hammered metal is complete. "According to Roswell, this equals immortality. I'm trying to see how it works."

It would never have occurred to me to spend time dissecting the firearm. I'm better with books, with messes people make with their minds. My ancestors and whatever spirits are around continue to whisper, but I'd swear they're talking to each other, not me. I can think, but it's not helping.

"I don't get it," I say. When Miranda's forehead wrinkles in question, I clarify, "Immortality."

She holds the gun closer to the lamp on the table, a gem on the grip flashing under the light from the bulb. "What do you mean?"

"It's such a bad idea. If everyone lives forever — well, just imagine it. Imagine if every person lived forever. For that matter, add every creature." I've never talked to anyone like this, not even Whitson, without wondering whether they'll think I'm nuts. "Earth would be overrun. We'd be out of resources to deal with it in a blink of geological time. And then you get all the doom and gloom. Rationing, wars, et cetera."

"Et cetera?" Miranda half smiles, but she's completely serious when she looks over. "I understand it — sort of. It's not about living forever. It's about not dying. To be able to keep the people you love around forever? I understand that." She shrugs and frowns at the trigger, rubbing her thumb across the hammered metal.

From what I understand of Dr. Whitson's journal, love isn't any part of Dee's motives. The alchemist identified the North Carolina coast as a place he could experiment on his band of witches and attempt to turn himself — and them — immortal using the weapon he made. If that worked, the island was to be his launching ground to lash out at the world, to take down the queen herself. When his plan went south, Dee and White hid messages in paintings and letters, messages Dr. Whitson has managed to tease out. He had a number of White's personal letters to Dee, but only a few replies from the alchemist-in-chief.

Some people believe Sir Walter Raleigh and Queen Elizabeth had a not-so-secret romantic connection, whether they acted on it or not. At least according to the reading I've done on the era. Watching Miranda, I decide Raleigh wouldn't have liked Dee going after his girlfriend's empire. Raleigh must have been Dee's unknowing pawn all along.

The page under my hand features a sketch of a doorway surrounded by trees, bald cypress trunks like fingers reaching out of the ground. According to the handwriting scrawled around the image, Dee had given the settlers — the ones who "followed him true and were promised" — detailed instructions for traveling past the veil of reality to the place of spirits. There, they could wait as long as they had to for someone to reassemble the plan, to bring them back and complete Dee's agenda. Their lives beyond were tied to the island, not so different than mine and Miranda's.

Dee intended to follow the colonists into the spirit waiting room after his own death, and he must have succeeded. I see shadows from beyond this veil, apparently, but as far as I can tell, they're not distinguishable as individual people. Still, I'm almost certain I've never seen *him*. He's playing a long game, and I'm afraid he's winning. There isn't enough here to come up with a strategy to even compete.

The sigh of frustration is out before I can stop it. "What's in here, it's not everything."

"How do you know?"

"These are mainly background details. Whitson must have another notebook somewhere," I say, drumming my fingers. "There are too many important things missing — like how to trigger the right conditions to bring the settlers back into our reality. And not much from Dee's own hand."

Even more telling, the Blackwoods are barely mentioned in this journal, which I don't want to say to Miranda. I'm still not sure how her family fits in to all this, what the traitor thing Gram wrote about translates to. Dee has a grudge against them — or does he? Was Mary Blackwood left behind just so he'd have a vessel to inhabit when he returned? Whitson claimed she was an alchemist like the rest. That makes it sound like she was on Dee's side, not any sort of traitor.

Or maybe that meant she was a traitor to humanity. I'm not about to voice that possibility out loud.

"You're right," Miranda says, peering over my shoulder. "There's nothing too specific in there — it's more chaos than theory."

"There's also nothing too specific about the weapon." Which means nothing about how to heal Mom from its effects. I suspect Dee is the only one who knows how the unpredictable gun in Miranda's hand works. His magic created it, after all.

"We can't put off leaving much longer," Miranda says. "It's too dangerous for your mom."

"Where will we go?" I ask, though I'm afraid I know the answer.

"Dee's got to be the only one who can help her. I think I have to go to my *new and improved* father and ask him."

"I don't want you to. I'll do it." After all, what if Dee can't or *won't* help? And even if he does, what will be his price?

Miranda doesn't respond right away, instead stashing the gun inside her bag and folding over the flap. She gets up and paces along a bookshelf at the other end of the library from the desk.

"Grant," she says, "I know this will be hard for you. You want to be my knight in . . . well, we don't have any armor, and that's part of the problem. We're way overmatched. I'm dealing with a curse hundreds of years old that makes this place loathe me and vice versa, and that makes you my enemy. You're sworn to put the island first."

"I'm not your enemy. I never could be."

At the end of the bookshelf, Miranda whirls to face me. The wide spines of reference works, dictionaries, and encyclopedias frame her on either side. None contain the answers we need.

"I have to go with you," she says. "And you'll use me to bargain for your mother's life. You know why?"

I don't want to hear anymore. "I won't."

"Because the part of me that shot that gun at your mother, that part enjoyed it."

I rise from the desk. The voices of spirits buzz — *Listen, listen — you have to* — but I do my best to accomplish the exact opposite of what they want. I don't listen.

When I reach Miranda, I tug her toward me gently. Our bodies touch, barely, the pressure slight. Pulling, repelling. I can tell she wants to run, but she doesn't. She stands, silent, waiting.

The raised voices of the spirits won't let me forget that we're not alone. I'm never alone here.

Why won't you —

Hear this —

It's too late —

The jumble of words swallows my own thoughts, leaving Mom's chalk-painted features. I release her. "You'll come then."

"I have to." Miranda looks away. Her eyes travel down the shelves of reference books, down to . . .

I'm confused when she bends, her hand exploring a gap between the bookshelf and the wall. She pulls on what appears to be a plastic tarp. But when I see the zipper, I understand what she's found. She drops the plastic as she realizes it too.

"Is that a body bag?" she asks.

Just then the hatch above us flips open, light from the living room above brightening the space. Miranda kicks at the body

233

bag, trying to get it stuffed back into the corner, and I shift to hide her motion from Dr. Whitson, who plunks down the steps. Bone is behind him, his face pasty instead of pink.

"I found your girlfriend's father to be much more polite, Grant," the doctor says. He walks closer to me, then looks around my shoulder at Miranda. "Of course, he was deceased at the time."

MIRANDA

Funny that *I'm* wearing the stupid snake when Roswell is one.

Sara's body lies across my and Grant's laps in the backseat of Roswell's hunter green Volvo. Bone rides shotgun. Heading across the island was our next move, but not like this. Not as prisoners.

Roswell forced me to hand over the gun first thing. There went my bargaining chip. I planned to trade it to Dee in exchange for Sara's health. I wasn't going to give it up until Sara was back to normal. Too bad.

Thick cords of rope, the kind used by fishermen in Wanchese, chafe my wrists. Bone pretended to take pleasure in binding me, but his shaking hands gave him away. He's wigged, but still taking orders from his dad.

Once Bone finished, I tested my restraints but quickly determined they were too tight to loosen. These ropes are made to withstand the pressure and high winds of the sound and ocean. I've used them to secure enough sails on the faux ship at the theater to know that all I'll accomplish by fighting them is ripping up my own skin.

"Doc," Grant says, raising his own bound wrists. "Why are you doing this?"

"After the time we've spent together, you don't have a guess? You know this is my research, my life's work." Roswell seems amused. "You've always been such a sharp boy, surely you can make a guess."

Bone shifts in his seat when his father compliments Grant, clearly unhappy. Does it have to do with his father's praise of Grant? Or was Grant near the mark when he theorized that Bone liked me? Doubtful it's the latter given the overkill on the rope, but still. We're going to need every edge we can get.

Grant taps his fingers together. "You've always been a crackpot, haven't you, Doc? Miranda was right about you. You trying to resurrect history won't change that."

"I'm not a crackpot." Roswell's voice is clipped. "And I've already resurrected *history*. One hundred and fifteen people, to be exact."

Right. Souls of 114 settlers inhabit the bodies of the returned, plus John Dee inside my dad. There might be others, Mary Blackwood or Grant's ancestor Virginia Dare in the mix. But these are the 114 people that history bothered to record as missing.

"Which means you're now killing one hundred and fourteen other people," I say.

"Well, in fairness, your father had to be killed for this to work, and technically the others are still alive. You've seen them for yourself."

Sara's breath hitches, shuddering in and out, and Grant turns toward her, worried. As I maneuver to check her pulse, her breathing settles into a more normal — if shallow — pattern.

"She's okay," I say. The words are a promise. Sara Rawling has to stay alive, even if it kills me.

Grant's fingers clench. *He'll never be much of a poker player,* I think. His body is too expressive.

"What's wrong with my mom?" He directs his question to the front seat.

"I knew you had the weapon," Roswell says. "It was obvious, once I considered it, that the Blackwoods would have it secreted away. And then fail to keep it safe, like they're destined to fail at everything." He pauses. "Sorry if that sounds harsh."

Roswell sure loves the sound of his own voice, I think.

"At any rate, the first stage is blackening," he continues. "Gunpowder — sulfur, potassium nitrate, and charcoal. They used to call it *black powder.* Grant had a hint of it on him at the courthouse, and that was when I began to suspect. Then, *albedo* — the whitening stage. Purification. Salt, chalk. The third is *rubedo* — well, we will all see that effect together. It is the Great Work. Only he knows its secret."

Grant sighs again. "This really is all about alchemy?"

I watch the edge of Roswell's face as it angles into an approving smile. "Nicely done, Grant. Such a bright one, you are."

I tilt my head toward Grant. Inches separate our faces. His criminally long eyelashes are so close I could count them. I almost expected him to forgive me in the library, in those last moments we were alone.

"Can you believe this guy?" I say softly.

"Magic and science," Roswell continues, "have never been in opposition the way we think of them now. Dee knew that and found the key to uniting them. To finally fulfilling the alchemist's greatest ambition —"

"Making the first home chemistry set?" I interrupt. I won't give Roswell the satisfaction of holding court.

"Eternal life."

He says it in a huff. I'm getting to him.

Grant clears his throat, flattens his palms together. "Alchemists were always looking for some kind of edge they could scheme out of the natural world. Making base metals into gold, sure, but their other great project was figuring out the secret to eternal life. Of course"— he rolls his eyes — "they should have known that eternal life is the opposite of natural. Why would nature provide a process to do that? It's a dream, nothing more."

"It's real enough," Roswell says. "The greatest discovery ever made. Does your mother look unaffected?"

I realize what Grant is doing — he's trying to make Roswell doubt the process will work.

"She doesn't look immortal," Grant says quietly. "Is a failed experiment worth all this death?"

"The experiment won't fail, my boy," Roswell says. "I'm sorry you and your mother had to be a part of this. But this is my life's work. No one in my family has ever gotten this close to bringing him back."

"What family?" I ask.

"John White's, obviously," Roswell says.

Grant's head drops, something suddenly clicking into place. "Whitson. White's son. That's why you had access to his private letters."

So Roswell is related to John White. I picture the stick-in-the-mud who overacts the part in the play. Figures.

Flashing lights up ahead distract me. A smattering of police cars are pulled off next to the roadway, a few cops milling around outside. No one else in the car has spotted them yet. If we can just keep Roswell talking, distracted, maybe we'll get flagged over. Grant's dad will help us.

"Why did you bring him back?" I ask.

"To finish his life's work, the greatest work of all," Roswell says, like we'd approve if we understood. "Now the time is right. None of those people were doing anything with their lives. Not like what he and his followers can accomplish."

"Lives aren't measured like that," Grant says. "Every person gets their own. One. Alchemy honors nature, and this is unnatural. It won't work."

I don't miss Grant sitting up straighter, and I know he sees the cops too. Roswell will notice them, but maybe too late. Morrison Grove isn't that far, which means the officers are at the entrance to Fort Raleigh and the theater. Odd place for a roadblock.

As we get closer, though, I realize it isn't a roadblock. It's just a cluster of police at the lip of the parking lot. A couple of TV trucks too. Hard to say what they're doing there.

"Dad," Bone says.

"Down," Roswell barks. "We're too close to fail now. Put your heads down." When we don't react, he turns to Grant and adds, "Your mother is in a very precarious state."

He sounds like a nasty professor threatening a bad grade, but we can't afford to ignore him. We both drape forward over Sara's body, ducking below the lip of the window. The flashing lights reflect on the glass, and I hold my breath, hoping for capture.

No one stops us.

I lose my breath as I realize we're out of options.

I'm going to see Dad.

It won't be Dad. Not really. But the body will be his, will move and breathe like he still inhabits it. A lie dressed up like a miracle. I'll never forget the sight of him on that metal table. He might not have been the perfect TV dad, but he doesn't deserve to have Dee wear his skin like a new suit.

Grant and I unfold from hiding as Roswell turns right into the Grove's parking lot and selects one of the few open spots. The packed lot stands in sharp contrast to the few abandoned cars left in a lonely tic-tac-toe the day before.

Roswell braces his hands on the steering wheel. "Dee's soul was waiting there for me. Hundreds of years he'd been past the boundary of our reality, and yet he slipped out of death and into that man's body like an egg from its shell. He understands how to unite the esoteric and the natural in a way the world has never seen before. He's used them to beat death. Think of the research we can do, the advances to be made."

"Research?" Grant snorts in disgust. "You are the worst amateur historian ever. Eugenics, anyone?"

"Perhaps research isn't what I mean, but knowledge," Roswell says.

Beside his father, Bone hasn't moved, gazing out the window toward the rental units that make up the Grove. Something in the set of his jaw has me suspecting he's been subjected to a number of these self-serving pep talks. Poor Bone. My sympathy is genuine, if not total.

"Knowledge," Roswell continues, "is all we have. All that separates us from lower animals. It is the basis of civilization."

I can't believe this jerk. "*Bullfrak.* This is about power. If you're pretending it's something else, even to yourself, then frak you, you delusional murdering excuse for a nutty professor."

There's silence for a moment. Then Grant says, "I'd applaud if I could."

I wriggle my wrists. "I understand."

"This is bigger than any individual one of us," says Roswell, his voice clipped. "He will build a shining city of light and knowledge. The New London. You'll see —"

He stops himself from finishing, and I know that deep down, he doesn't know if we will. He doesn't know what Dee has planned for us. Maybe we aren't going to see anything for much longer.

I look at Grant, stung by the fresh reminder that Roswell doesn't matter so much anymore. He's just a henchman, the equivalent of a faceless storm trooper in *Star Wars*. The mastermind behind everything, the man who defeated death, is the one wearing my father.

Getting out of the car is awkward thanks to Roswell and Bone's lack of skill in dealing with captives — particularly with Sara out cold. Bone is surprisingly careful when he lifts her limp body from the car. I'm thankful for that, anyway. Otherwise, Grant would need immediate payback, and I need him busy generating one of his grand schemes to end all this, to crack Dee's stolen shell and send him back to Eggville.

It doesn't feel like something a traitor would want.

Still.

Dr. Roswell heads for the trail that leads through the trees to the houses. We march behind him. There's no point in trying to escape. All paths would lead here eventually. Bone follows us, his steps landing heavier with Sara's weight in his arms.

Dust particles fly in the millions wherever sun pierces the canopy of trees. What do they call twilight on movie sets? Oh right — magic hour. Ha.

This is my chance. I have to test Grant's assumption, see if I can sway Bone to our side. I meet Grant's questioning glance when I slow and nod my head for him to go on ahead. He hurries to catch the none-the-wiser Roswell, and I spin to face Bone. He's paler than usual, if not as chalky as the woman in his arms. He wears another Tarheels shirt, this one with long sleeves pushed up to the elbow.

"What?" he asks.

"Bone, I just want you to know that I understand why you've always treated me like you have. If it wasn't me, it would have been you." *Him with his crazy dad, him with no mother, him getting mocked.* "But I don't believe that's all you have in you," I continue. "You're not just your father's son."

Bone blinks. I don't need him to respond right away, so I trot back to rejoin Grant. Roswell continues to barrel ahead, eager to reach his alchemical crush.

The trail is damp, though I can't recall the last decent rain we had, and leaves stick to the packed earth. The trees' shadows made the trail dark, and the houses are quiet given the number of cars in the lot. I don't even hear any birds singing to each other. The forest could be dead.

That is until a rich, throaty bay pierces the quiet. I'd know that lonely howl anywhere. *Sidekick.*

I dart around Roswell. "Stop!" he calls, but I lope clumsily on, my tied wrists at my waist. I track the howl through the open door of Polly's apartment. I stop just over the threshold, uncertain how to proceed.

Dad stands in the middle of the common room. He's bent, a hand curled in the fur of Sidekick's neck.

The coffee table has been moved, along with most of the other furniture, turning him into a circus master at center ring. Women I vaguely recognize crowd the edges of the room, sitting in chairs raided from a variety of kitchens. Their backs are hunched over some task. Needles flash in their fingers, sweeps of gray fabric draped across their laps as they sew. Several of them look up, but none set their work aside.

Sidekick struggles and whines against the fingers of the man in the suit. If I harbored the smallest doubt that Dad is really gone, I now know for sure. Dad might have complained about "that fool dog," but Sidekick adored him, and he quietly rewarded that affection with belly scratches and the occasional table scrap. A piece of bread here, a crumble of bacon there. The worst thing is that this man in front of me, the one Sidekick is desperate to escape, is a perverse picture of the sober, cleaned-up version of Dad I wished for a thousand times.

John Dee gazes at me through my father's face. "Mary," he says.

Well, maybe not the worst thing.

Dee gives my father's head a slow shake and releases his grip on Sidekick. Sidekick immediately scrambles to me, his nails scraping the floor, and cowers beside me in a way that makes me ache. Tail between his legs, ears and head down. As if he's done something wrong.

Kneeling, I bury my face in Sidekick's fur, managing to loop my arms over his head to hug him in spite of my tied wrists. He shivers against me.

Dee's footsteps approach, measured. I should cringe in fear. I shouldn't provoke him. I have to remember Sara, unconscious. We have no way to wake her that doesn't rely on Dee's assistance.

But I can't help myself. I want nothing more than to send this devil back to whatever hell he's been hiding in for the past four hundred years. He scared my dog.

"Wrong girl," I say. "I'm Miranda."

GRANT

I should make some effort to hide my shock, but the scene in the house Miranda raced into is not something anyone could expect. No matter how weird the past few days have been. No matter the shadows that surround me, speaking loudly.

The devil is HERE —

He will know you —

You must listen!

But the minute I step inside, they quiet down. For once, I see no shadowy movements. Maybe they're afraid the man presiding over this tableau will sense them.

A bunch of women are sewing — yes, *sewing* — or, rather, they've stopped sewing to watch the drama taking place in front of them. Miranda stands from a crouch next to Sidekick. Her father stands opposite her, a sympathetic expression on his face.

John Dee's expression, Mr. Blackwood's body, I remind myself. What surprises me is that the sympathy the man radiates toward Miranda actually seems *sincere*.

"I would never hurt your pet," Dee says. "Animals are more sensitive than most humans" — he looks over Miranda's shoulder at me with curiosity — "and can sense when the forces of nature are in flux."

Miranda gapes at John Dee inside her dad. She's clearly furious, and I don't want her talking to him when anger is in control. I don't believe Miranda shot at Mom on purpose, no matter what she said. It's the snake, the curse. I'm still on her side, even though I have no idea what Gram would say about that. Protecting the island should come first, according to her letter. Thankfully, the whispers of the spirits — and they *are* whispering — are so quiet I barely hear them. If Gram's among them, I can't hear her either.

"You're Dr. John Dee, then?" I ask.

Sidekick's tail thumps a couple of times in acknowledgement of my presence. Even the dog seems nervous.

Bone has stopped next to me, still cradling Mom's body. Dr. Whitson pushes past his son to get to John Dee. "I'll do the introductions," he starts, but Dee sidesteps the doc without a hint of interest in him.

"I had no idea Eleanor's Virginia had survived," Dee says, wonder and disdain mixing. "She was a seed of a thing, and the natives were . . . what's the expression? Restless. Owing to you." He focuses the accusation on Miranda, whose only reaction is to continue to scowl at him. Finally he turns to me, frowning. "Why have you bound the hands of Virginia Dare's descendant? Why is he here at all? The child is not one of mine. Her parents are."

"*I'm* not one of yours either," Miranda points out.

Dee only looks at her again.

I need to distract him. I hold up my tied hands, jerk my head toward Bone. "I'd like to take my mother now, please."

Dee reaches into the pocket of the jacket he wears. When his hand emerges, long fingers hold the handle of a short, sharp knife. He moves forward, smooth as a shark, and slices through the ropes that bind me. The thick cords fall away. A single cut shouldn't have done it.

Dee untrusses Miranda with the same quick motion, and she quickly backs away. Despite that, Dee appears pleased. I watch the way he studies his hand with approval before returning the knife to his pocket.

"Getting comfortable in there?" I ask.

Dee turns to me. "It's a process. Like all transmutations, one does not simply achieve success in a moment. After being in the starless void for so long, I find I am in no rush. Each sensation is a new discovery."

Whitson lets out a murmur of approval, and the adoration he manages to cram into the sound turns my stomach. How did I ever trust that guy?

Miranda is edging slowly further into the house with Sidekick. I don't know where she's headed, but I can keep Dee occupied a little longer. Hands free, I accept my mother's weight from Bone.

"What's wrong with her?" I ask Dee.

Dee reaches out with his borrowed fingers and tenderly touches the side of Mom's chalked face. "She is unaffiliated," he says, "which means I can aid her, if you wish." He finds Dr. Whitson then, and the professor squints like the sun is shining in his eyes. Like he's seeing something holy.

"You have the invention?" Dee asks him, sounding irritated.

"Right here." Whitson snaps open his leather valise and produces the bundle eagerly. He's wrapped the heavy metal weapon in a fusty afghan throw.

"Remove the cloth," Dee orders, his nose wrinkling.

Dr. Whitson quickly complies, and the gun lies flat, exposed, against the nubby plaid throw. It's a dream made in metal. This man's dream.

One of the sewing women gets up and walks to Dee's side. She wears a summer dress, long and flowing, and small sandals that seem out of place with such a stiff gait. The gun must be difficult for her to ignore, but she does.

"Master," she says, "I need to go now, or he will suspect."

"Of course." Dee raises his voice. "Any of you whose vessels possess family should go to them now. You can return here tomorrow."

"I would rather not go back there," says a woman who can't be older than her mid-twenties.

"I understand that what I ask of you is not easy, but one more day and then such concerns will leave us."

The woman nods, and all but two leave through the front door. They drape the materials they're working on over the chair backs on their way out, giving the furniture the appearance of cloth gravestones.

Dee gestures for me to follow him. "Bring her this way."

I can't believe I'm taking this guy's orders. I also can't believe Dee is being so calm and rational. I expected a fiery, beyond-the-grave menace. *Don't trust*, the shades whisper, *don't trust — don't trust — don't trust*. Sometimes it's hard to tell the difference between the other voices and my own thoughts.

This is one of those times.

As we pass a kitchen, I spot three doughnut boxes — nothing but a few crumbs of frosting left inside — on the counter. No doughnuts in the starless void, then.

"Eleanor," Dee calls, his voice carrying through the silent house, "keep an eye on my M . . . Miranda, please."

A woman answers from a room at the far end of the hall. "She's right here," she says.

Satisfied, Dee motions me through a nearby door. Inside the room, I put Mom down on the bed. I straighten her legs on the pink bedspread, wishing again for her not to be part of this.

Dee eases down onto the side of the bed beside her and touches her face again. The bedside lamp's light gives the white mask she wears hollows and shadows, like she's already becoming one of the spirits.

"Miranda shot me with your gun too," I say. "All it did was coat me with black dust. Why didn't this happen to me?"

Dee spots Whitson lingering in the door. "Leave us," Dee commands.

I watch the doctor swallow his protest. Obediently, he goes. I figure Bone must be hanging out with the women who stayed. He probably isn't much for sewing, though.

"She shot you?" Dee asks, his pupils large and black. "Of course, she did."

I note the moony quality that crosses Dee's face when he's talking about Miranda. Maybe he and Mary Blackwood were closer than I previously assumed. I'm relieved when all traces of creepy adoration vanish as he goes on.

"You were never in danger because Virginia was too young to follow her parents through the veil, into the void. She stayed behind. Too young for a decision, so the decision was made by her inability. You share her blood . . . with a curiously strong tie given the years that separate you. Regardless, it protected you."

"Her parents just left her behind?"

"Mortality is fleeting. Immortality is a promise of the eternal, pure as light itself."

I imagine a tiny girl on a huge beach, a wilderness surrounding her. They must have assumed she would die in minutes, hours, days. That's some funny idea of light and purity.

"But my mother — she hasn't chosen?" I'm solving the riddle. "You said you can help her because she's unaffiliated."

Dee says nothing. He watches as I put things together.

"You can help her if you offer her a choice. If she chooses you." I draw in a shaky breath. "You can only help her if she becomes one of yours."

Dee strokes Mom's chalky skin. She's so pale, a ghost, fading fast into nothing.

"Yes," he says. "That is correct."

He's the devil, one of the voices whispers. But it's not like I need the spirits to tell me that. I already know.

MIRANDA

I find Polly easily. She's in her room, sitting on the bed and bent over a long swath of fabric like the other women. As I watch, she curses, and her lips pinch in a universal *ouch*.

Sidekick stays so close to me I can feel his cringe at the word. I wish I were better at protecting what I love, better at understanding that my circumstances are not of my own making — or of Dad's. I wish I could have seen all this coming early enough to stop it.

Polly has angled the shade of the lamp to give herself as much light as possible, but it clearly isn't enough. She doesn't appear to notice my presence until Dee's voice — Dad's but deeper and more commanding, with a clipped accent — calls out for Eleanor. At the word, Polly's familiar face looks up, exhaustion painted on it, and confirms I'm with her.

"You knew I was here," I say.

"This body has excellent hearing." Polly jams the needle through the fabric, cursing again as she sticks herself. It's the most inept attempt at sewing I've ever seen.

"You came in here because you didn't want the others to see how much you suck at this," I say.

"Perceptive," Polly says. "I was neither a housewife nor a tailor nor anything else but my father's protégée. The favored daughter of Governor White. Of those of us who traveled to make the New London, to bring about the great transformation, I was the most skilled next to Master Dee."

I'm close enough to see the tips of Polly's fingers are coated with red where she's repeatedly stabbed herself. I now know that Eleanor Dare — Virginia's mother, a speaking part, not a footnote — is inside that injured skin, but somehow that doesn't matter. It's Polly's body.

"Let me," I say, taking the fabric before she can protest.

I sit on the bed and hold out my hand for the needle and thread. I start to ask what they're making, but then realize, with a stroke over the cloth, that I already know. A vision crosses my mind — the returned people in the square, arms drifting through the air, reunited with flesh and each other after so many years.

Cloaks. They're sewing the cloaks from my dream.

After a moment's hesitation, Polly hands over the needle, the rough red of her fingertips painful to look at.

I accept it and fit the needle through the cloth again and again. I've helped the costumers enough on similar pieces that it's old habit. Sidekick slides down at my feet, letting gravity pull his eyes closed. Polly watches with a puzzled expression.

"Why are you helping me? Your friend is not in here. She is in the void."

"My friend," I say, focusing on the easy motion of the needle, the satisfying push through the fabric, "still exists. That's enough."

If only it was true.

We sit in silence while I sew. I know she's only staying here because Dee told her to keep an eye on me.

At last, I bite the thread loose and tie it, then hold up the garment. The fabric billows like a storm cloud in miniature when I shake out the cloth. It's about the best a sinister gray cloak can be, in my opinion.

Polly plucks the cloak from my fingers and sweeps it around her own shoulders. She hooks a wide loop over a button she must have struggled to sew on. I didn't do it.

"Very Salem," I say.

"There is much to complete before tomorrow evening," Polly says. "Will you do another?"

I find myself nodding yes before I recall that this isn't the real Polly. This isn't the person I usually help without thinking, the person who lets me have a stage-side view of every show. The cape flutters behind Polly's body as she leaves the room, before I can take back the yes. What is tomorrow evening? And where has Grant gone?

Before I can wonder the same thing about my father's body and its make-nice hitchhiker, he materializes in the doorway with a bolt of gray fabric. He raises his brows skeptically. "Eleanor said you asked for this."

Sidekick wakes from sleep and scoots behind my legs. I can relate. I'd like to get out of his sight too. I settle for staring at the floor. "I agreed to sew another for Polly's sake."

Why do I feel the need to provoke him? This guy came back from the grave. I probably wouldn't like him when he's angry. But the insult of having to deal with Dad's form is too fresh. I refuse to look at him.

"Who actually killed him?" I ask, keeping my eyes down. "Was it you or Dr. Whitson? Or was it the ship?"

Dee places the bolt of cloth on the bed beside me. He's too close. I don't move.

Finally he backs off, settling into a wooden chair near the foot of the bed. I resist the urge to put more distance between us.

"What if I told you it was none of those? That it was the curse he bore?"

I pick up the cloth and shake it into position. The snake on my cheek feels like it's crawling. "Then that means you — you or your ship. It's *your* curse."

I unspool a bit of thread — filched from the costume department, without a doubt — and thread my needle. The fabric flows before me, a gray flood. I *won't* look at him.

"It must be difficult," he says.

Needle through fabric, needle through fabric, needle through fabric. I picture Mom hand sewing and long for the machine I inherited from her.

Dee goes on. "Difficult to be so skilled but to continually experience setbacks. You do, don't you? The other night at the theater must have been one."

You haven't answered my question, I think. *Why would I answer yours?*

I focus on folding a length of cloth over on itself to make a hem, a flash of silver as I poke the needle through. But the words are out before I can stop them. "How do you know that?"

"You'll have to forgive me," he says.

I hear echoes of Dad in those words, memories of all the times he said: "Forgive me, Miranda-bug." "Forgive me, sweetie." Or just: "I'm sorry." But Dee's words come with his clipped accent and crisp delivery.

I stare at the cloth. I can feel him waiting for an answer, but I won't look up. I refuse to. My fingers are so dedicated to their task they ache.

"Forgive you for killing my father?" I ask. "I deserve a straight answer. You got his body somehow."

He doesn't respond right away.

Then, finally, "You were conflicted, weren't you, when you discovered he was missing? We are not blind beyond, not unless we wish it. Where the veil thins, we can see light leaking through, can watch the lives on the other side as if through a curtain made of glass. Part of you was relieved, in that first moment, to discover your father might have passed beyond. I was watching."

My teeth grind together. So what if my whole body rose like hot air when I understood what Blue Doe's reporting meant — that Dad might be missing? It was one stupid moment, passed in a heartbeat.

"I didn't know he was dead. I'm not that kind of person."

"You are a strong person. You knew it meant you could be free. And isn't that what you've always longed for? For freedom?"

I look up and over at him, finally. The sight of Dad's face comes as a shock, even expecting it. Talking to him isn't like talking to Dad. Looking at him is different too. He leans forward, watching me, his elbows on his knees and his hands clasped. He's like a preacher waiting for a confession. My dad never sat like that in his life.

"I *never* wanted him dead. Answer my question — which one of you killed him?"

My attention goes back to my hands.

"I wish I could make the answer simple. But it isn't. Your father had to die. He bore the mark, the one that allowed me to return to his body. The reasons he bore that mark — the one now passed to you — are complicated. Suffice to say, your family owed me a debt. I consider that debt paid."

I hesitate, then stand, letting the cloth fall, tossing the needle onto the bedspread. "Then I can go, right? I can leave right now, and you won't follow me? None of this will follow me. My debt is paid?"

Dad's eyes burn with regret. "I'm afraid not, not so long as you hold the mark. Your family will be a part of this as long as you wear it, as long as my soul lives."

"That's what I thought." I drop back, defeated, onto the side of the bed. I leave the stupid cloak-in-the-making where it lies.

"No," he says. "You misunderstand."

Dad — Dee — moves at the corner of my vision. My cringe away from him is automatic, but he sits down beside me on the bed anyway. The snake burns and squirms against my cheek, and then my entire skin becomes the snake. Surely, with the way my arms and legs crawl at his closeness, I will shed it. This is the opposite of what being close to Grant feels like. Every instinct screams at me to exit, leave, run.

Sorry, instinct.

I sit my ground, keeping some pride by making no effort to disguise my discomfort. He won't need to spy through any glass curtain or veil to see it.

"You look so like her," he says. He lifts a hand.

I hope he doesn't have any designs on touching me with those fingers. I won't meet his eyes. Sidekick whines.

"Don't," I say. But I realize from his slip at the door who he must mean. "You're talking about my ancestor, Mary?"

Dee nods once. "It tells me that the grand design brought us all here. The angels spoke in my ear when I was alive and told me it would all come to pass as it was meant to. And now the boy with his connection to Virginia is here. And you, so clearly of Mary's line. The fullness of time has brought us to perfection. This moment was always the right one."

I miss the meaning of some of what he says, but his joy is unmistakable. Maybe his inappropriate good mood will make him more inclined to help Sara. I assume she's still somewhere in her unnatural sleep. Grant would have found me to tell me if she woke up.

"If you help Grant's mom, Sara, it would make up for what you did to Mary. At least some." I hesitate. "Why did you curse her?"

And my family. *Me.*

"I was angry then," he says. For a long moment, he says nothing else. "You are a fresh chance to be better than that rage. A gift for our homecoming. An auspicious sign."

"No, I'm not." I don't trust the soft tone of sympathy, of care, that he uses. He's making it sound like he cares for me.

"I can take this away." Dee's finger traces the mark down my cheek, a bolt of heat smashing into me like a wall of fire.

My skin must really be coming off this time. It will melt onto the floor at my feet, and I'll be nothing but blood and bones, like the story Mom told at the Halloween bonfire the year before she died, the flickering light playing over her features and making them unfamiliar. *Bloody Bones, coming for you. Bloody Bones takes naughty children to his dirty pen, and they are never seen again.*

"I can take it away," he continues. "I can give you freedom."

Bloody Bones, coming to fetch you . . .

The feeling of being on fire fades as soon as he removes his finger, until the sensation subsides to a scoured-raw feeling. He leaves the room without another word. What he said lingers.

If he takes the curse away, what will be left of me?

*

Grant is outside on the deck when I finally go in search of him. His forehead presses against the middle bar of the wood railing, his feet dangling in space. He looks out into the tree house world of the Grove.

I admire him for a stolen second, unnoticed. He's been kinder to me than anyone ever has. Hope is an unfamiliar thing for me to feel, but that's what I most associate with him. Dee is killing that hope. Maybe it's already dead.

Sidekick breezes past me and over to Grant, wiggling his head under Grant's arm. "Hey, boy," he says, glancing over his shoulder at me. "Join me."

That's the best offer I've had in hours.

"What's tomorrow?" I ask, slipping down next to him. I leave Sidekick between us, without letting Grant be too far away. Every moment we have feels like one where I'm saying goodbye.

"How'd you know I'd find out?" he asks.

"I didn't bother trying — I knew you'd figure out what they're up to." That wins a flash of white teeth in the dark, a brief smile.

"They're going to put on the production and conduct some sort of ceremony," Grant says. "It will make all this permanent, from what I can tell. I think they need the townspeople there. They're calling it a *special Dare County night*. This is from Bone, but I believe him."

So I swayed Bone's allegiance after all. "Wow. That's perfect."

"Why?"

"We have Dare County Night every year at the beginning of the season." My vision has adjusted to the dark enough that I see his eyebrow raise in question. "The play isn't exactly the same every year — it changes. Sometimes big changes, like the year the director inserted a bunch of people in animal suits, but usually smaller ones. Anyway, we have a town night every year, a free show, because the locals are the ones who make or break it. They're the ones who talk it up to the tourists . . . or not. It's a big deal. A special thing the town and the theater have together. This year's season is almost over, and tomorrow's an off night. No ticket holders to piss off. They can do a special one."

Grant turns his head toward me, temple against the railing. "You're right. It *is* perfect. This one, this performance, is supposed to be to celebrate the return."

"Everyone will cover it." That must be why the cops are staking out the theater. Security to keep everyone out until the big night. "When Dee does . . . whatever, won't they just think he's crazy?"

"This is John Dee we're talking about here. Crazy is just the beginning."

"Point taken. I've been sewing gray witch cloaks for the past two hours." The moonlight wanes over us, its light thin, and we're both quiet for a moment. Then I say, "He told me he watched me when they were . . . wherever they were."

Thin moonlight or no, Grant's scowl is unmistakable.

"What?" I ask.

"I *bet* he was watching," is all he says.

I let it go. Minutes squeeze by before he speaks again.

"What did he offer you?" he asks.

Freedom. "The one thing I ever wanted."

"Oh," he says. "He offered to make my mom one of his minions."

"But he'll save her?"

"So he says."

I don't believe Dee either. But the hope . . . I have to honor it. "I can convince him to help her."

Grant shakes his head. "No."

"I'm doomed as long as I wear this mark, anyway. I can convince him. He wants me."

Saying it out loud makes it worse. Realer somehow. There's my skin, crawling again. He does want me. Maybe he wants me as much as he wants his New London. His followers. His alchemical madness. And he's dressed up in my dad.

Ewwww doesn't begin to cover it.

"He's the devil," Grant says. "He is."

Sidekick moves his head over onto my leg. I think I could sit here forever with my dog and Grant and be happy. If none of the rest of this existed.

"I know."

GRANT

I wake up to discover my legs tangled with Miranda's. Whispering leaves frame a soft blue sky. She fell asleep sometime after we stopped talking, oozing into unconsciousness on the deck. I vaguely recall giving in and stretching out beside her, closing my eyes. . . . But how we ended up sleeping so close together that I can't move without jostling her awake is a mystery.

Miranda's fists are curled to her chest like she's ready to fight dream monsters, her hair tossed in messy fronds. From this angle, the snake mark on her cheek doesn't exist. I can almost pretend that none of what's happened the past few days exists. That we're normal people doing normal things, and I came home for a visit and saw her again. That we stayed out all night and soon we'll have to deal with overreacting parents.

A shadow flickers across the edge of my vision, and I hear voices other than my own internal one.

No longer sleeping —

Wake up —

She's awake —

Maybe you'll listen —

Reality sinks sharp teeth into me. I need to check on Mom.

I intend to scoot a safe, non-awkward distance away before I get up, but as soon as I move, Sidekick whines. I never had a dog growing up, but figuring out this is a plea for one of us to take him off the deck to the bathroom isn't rocket science. Still, I regret not being able to freeze this moment. Slow down the clock.

Sidekick's whining jolts Miranda awake, and she blinks, then slides her legs from mine and stiffly sits up. She stares out into the forest instead of looking at me. Is she blushing?

"I better take Sidekick down," she says, the dog nosing her arm.

Since the moment I want to freeze is now past, I now wish for the ability to snap my fingers and make things not awkward. I search for something to say that will make her laugh, relax. But what comes out is, "I don't know how much sleep we got, if you're wondering."

Why did I say that? All we *did* was sleep.

Miranda climbs to her feet and stretches, her back curving a long arch beneath her T-shirt. "I can't believe I slept at all." Then she pulls the screen door open, and Sidekick trots inside. His tail tucks down between his legs as soon as he enters the house.

Miranda pauses. "You hear that?"

The trees rush like water in a gust of wind. Nothing else.

"No. What is it?" I ask.

"Nothing. That's my point. No birds or insects . . . it was quiet when we got here last night too, aside from Kick's howling. It's like they're all in hiding. Or maybe took off for less-messed-up pastures."

I push to my feet as she disappears into the house. How did I not notice the unnatural silence? A forest should be full of sounds. I'm totally off my game, officially plan-free. And I forgot all about getting news to Dad. He's sure to be way past freaking out at this point.

Just then a voice speaks, remarkably clearly and unfragmented: *Don't worry about him. He's safe. Unlike you.*

Great. Even the dead's *comforting* messages are troubling.

At least Dad is safe, unlike me and Mom and Miranda, lost in this too-quiet forest. Dee said the natural world can sense flux, but maybe animals are just smarter than people. You don't see them trying to outwit death and build immortal societies.

Inside the house, I encounter a handful of girls and women, dressed normally and back at the sewing. Several more people — men and women — crowd into the small kitchen, involved in some other weird activity. Water steams, and there's the smell of burning . . . is that wax?

Spying four fresh cartons of doughnuts propped open on a short bookshelf beside the kitchen. I grab one. "Morning, creepy, doughnut-loving alchemists," I say.

No reaction whatsoever.

I head to the room where Dee stashed Mom, taking a bite of what tastes like sugar and cardboard. The doughnuts are from Stop and Gas, for sure.

The bed where Mom should be unconscious is made, the puffy pink comforter smooth and vacant. Bone, wearing another of his seeming lifetime supply of Tarheels T-shirts, sits in a corner of the room staring at it. I swallow, my throat stuffed with dry dough.

Shadows loom on either side of me and whisper: *Worse than you think — much worse.* I'm fighting to keep my panic theoretical.

"Where is she?" I demand.

Bone rubs a hand over his cheek in a gesture that makes him seem older than usual. Maybe his actual age. "She's fine — I mean, awake. Doing better. A lot better." Bone stops and chooses his next words carefully, possibly the most frightening thing that's happened yet. Finally, he says, "She's with him. The 'master.'"

"What?" I can't understand.

Dee enters the bedroom at that moment. He's changed into a fresh suit, and his skin glows like a commercial for skin cream.

He's getting stronger.

I waste no time on being polite. "But I didn't choose. You said it was my choice."

"I believe I told you I could offer *her* a choice, help *her*. I could not stand by watching the poor woman suffer through the purification cycle any longer. Now she'll have time to build her strength before tonight."

"Where is she?"

"Come see for yourself. She's much improved." Dee sweeps out his arm and leaves the room, obviously meaning for me to snap to and follow.

Bone gets to his feet. "This is bad, isn't it?"

I nod. I feel like I'm hovering inches off the floor, the surfaces around me distant and unreal. As I leave the bedroom to see Mom's miraculous recovery, I feel like one of the ghosts that glide quietly around me.

Dee preens on the tree-shaded central lawn outside. He lifts a hand to point out Mom in the swarm of people gathered there.

Mom's health *has* improved greatly. There's no arguing that. She chats and gestures, her energy at odds with the subdued people around her, all members of the returned, I assume. Maybe some of them are even from her rook club.

I scan the scene. Between the people outside and the ones in the kitchen, all 114 settlers must be accounted for.

At the edges of the main group, a few uneasy people lurk. Confused family members? I consider trekking over to them and casting my own confused lot with theirs. There's also a smattering of other people. They give a wide berth to the lawn, to-ing and fro-ing among the houses like they belong. They must be the regular theater workers.

Dee really is going to put on a show.

Miranda stands near the door with Sidekick. She's staring at my gabbing mother. Scratch that — Dee already *is* putting on a show.

Mom spots me and smiles. I lift my hand and give her a forced wave. I'm glad she's awake and smiling. But not like this. Not if it means she's cozied up to these body thieves.

Mom crosses the lawn to me, the members of the group moving to let her pass. She looks like this is some sort of town event, and she's heading over to say hello and catch me up on the gossip. She still wears sweats, her clog straps dirty around her heels.

It pains me, but I have to admit . . . she looks great. After we moved to the island, too often she wore exhaustion like a second skin. The weight of her worry as plain as coffee stains and cigarette smoke. All because of me.

That weight appears not to exist anymore. Her happiness taunts me. Dee gave this to her. Dee repaired the damage I did.

"Grant," Mom says, pulling me into her arms.

I let her, but it doesn't feel right.

"I called your dad," she says, speaking louder than necessary. She pushes me back to arm's length, a hand on my shoulder. "He knows we're both here and that everything's okay now. He'll keep the others away until it's over."

Dee grins at Mom, who returns a stiff smile. Getting a closer look at her, I decide that what I initially read as happiness is simply relief. She made a deal with Dee.

Miranda walks over, Sidekick close on her heels. The other people outside pretend to be ignoring us, but they're as nosy as the people whose bodies they wear. And the normal people at the fringes, they're nosier. Their town drunk commands the scene.

Then again, he's supposed to be dead, so they must have convinced themselves this is some stranger. People are used to that. But they'll still want to know why their mothers and sisters, brothers and sons want to hang out with the theater people. Dee must have conjured up a convincing story if they're content to stand by and watch.

"Everything is most definitely not okay," I say, finally.

Master Dee chuckles and says, "Does your mother look harmed? She will be one of mine now, Grant, an immortal. It's almost like Virginia has come back to us — not in blood, of course, but you are her family. It's as if you are one of us too. There will be a place for you in New London."

The stiff smile remains on Mom's face. I want to grab her shoulders and shake her.

Miranda appeals to her. "Sara, please. Think. You know Grant can't be part of this."

Mom dismisses Miranda's objection. "He can't stop it either," she says. "We are all a part of this now, and we've come too far to stop. The world is going to change. Tonight. And no one has to be hurt for it to happen. We can all get what we want."

Her certainty sounds like a little kid's. So does her logic.

"What about your rook club?" I ask. "Your friends."

"There are some things I'm willing to let go of and some things I'm not. You are my son. They would understand."

Doubtful. But Mom is too scared to listen. Nothing I can say will change her mind. I can guess just how Dee managed to manipulate her to his way of thinking. As long as Mom thinks Dad and I will come through this unharmed, she'll go along.

I have to try anyway. "Mom, you can't give up your soul."

Dee steps closer and places a hand on my arm. "I value those who are mine, Grant. You need not worry for your mother any longer, unless you try to disrupt the ceremony. I would never willingly give up anyone who belongs to me."

I don't miss where Dee's eyes land — on Miranda.

"You see, Grant. This is fine." A slight falter in Mom's voice gives her away, but I don't believe she'll do anything to cross Dee, even if she changes her mind.

Just then a short, square-jawed man joins our small, unhappy group. His face is tight with barely concealed anger, and a gray-haired woman I've never seen before is at his side, frowning at him.

"Master, I apologize for the interruption," the woman says.

"No need, Eleanor," says Dee. "What can I do for the director?"

The voices have stayed quiet, the barest suggestion of being present. *They are trapped,* they whisper, soft, so soft, overlapping. *We feel them.* They whisper as if they're afraid Dee will overhear. What they're saying makes zero sense to me.

"Who is Eleanor? Wait, I don't care." The director is clearly used to holding court. "You have to understand one thing: I won't have my name associated with a sham production. Not while the whole town is watching. If we're going to put on

267

the show, I need my employees back," he says. "That includes my intern too." He looks past Miranda, to where Bone is lurking. "And my other intern, the screwup. I need all my people. Now."

Beside Bone is his father, holding his leather valise. Whitson smirks at the director trying to direct the dead man.

Dee smiles, slow and cold. "They are not yours any longer and —"

"This is Polly's support group," Miranda interrupts. "And Kirsten's and Gretchen's. Surely you can sub in someone for them this once?"

Dee watches Miranda with naked admiration. He stays silent.

The director cracks his jaw. "And you? You need a support group?"

"Me, well . . . I . . ." Miranda's shoulders tick down a fraction, but I'm probably the only one who catches the movement before she lifts them. She shrugs. "I quit."

"Me too," says Bone, though he sounds happy about it.

The director isn't trying to conceal his outrage anymore. He opens his mouth to respond, but Dee lifts his hand and touches the man's shoulder. "Leave us in peace. You have work to do."

I brace for a fight, knowing the director can't have a clue who he's dealing with, but he gives a simple nod. "I agree," he says, scowling like he wants to argue with what he just said. He turns on his heel and leaves.

What just happened?

Dee must not want any of us thinking about it too hard. "Now, Sara, you'd best continue with the others," he says. "The director is not the only one with work to do. Today is all we have to finish the preparations." With that, he ushers Mom away, Eleanor trailing them like an obedient puppy. Bone and Dr. Whitson do the same.

"I can't believe I quit," Miranda says once we're alone. "Or that your mom's decided to go along with this. What are we going to do now?"

Before I can answer, music begins and swells into something like a waltz, swooping and old-fashioned, grand and polished. The song comes from within the crowd. As the gathered people move back, I see a handful of the returned men are playing instruments while Dee looks on with approval.

He pivots and strides back to us. Before I can stop him, Dee grabs Miranda's hand in his, puts his other on her waist. Miranda stumbles but manages to stay on her feet as Dee drives her in a clumsy dance around the circle formed by the crowd. Mom looks worried, and Whitson disapproving, but the rest smile in muted approval. Dee is blissed out.

Turn after turn, the dead band plays on. When Dee and Miranda near my side of the cleared space, I take a step forward. Miranda's eyes are wide and panicked when they meet mine. She shakes her head slightly, mouthing, *No.*

I ignore her and migrate closer, dodging Dee's practiced step to avoid getting mowed down. "Mind if I cut in?" I ask.

Miranda stumbles again.

"I do," Dee says, wheeling her away.

I'm unsure how to force the issue. Mom walks over and loops her arm tightly through mine to prevent me from trying to interfere again.

At last, Dee circles Miranda back to where he grabbed her. He bends to drop a light, respectful kiss on the skin of her hand, then deposits her at my side. Mom says, low, "Just one more day. One more," and is gone before Dee's attention falls on her.

I don't know what to say, and clearly neither does Miranda. She opens and shuts her mouth a couple of times. The crowd retakes the lawn. The music wavers and halts. Finally, she says, "Did that just happen?"

I hold her hands in mine. They're cold as seawater in winter. "You know, insects can't just stop making noise. And a lot of them have no way to get out of here. They can't fly or swim."

"Then where are they?" she asks, seizing on the change of topic.

"There's another possibility. They might be dead."

MIRANDA

I follow Grant along the path to the furthest edge of the Grove's property. Sidekick lopes ahead of us. My hand vibrates with invisible ick I will never get rid of. Dee touched it . . . with his lips. *He* danced with me. *He* wants me.

I officially have devil cooties.

After the nightmare dance, the body snatchers and the theater crew got back to work. Mounting the production after a few days off is always harder, and preparing for the *transformation* apparently has its own pages-long to-do list. Dee abandoned us to our own devices. It annoys me that he's so sure we won't try to escape, that we won't be able to do anything worth preventing.

Especially since he's right.

Where could we go? I have no way to be anywhere but here. This island. This day. And if Grant tries to stop the preparations, he's risking his mother's life.

Maybe it's a good thing I never made life plans.

Grant wants to test his insect theory, so that's what we're doing. I also suspect he wants some distance. So do I. Breathing the same air as Dee is like having *FREAK* written on the outside of my car a million times in a row.

We reach the final house of the Grove. Just past it is a stretch of mowed grass that leads down to the shore, thick forest bordering its other side. Grant kneels at the edge of the trees and rummages around in the undergrowth.

"Got one," he says. He removes his hand, cupping it to brandish a dead insect at me.

"Dead bug," I say. I pretend to fan myself. "For me?"

Grant kneels again and rummages some more. When he opens his hand this time, there are several tiny bodies, like small damaged robots.

"Oh," I say. "You think he killed them."

"He has to be getting energy from somewhere, enough to keep himself breathing in that body until it's really his. I think he's pulling on nature to get what he needs, for him and for the rest of them. I have nothing to back this up, not really, but" — he holds up the handful of bugs — "this. And you said animals were being all weird that first night too, right?"

I eye Sidekick, worried. "The dogs all went crazy. It was like they were barking mad about something. Even Sidekick. Do you think Dee hurt him?"

Sidekick thumps his tail at his name. He looks fine.

"You said he told you he's been watching you. I don't think he'd hurt Sidekick, because he'd be afraid you'd find out. And I'm afraid he has control of this. Killing these insects, no one will care or even notice. The birds, they'll make up explanations for. He needs everyone to hang around until he's really in power. He can't go scaring the locals too much before then. I'm thinking he can't — or won't — directly affect the real world, not until he had a body again."

I flex and unflex my fingers. I need to tell him about the dance.

"I don't waltz," I say. "Or foxtrot or whatever that was."

Grant's eyebrows draw together. "You didn't have much of a choice."

"I didn't have *any* choice, actually."

"What do you mean?" he asks.

The dead silence around us doesn't make this nightmare any easier to talk about. I walk a little further around the side of the last house, through the patchy trees. The waves of the sound flow in, then back out from the beach nearby, almost visible from where we are. The cadence is usually soothing. Not now.

"I mean that he was controlling me. Like some puppet. A marionette. I wasn't doing the moving."

Grant stands there, not doing anything. Finally, he says, "When I tried to cut in, you stumbled. Because I distracted Dee. You were fighting him?"

"Trying, especially at first, but he was too strong. The mark . . ." I raise my fingers and flutter then alongside the snake, then drop them. "It burned on my face the whole time."

Grant lays his hand lightly across the snake, and I suck in a surprised breath. Not a bad surprise. We look at each other.

"He said he could take it away," I whisper. "That I'd be free."

Grant's hand stays on my cheek, and he inclines his head. "But he didn't, did he?"

"It wouldn't matter if he did, I don't think."

Our foreheads rest against each other, and I experience a weird sensation — an easier time breathing, a harder time breathing. The sound washes against the shore behind us in its own easy rhythm. I lean into the pressure of his hand, and I kiss him. A hungry kiss, full of my need to get away from dead bugs and dead fathers.

Then full of something more, something that only belongs to us.

Grant's hand slides into my hair, gripping lightly at the roots. Mine gathers the cloth of his T-shirt in my fist, holding him to me.

"Uh, sorry," Bone says from somewhere nearby. "Seemed like the best time to talk. They're all busy."

At least one thing hasn't changed — Bone's terrible timing.

Heavy footsteps clomp toward us, and I release Grant's shirt. But he doesn't turn to Bone right away, watching me instead. His face is still near mine.

I'm blushing. I know I am. But it helps that he doesn't jump away from me. That he stays put.

Grant touches his forehead to mine again. "I asked him to come," he says, making it clear he now regrets that.

I nod, "It's okay."

He steps away from me, motioning Bone closer. "What can you tell us? Anything?"

"Well, my dad is nuts," Bone says. "I never thought any of it was real. Dude, I thought he was *just* nuts."

"I liked your dad," Grant says.

"I didn't," I say.

Bone becomes solemn. "I'm sorry about your dad," he says. "I never thought mine would do something like . . . that."

Interesting. "So it *was* him who killed Dad? Not Dee?"

Bone shrugs. "I only know from the bragging, but I think he . . . called Dee here somehow. I don't know how they did it, but your father had to die and lie empty for so long. Then . . ."

"He went to the body and helped Dee take possession of it," I finish.

Bone nods. "I'm sorry. Until I saw the body bag when we came downstairs, I thought it wasn't real. But that's the kind of thing he'd keep. For his collection. I didn't know."

I can't deal with the idea of Dad's body bag as part of someone's collection. "Do you know what they did with the gun?"

"Dee looked it over last night while Dad told him what a genius he is. He put Dad in charge of it until tonight, his reward from 'the master,'" Bone says. "I should have known he was like this. I should have done . . . something."

Shame is clear on Bone's face. I hate feeling sympathetic toward him, but there it is. I understand him too well at this point not to. "I just danced with the devil. None of us have choices here."

Grant raises his hand. "About that. You don't think Dee's been able to control you all these years, do you?"

I wondered the same thing, but I answer, "No. And I don't think he could control Dad before either. But the mark has its own influence too. Our curse. I wonder if it's why Dad drank so much. You can feel it, when it takes over, makes you do things you wouldn't. You can feel that it's not really you, but it's hard to fight."

"It's hard to believe your dad stayed sane," Grant says. "I can't figure out why Dee would curse you, given how into Mary he was."

"He likes controlling people?" I shrug. "I stopped cutting Dad slack so long ago, gave up on him. And I was wrong."

Maybe he's watching you through the veil. Maybe he knows you're sorry.

Grant comes closer to me again, and I let him tuck me against his side. He's the one good thing in all this mess. One more thing I'm going to lose and never get back before this ends.

His nose crinkles. "You smell that?"

I sniff and, even with the wind blowing in the other direction, inhale something rotten.

Bone says, "I do."

We hurry toward the smell. After a few more feet, Sidekick lies down on his belly and whines, refusing to come along.

The scent trail leads us to a small bank that overlooks a slice of beach. When we reach the overhang, I turn away almost immediately. I've seen enough.

Dead fish cover the shore in heaps. Silver, black, and red scales shine in the sun. Their empty eyes stare, sightless.

"They weren't here yesterday," Bone says.

The smell shouldn't be so strong, not so soon. Dee killed these fish. I know it. He sucked out their lives. The bodies are decomposing faster than normal.

I stagger back toward the forest. I hear the boys behind me. Grant catches up and touches my shoulder. It's a small comfort against the sight of that shoreline.

"Dee went into a room alone 'to prepare,'" Bone says. "My dad says he talks to angels."

"Satan was an angel," I point out.

"No," Grant says, "this isn't something any god would be involved in. Or any fallen angel, for that matter. The devil is just the kind of word my gram would use."

"What do you mean?"

"The forces he's calling on . . . you've felt it when he looks at you, when he touches you. He was just a man once, a mad scientist who wanted to believe he was talking to angels. A man who believed in progress, in the dream of a New London on this island. But he's become something else. Worse. More."

"Death," Bone says.

We leave it at that.

*

I sit beside Grant on the sidewalk in front of Polly's place, the house that forms the main hub of activity for the returned. We watch in silence as the secret alchemists and the regular theater types bustle around. I asked Bone to fetch my messenger bag from his dad's car, and I get up when I see him carrying it toward us.

"Where are you going?" Grant asks.

"Just to freshen up," I say. "A girl needs her secrets."

Grant smiles at me, but it's nervous. And that's why I can't tell him where I'm going. He'll only worry more. He'll want to help. This is a last-ditch effort anyway. It's better for him to stay out here in relative safety, in case I'm caught in my attempts. Who knows what Dee might do to Grant if I give him an excuse?

I meet Bone and take the bag. "Thanks," I say. Lowering my voice I add, "Follow me inside. I need one more thing."

Bone does as I ask without drawing attention to it. He really isn't so bad after all.

In the apartment, the bizarre prep continues. Women sew their fingers raw. A mix of men and women in the kitchen dry freshly made candles. The smell of burnt wax is everywhere. A couple of the women glance up at us as we enter, then go back to work, unconcerned.

And why should they be? I think. *What threat do I pose to them?* That's the mindset I'm counting on.

"What is it?" Bone asks.

"Your dad, where is he?"

He nods toward a hallway that goes in the opposite direction of Polly's room. "He's in the bedroom next to the one Dee's in, I think."

Good. "Can you give me a couple of minutes, then distract him?"

Bone looks at me. "What are you going to do?"

"Better if you don't know." When he doesn't answer, I lean in close to his ear, "You said you should have done something."

He hesitates, then says, "Two minutes?"

"I have to duck into the other bedroom. Then I'll wait in the bathroom across the hall."

Bone nods and pretends to be examining a magazine on a nearby end table. I saw Eleanor-slash-Polly outside a few moments ago and slip into her bedroom. There's no one in here. *Whew.*

I look around to see what I can score that might help. Not much, but there's some stuff. My heart pounds as I shove two small spools of thread, some stray needles, and a thimble someone must have finally given her into my bag.

I don't trust Bone to give me more time, so I slip out of the room. I catch his eye, and we head up the little hall to the other bedrooms, me in front.

I nod to a frowning woman as we pass her. "Bathroom," I say, though she didn't ask.

I keep my bag tucked against my side and let myself inside the small bathroom, softly shutting the door, while Bone breaks off into the room across the hall. The mirror calls out to me, and when I see what a mess I am, I swipe at my hair in an attempt to smooth it. I position my face so I don't have to see the snake. Then I move closer to the door so I can listen while I get ready.

Bone and his dad are arguing. Bone raises his voice, no doubt so I'll hear him. "Dad, I get that you have things to do, but I need you for a minute outside. Just a minute."

While I wait, I scoop out the things I took from Polly's room and transfer them to my pocket. I add a handful of change from the bottom of my bag. I resist a victorious fist pump when I hear Bone and his dad enter the hallway, Roswell complaining loudly the whole time.

Once it sounds as though the coast is clear, I open the door by degrees and rush across into the bedroom. I hope against hope that Roswell didn't take the gun with him.

He didn't.

It rests on the center of a pillow on the bed, like a crown in some king's chamber. I put my bag down next to it. I don't have much time, and this is a long shot at best. The gems on the grip flash as I pick it up.

I stuff the loot in my pocket into the long barrel, one thing at a time, starting with the needles, thimble, and thread. I use a pen from my bag to press them deep inside. I do the coins after that. For the capper, I crumple the page with the picture of Dee I ripped from Roswell's book earlier and add it.

When everything is in and I'm satisfied a casual examination will reveal nothing, I hurry back to my hiding place. Roswell harrumphs his way back up the hall seconds after I close the bathroom door.

I have no idea if what I did is enough to jam Dee's weapon. Probably not, and so I'll keep the fact I did it to myself. I don't want to give Grant false hope. But I tried, and that's worth something.

GRANT

Miranda is off freshening up, so I decide to give another shot to convincing Mom her plan is the worst possible approach. I find her helping with the outdoor division of the candle squad. They place freshly made candles with long black tapers on a sheet with a silly Christmas pattern and trim the wicks. It's a surreal sight.

Mom knows I'm standing here, off to the side of the cluster, but she does her best to ignore me. Sorry, not happening.

"Mom, can I have a word?" I say finally, smiling a good-boy smile.

The other women look at me for a heartbeat before returning to their work. Mom steps away and scans the yard, and I know she's looking for Dee.

"He's not out here," I say. "He's preparing for whatever awful thing he's about to do — you know he's killing the people who these bodies belong to, right?"

The spirits around us are waving gray lights. They whisper:

That's right —
What he means to do —
It's a trap —
Can't let —
Can't —

Mom takes my arm, hard, towing me away. "Careful," she says. "He'll find out, Grant. We can't be talking. I'm doing this for you. Stay out of the way, and don't cause trouble."

And with that, she's gone. I could make a scene — I'm good at that — but I can't risk Dee banishing me. I have to at least stay in the game. And that means essentially following my mother's orders. For now.

I retake my seat on the sidewalk, and Miranda comes back before long. We sit and observe, watching from the edges. I wonder if this is what the spirits feel like. Useless and desperate.

It must be.

I envy their nonsense chattering. If I indulged in that, it would at least break the silence that keeps falling between Miranda and me. Beside me, she strokes Sidekick's head. I can feel her nerves growing as time passes.

I don't blame her. The desiccated insects in the forest and the rotting fish washed onto the beach are never far from my thoughts. The voices of the spirits whisper insinuations —

Death's here —
We're here —
You need to hear —

As usual, details aren't provided.

"I should be helping the techs," Miranda says. "They'll be down several staff. And Polly . . . it's still the show."

I gape at her. "No way. That's nuts. You can't help them with this."

"I know. It's just . . . the theater, it's always been an escape."
She shakes her head. "Figures Dee's wrecked that too."

"You did quit, at least."

"I still can't believe I did that."

"I can," I tell her, nudging her with my arm.

We lapse back into silent worry. I consider calling Dad,
but I can't figure out how that will help. So I sit and watch
and try try *try* to locate an exit strategy we can use later. Dee's
soul is a wrong thing, unnatural, and we'll regret forever the
moment when he gets what he wants, what he's waited for all
this time.

Immortality.

He must not succeed —

You must stop this —

Must stop —

Must —

I press the voices away — either I'm getting better at blocking them out, or being near Dee makes it easier. I'm not sure
how I feel about either possibility. I also don't see how these
chattering spirits are supposed to help me; Gram's gift must
have acted differently. I'm about to fail my ancestor, who apparently gave us this capacity for a reason. But how am I supposed
to think with so many voices talking at me? What strength do
spirits have to give?

The early evening steals in like a cat burglar and with it
comes Polly. She emerges from the house in a long cloak that
matches her hair. Her fingers are red, bloody raw, and she sucks
on one absently, as if she feels the hurt from far away.

"Dinner inside," she says. "Miranda, I need you to come
with me."

"You're Eleanor, right?" I ask. "My ancestor?"

The gray-haired young woman nods. "You're one of Ginny's descendants. Such a surprise that she survived."

"She hated everything you stand for," I say. "She passed that on down the line."

"We have been misunderstood all along. I'm not surprised to hear it from my daughter's spawn. Come inside. Soup for you. And Miranda gets a bath."

Miranda climbs to her feet and turns to me. "Have your soup. I'll do the bath because I smell." Eleanor-Polly smiles again, and Miranda adds, "But if you try to stick me in some wedding gown or something, it will not happen. Got it?"

My smile is real but gone as soon as Miranda is. What if they *do* try to put her in a wedding gown?

Sidekick stays with me, looking hopeful.

"All right, boy. Last meal, it is."

In the kitchen, a few fat candles sit on wax paper, burned down to their wicks. They're black, just like the ones outside. "Subtle," I mutter.

I discover an enormous kettle of normal-smelling beef-and-vegetable soup on the stove, and a stack of bowls beside it that must have been collected from several kitchens. I scoop soup into one, noticing how loud every noise seems in the lack of bustle. I eat a bite and realize I'm starving, but pause, just to make sure I don't keel over. I don't, so I put the bowl on the floor for Sidekick to slurp in gulps. My own bowl goes almost as fast.

I expect Polly and Miranda will be the first to reemerge. Instead, Dee joins me.

If Dee was a skin cream commercial before, now he's an ad for youth itself. Vitality. Strength. Even the body he wears seems in better shape.

He's also wearing yet another suit. This one has thin gray pinstripes. Some devoted follower, or maybe his lackey Whitson, must've shopped until they dropped to make sure he coordinates with his coven's capes. Dee's own gray cloak remains folded across his arm.

"So, what's your big dastardly plan?" I set down my bowl on the counter with a clatter. It can't hurt to ask.

Dee looks at me, eyes as black and blank as if he's a painting that walks. In that moment, I'm sure I'm right about the forces he's accessing. They are unknowable, beyond my understanding. Maybe they're using Dee. Maybe he isn't fully in control either.

Those eyes make the whispering voices around us go quiet. They make it hard for me to breathe.

Or maybe that's the invisible fist squeezing my lungs.

I can't breathe. My lungs burn. My mouth is open, but no air comes in. I can't force myself to suck in a breath.

I start to panic. So do the spirits.

Strong —

Breathe —

You can't let this —

No —

"Shall we go?" Dee's lips form the words, and the flatness vanishes from his eyes. A boundless dark energy replaces the two-dimensional death glare.

I know who I'll see before I turn, gasping, lungs released.

Miranda stands in the middle of the common room with her arms crossed over her chest. Her hair is loose and almost dry. She wears a fresh outfit — a vintage western shirt, a pair of jeans, and dusty sneakers. This is the girl I want to go anywhere with, anywhere except wherever Dee is taking us.

Beside her, Polly and a couple of women I don't recognize sport heavy cloaks. Polly — or rather, Eleanor — says, "Master, I apologize for the state of her. She wouldn't consent —"

Dee holds up a hand. "Mary —" He pauses. "That is to say, *Miss Blackwood* is a vision. It will be my honor to escort her to the birth of New London."

Polly's mouth closes, and she nods.

"I'll walk with Grant." Miranda crosses the room to me.

"That will be fine." Dee responds with a don't-care elegance; he can afford it with everything else going his way.

I cannot fathom how the man is so divorced from reality that he not only thinks Miranda is into dead guys, but that she'll ever be attracted to someone who looks like her dad. Merry olde England wasn't that backward. Was it?

My thinking must show on my face, because the squeeze of my lungs is worse this time. I cough, hacking, struggling to breathe.

Miranda grips my arm, concerned. "What's wrong?"

The pressure vanishes at Miranda's question, and I suck in air. Dee is waiting to see how I'll respond. I choke out an answer, "What isn't?"

Dee's black eyes leave me.

Still, I'm not breathing easy.

MIRANDA

The trek to the theater begins at sunset. Dee, Polly, Roswell, and Sara are in the lead, followed by Grant and me. The rest of the returned form a dark cloud behind us. These familiar figures wearing the unfamiliar gray cloaks are guaranteed to freak out any friends and loved ones attending the Dare County Night to end all Dare County Nights.

We don't walk along the main road but rather take the back way. I've always considered this path somewhat enchanted, because only people in the show use it. It hugs the coast, the waters of the sound in full view, and runs all the way to Waterside Theater's backstage. Sure, it's infested with snakes — though tellingly we don't see any tonight.

The actors and technicians left a few hours earlier. Dee wants them to put on the show, though I still don't understand why. Can't he just clap his hands and make thunder and lightning and drop birds from the sky and then take his stupid gun and force me to betray everything I am?

I don't know about the other stuff, but the last one is coming. The moment when I'm transformed into the traitor he branded me as. I touch my cheek, an absent gesture that's becoming habit. My last-ditch effort at sabotaging the gun strikes me as little more than a bad joke with this entire parade of body-snatching alchemists around us.

"What did they want you to wear?" Grant asks.

These are the first words he's spoken since we left Polly's, since that weird choking incident.

"Gray isn't my color," is all I say. Back at the apartment, Polly and Kirsten presented me with a tray of makeup from somewhere, along with a too-long sack-like baby doll dress made in the same gray of the cloaks. Polly attempted to at least force a cloak onto my shoulders, but I locked the bathroom door and put on my own clothes.

The wind tosses my hair around my face. I'm not even going to look over at the sound, in case it's a dead fish fiesta from here to eternity. Dee seems far too strong, leading his favored companions toward the theater. Or Eleanor is favored, anyway — Sara is as much a pawn in this as me, and Roswell just has a bad case of hero worship.

I want to tell Grant how much his sticking with me means. I want to tell him lots of things. But I don't. He doesn't say anything more either. I hope he hasn't forgotten that he promised not to let me betray my principles, this town, this world. I don't want to be the bad guy.

I pause and pat Sidekick's head where he trots along beside me. I was afraid to leave him behind. If I never made it back, I didn't want him trapped with them.

Our silent party finally reaches the theater and heads backstage, winding along the stone path between tall trees and the small buildings that house everything from costumes and props to lighting gels and tools. A stagehand leaving the costume shop calls out to Polly. "Poll, where have you been all day?"

Polly ignores him, fixated on her master.

Dee doesn't pause until we're to the amphitheater. He stops in front of the stage and waits for the mass of his followers to file out from behind him. The event has packed the house. Every seat is taken, aside from a large vacant section down front blocked off by strands of police tape. The audience, already in their seats, watches, murmuring questions. I even glimpse Blue Doe at the back of the house with her cameraman. She beams in our direction as they film the big event.

Once his cohort is complete, Dee crosses to the first row of empty seats. He sweeps on his cloak with a flourish. He calls out, loud and clear, as if his words are being broadcast through a wireless microphone: "Welcome tonight's guests of honor. Your beloved have returned to you!"

Confused applause quickly gathers force as the returned claim their seats. Most of the people here will likely see their annual income triple thanks to the interest caused by the disappearance and reappearance, the all-new lost-and-found colony. The show's next season will probably be the biggest ever. This night is about dragging out the attention on the new mystery, adding to the local legend. Next year's dollar signs are in everyone's eyes. Except they don't know we'll be living in "New London" with our creepy mayor, aka the devil of Roanoke Island.

When I finally look at him, I realize Dee is waiting for me. He leans forward, giving me a small bow. "You will do me the honor of sitting at my side," he says.

It's not phrased as a question. The snake burns, and my lips open. "Yes, delighted." I hear the words come out of my mouth, not of my own accord. He made me say it.

I guess that freedom promise is officially off the table.

"I'll stay with you," Grant says.

"Yes, and our Sara will be right beside you," Dee says, scanning for Grant's mom, "in case you need motherly guidance."

Dee finds his wayward recruit at the same time I do. She's engaged in a heated conversation with Chief Rawling, who's there in uniform. Sara meets Dee's gaze and walks back to us without another word to her husband.

The chief shoots a worried look in Grant's and my direction. I match it as Dee's cloak whips in the air. He urges us into our seats. Front row center, of course.

Blue Doe appears as soon as we're seated. She teeters on high heels directly in front of Dee. Her eyes narrow on me as if she can't quite place me. I crane my neck in the opposite direction to avoid her scrutiny.

"Sir, ah, sir, can I have a moment of your time?" Blue Doe asks. When there's no response, she raises her voice. "Anyone care to do a quick interview? Come on, now. Don't be shy. America wants to hear your stories. . . . What is that *dog* doing here?"

Without looking at her, I reach down and tug Sidekick more securely in front of my feet.

"What do the capes symbolize?" Blue Doe asks, exasperated. "At least give me that much."

"Ceremony. The connection between souls who have been among the lost," Dee answers, nailing the reporter with a look that would shut me up.

Apparently Blue Doe and I have that much in common. She clicks away on her high heels. I can't even enjoy her retreat, because Dee places his hand over mine. The hunk of flesh is cold as ice cubes. The summer night's humidity is sticky, and I half expect mist to form where his hand makes contact with my warm skin.

The lights swell, then dim. The crew is getting ready for curtain.

"We're really watching the show," I say, disbelieving.

"I know this version of history means much to you," Dee says. "And what better way to bring reality to our new home? We will show it to them."

I open my mouth to ask what he means — not that I think he'll answer — but His Royal Majesty strides out on stage. I don't miss the dirty look he shoots at Polly and me in the front row.

Fabulous. Now he really hates me.

"Welcome, friends, neighbors, and strangers," he begins. "It's such a relief to have everyone home safe. We here at Waterside Theater wanted to mark the return of everyone's loved ones in a special way, with this special island tradition. Enjoy."

I hear every word, but process little of it. What does Dee mean, *We will show it to them?*

The director exits stage right to another round of applause — this one merely polite — and the show starts. I try to lift my hand from Dee's under the guise of covering a yawn, but he exerts a steady pressure that keeps it under his own. Noticing the struggle, Grant props his forearm on the armrest, so his shoulder rubs against mine.

Death on one side, life on the other.

The first group of actors marches onto the stage, decked out in the most elaborate Elizabethan costumes *The Lost Colony* has to offer. They bustle with pomp, and despite the reality of what's happening, I settle into my seat, dipping my head back to take in the sky above. Familiar clear pinpoints of light stare down. The stars are watching tonight's performance too, and I want to warn them.

New scenes, little rehearsal. This night may well go down in flames.

The play begins with Queen Elizabeth and Sir Walter Raleigh in London, both in agreement that he should colonize the new world. The settlers come on next. They voyage and arrive, argue and suffer. The musical numbers hit in perfect time, the chorus not a note out of tune. No one forgets a line or steps on a cue. Mean little Caroline is a rosy-cheeked angel.

It's one of the best performances I can remember.

And none of them know what lies ahead.

I chance a look next to me, resigned not to hold it against Grant if he's smirking or bored. But by all appearances, he's into the production too. I'm oddly glad. I'm more tied to the theater than any other part of the island. I've always belonged here more than anywhere else. This has always been my best escape.

The show is also long, too long for Dee's patience to hold, apparently. Just as the second act closes — after the actors exit the stage, but before the lights go down and intermission starts — he releases my hand.

Watching the play has been a reprieve, but that ends when Dee rises to his feet. The rest of the returned stand on his cue. The mark on my face burns again, as I get to my feet, not of my own volition.

Sorry, stars in the sky, we have to interrupt this program.

Grant gets up, and says, "Miranda . . . Mom . . ." But Sara is already walking away with the others.

The returned file out of their rows in neat lines, as choreographed as if they've been rehearsing for a few hundred years.

They climb the stairs on either side of the stage. Some linger on the steps, facing the audience, while others take over the back half of the stage itself. All of them leave space for someone else to pass by. I realize it's a makeshift promenade.

The crowd buzzes in confusion, not sure how to react. But they stay in their seats.

I fight as hard as I can, willing my limbs to be under my own control, but it's no use. My elbow juts out at a wide, proper angle to allow Dee to slip his through it. My feet walk me forward, my pace matching his perfectly.

The cloaked figures curve in a generous half-moon as Dee parades me past, a cupping shell that mirrors the top of the *monas hieroglyphica* symbol. We climb the steps onto the stage.

When we reach the top of the short flight of stairs, I look into the crowd. Locating Grant is as easy as finding the flash of movement. Agent Malone and Agent Walker are also at the show and busy hauling Grant up the aisle in slow degrees. His father attempts to intervene while Grant argues, but neither of their protests seem to be meeting with success.

The crowd barely notes that disturbance, even with the busiest busybodies in town in attendance. They're too busy watching the stage — there are a few confused murmurs but far more wide smiles that assume this is all part of the show. The disappearances themselves were probably part of it, they must be thinking. What a grand idea.

No one is going to intervene. No one is going to save me.

My head turns back to what's ahead of me, and my feet continue to move forward. Cloaked arms extend. They make a gray path across the stage for my father's body and me.

The audience murmurs kick up a notch then. People won't think *this* is part of the show.

"That's the Blackwoods!" someone says. The man is in the middle section, starting to rise from his seat, gesturing toward the stage. Is that Mike from Stop and Gas? As the seller of the cheapest six-pack in town, he would be the other person besides Chief Rawling to finally recognize Dad.

As quickly as the words are out, the man's mouth clacks shut, his seatmates shrinking away from the loud noise of his teeth colliding with each other.

Dee calls, "Stay in your seats."

The audience does, obviously bewildered that they can't do otherwise. The feds and Chief Rawling trot back down the aisle, sinking into seats left empty in the returned's former section.

The breeze brings a rank smell to my nostrils. *More dead fish.* They must be washing up on the beach behind the theater.

His Royal Majesty appears at stage right. "What is this?" he demands. The director is silenced as quickly as the others.

The words Dee speaks next aren't in any language I recognize.

A trembling-in-ecstasy Roswell joins us onstage, though. He doesn't rate a cloak, but he carries the pistol. The dulled metal with its bright jewels lies flat on his extended hands as he walks up the stairs. A paler-than-ever Bone peels off behind him, not climbing onto the stage, but taking a seat down front instead.

Roswell crosses the stage, stopping across from us. We're obviously the main event, isolated from the mass of gray cloaks. My position places me at exactly center stage under the main spotlight. Dee is gazing at me.

I cringe at how loud my voice is when I'm made to speak. "I have a story to tell, of a night much like this, on a shore not far from here, many years ago," I say, only it's not me supplying the words. "A young woman, Mary Blackwood, was brought out from the safe walls of the colony's fort at night to meet the ship of the man who loved her. A man who had spent long months traveling, navigating by patterns in the stars, on the most auspicious of schedules. A great man who would have given up his greatness had she but asked. A man who was coming to deliver his promise to the colonists sent on Raleigh's voyage. To deliver his promise to Miss Blackwood herself."

I'm held as rapt by the story as everyone else, despite the fact I'm being used to tell it. Once I stop fighting for control, my tongue moves easier. The words slip freely from my lips.

"She was an enchantment, a brave dream, emerging from the night forest in a dark, hooded cloak. The girl met him with a kiss — as beautiful as she had ever been, even after those long months away. The colonists were ready, she said, ready for their final journey, the journey of forever. She asked to see the mechanism of their transformation."

I pause, not of my own accord, because Dee wants a pause. Apparently a sizeable one.

The surf sloshes behind us. The wind sings in my ears.

"The weapon was a variation on a new creation. A pistol. No wondrous thing now, of course, but then the processes were still being perfected. And the man had let the words of angels and pure intentions guide him as he perfected this weapon, so that it gave not death, but life. Eternal life. The alchemist's — humanity's — final challenge. His love asked, and he showed her the product of his work. He placed it in her hands himself, to let her hold it."

If any insects were still alive, they would be loud in the hush of the theater. But there's nothing. The crowd listens in silence.

"But Mary had not — as the others — agreed to the voyage, to the prospects ahead, with a pure and true heart. She was pledged to the queen's stooge, Raleigh, the purse behind the colonist's voyage, but not the power. The man before her had always been the power. Mary stole the weapon and hid it. The stars were only auspicious that night, the preparations in place nearly impossible to re-create. She made his promise a lie. Even so, the alchemist was too noble to let her meet the punishment she deserved. Instead he joined their fates forever, with a simple mark. Made it so he could never lose her. She would still have the weapon, and one day she would bring it to him, and assist in the last great work that ever need be done. She would do so willingly. She would keep her promise."

I want to protest with some comments of my own here, but of course I can't. There's no *willingly* about any of this. But one thing is electric and clear in this moment:

I'm not a betrayer of good — I'm a betrayer of *evil*.

My ancestor Mary Blackwood tricked John Dee. She beat him. Winning is possible.

It. Is. Possible.

When Roswell comes closer, my hands reach out for the pistol and grip it. Grant's shout of, "Miranda, fight him!" is sweet but meaningless. The surf and air and night around me feel as unreal as my ability to exert my own will.

I level the pistol, arm steady, and point it at Dee. My lips form a final pronouncement: "And now I will make this great man, and with him these colonists, the first immortals in a new world."

My finger curls around the trigger, and I pull hard. The gun vibrates in my hand, with hard enough force to push me back, and I wait to see the spray of dust emerge.

But nothing else happens. Nothing.

The barrel is blocked. Not even magic can force the contents out until it's cleared. My stupid last-ditch sabotage *worked*.

As Dee understands there's a malfunction, his face — Dad's face — twists, and he roars in ugly rage. The colonists shout to each other — "What is happening?" "Master?" — and surge forward in their borrowed bodies.

To my profound relief, I can move again, enough to fling the gun off the stage in Grant's general direction. I can only hope he'll take it behind the theater and throw it in the sound to drown it in the waves, lost forever, carried out to the ocean beyond.

Dee lunges at me, and my heart freezes into ice. But it's not him that causes my fear — it's Sidekick. My dog dances across the stage, barking and snarling, snapping at Dee's legs, trying to protect me.

"No, boy!" I say. "No!" I intend to get Sidekick behind me, but he begins to wheeze.

Dee must be the cause. He stands blade straight in still concentration, his black eyes fixed on Sidekick. Death rattles twist my sweet dog's long torso, and he suddenly seems nothing like my big, goofy dog at all. He seems so very small and fragile, so easy for Dee to break, to end forever.

I think of Dad and how he would *never* hurt Sidekick. I think of Dad, who didn't go crazy after all, and I hope he's on the other side of that glass wall, watching through the veil. I hope for him to break through.

"Dad!" I scream. "Dad, you have to stop him! He's killing Sidekick! *Dad!*"

GRANT

When Sidekick leaps onto the stage, snarling, I know that no federal agents will keep me off it. "Dad, I have to go," I plead.

Without hesitation, Dad thrusts an arm across the feds' chests and says, "Let him," in a tone with no room for argument.

I bound from my seat, pausing to say, "Sorry about that whole drugging you thing. Desperate times, desperate measures." The agent starts to respond, but I don't stick around to hear what he has to say.

As I rush the stage, the spirits rush with me. They're everywhere; shadows that almost blend into the gray cloaks the returned wear. Their voices are a raging river of sound. It's all I can do to stay focused on Miranda, on building a wall and trying to shove them behind it. I need my mind clear. Or clearer, anyway.

The crowd is on its feet, but I'm the lone one heading into the action on the stage. The audience sounds more confused than anything, thrown by their inability to move during Dee's pathetic monologue using Miranda as mouthpiece. Invisible hands held us all in our seats.

But Miranda messed with Dee's magical weapon somehow. I have no doubt. She's amazing.

I put my hands on the edge of the stage and vault onto it. I immediately have to dodge a few angry cloak wearers, who are forming a protective circle around their outraged master. The returned will hold a grudge against Miranda, won't they? Her ancestor trapped them in mortality, was the reason Dee put them on hold behind death's veil. He's essentially a jilted fake boyfriend.

I'm not comforted by the thought. Anyone who carries an unrequited torch after this long is dangerous — even without the power over life and death.

A middle-aged cloaked woman attempts to block my path, but Mom pushes her aside. I wait for Mom to try to stop me, but then I see how watery her eyes are. They gleam under the stage lights. "I just wanted to protect you," she says. "I'm so sorry."

So Mom is free enough from Dee's influence to think clearly. Too late is better than never. "You need to get out of here," I say. "Go find Dad."

"I'm a bad mother, the worst. You help that girl. You . . ." She squeezes me into a brief hug. "You be careful. I trust you."

Mom releases me, and I maneuver through two more cloak wearers, past the boundaries of their imperfect circle. I'm just in time to watch Miranda lunge at Dee and beat his chest with her fists. She's screaming. Dee doesn't fight her. He accepts her blows, vain and proud and tall.

Sidekick isn't fighting either. He's rolled onto his side. From this angle, it's impossible to say whether he's still breathing. Maybe Miranda managed to distract Dee before he could do permanent damage to the dog's lungs or heart. What he did to mine hurt like hell. Poor Sidekick wouldn't even know where the pain came from.

As I watch, Dr. Whitson launches himself at Miranda, latching on to her like a tick. He's trying to pry her off his hero. She elbows him in the face. Good for her.

I run the rest of the way to her and shoulder Whitson away with as much force as I can. "Time out, Doctor," I say, satisfied when Whitson skitters back several feet.

With Miranda no longer pummeling Dee, the alchemist doubles over, the pinstripes of his suit folding in a crease at his waist. I wonder if she's actually injured him. But then Dee abruptly unfolds to a standing position, his arms flinging out. The motions remind me of a puppet on jerky strings. They aren't the least bit fluid. Is Dee not able to control the body anymore? Why?

Miranda sucks in a breath. "Dad?" she asks. "Is it you?"

Dee's form — no, Mr. Blackwood's form — makes two sharp bobs of the head for yes. His limbs fly into the air in a fight with himself. No, not with himself. With *Dee.*

Miranda's dad is back inside his body, but Dee must still be on board too. The body turns, and looks at me. The chorus of the spirits erupts from behind the flimsy wall I tried to press them behind.

No —

Don't let this happen —

You have to listen —

You have to fight —

Use your strength —

The man's eyes go flat and black for just a moment, and he says to me, "She wants you. She gets what she deserves."

I don't have time to prepare for the force that slams into me. Not that I could. All the air leaves my body. The spirits roar in a rising cocoon of sound, shadows everywhere around me until suddenly it feels like *I'm* the one behind a wall. I'm the one clawing to get to the surface, trapped.

John Dee has occupied my body.

"Dad? Why would you say that? Dad!"

I barely understand I'm hearing Miranda's voice. I watch from what feels like a great distance as a ribbon of dark energy, like an arm or a tentacle, emerges from my body. No one else seems to see it. It's searching . . . seeking . . .

Dee lifts my arm. He waves the hand at a cloaked figure blocking the crowd. "Step aside," he says with my voice. "This body is much more . . . receptive."

The man drops his cloak and moves, saying, "Master."

Dee sweeps his eyes — *my* eyes — over the audience, and I'm looking too. What does he mean I'm more receptive?

Nice, brave, loyal Officer Warren doesn't look afraid. His weapon is in his hand, and he's in the aisle heading straight for us. The ribbon of power — Dee's power — extending from my hand smashes into him, and the officer falls to his knees like he just crossed a goal line.

Officer Warren's death fills Dee with a rush of power. I can feel it coursing through my limbs, even trapped in here while he uses me.

A woman wearing a long dress crumples as Dee moves on to her, adding the energy of her life force to his ribbon of power.

I can feel Dee reveling in the rush of it. I feel everything he does. It's awful.

Dr. Whitson wobbles into the edge of my vision, and Dee notices him. I know he's next. The ribbon of energy only Dee and I see enters Whitson's chest and stays there longer, Dee wringing every drop he can from the man as he kills him.

I know too that Whitson's death is a punishment for touching Miranda. Inside Dee, I sense a vast rage that must once have been love. It's cold and absolute and centered on Miranda. Dee can't separate her from her ancestor. Mary, Miranda. Both are Blackwoods.

I hear Miranda's voice, still distant, talking to her father. "Dad . . . is he still inside you? Dad?"

"He . . ." The man's response is weak, shaky. But his words get stronger as he goes on. "He left. Miranda, my sweet Miranda. Let me fix this for you. Let me be there for once. I'm dead. I'm already gone. I can go out, off the island. I just need him in me. Back in me. If I leave with him in me, we'll beat him. Listen . . ."

"I'm listening," she says, clearly unaware Dee has taken over *my* body instead.

Whitson collapses then, wearing a dreamy smile as he dies. Crazy as he was, he didn't need to die. No one else needs to.

At first, Miranda doesn't move, too busy gaping at Dr. Whitson's glassy dead eyes. But then she turns to me in confusion. "What happened to him?"

Busy making his way through every cell of my body, Dee is barely aware of her question. I can hear the dull roar of the spirits. They're trying to reach me, but I can't understand them.

Dee learns his new vessel quickly. When he notices Miranda's attention, it's like a spark flaring into fire. He wants her. He shifts my body toward her, close enough to use one of my arms to grip the back of her head.

Miranda frowns, still confused. I hear my voice say, "Such a beauty," in a weirdly clipped accent. I feel my arm pull her close to me.

The spirits are talking and talking, and I have no way to warn her.

I don't need to. Miranda figures it out, tearing free of my grip. But she doesn't run, not this girl. She puts her hands on my shoulders and shakes them. She snaps her fingers in my face. Dee's cold rage surges. I feel it.

"Grant. Your grandmother, remember what she said — you need to use your strength, all the strength you have. Don't let him win. Dad thinks we can beat him." Her lips are still moving, but no matter how I scratch and claw I can't hear her anymore.

Dee is ready to punish Miranda now. I feel the thoughts almost like they're my own. She's rejected him for the last time. He takes that power, that ribbon of dark energy, made stronger by the lives he's stolen, and turns it on Miranda.

"You may not be her," Dee says, using my lips to deliver Miranda's death sentence, "but you are just like her. I had hoped for redemption for you. But it is not to be." The last words are whispers. "Alas. Good night."

The wide ribbon of energy floods out of my body and into Miranda. She gasps, her father's hand still clutched in hers. He's ashen beside her.

Miranda chokes out, "Grant, the letter," and bows like a weak branch under the onslaught.

Dee is using me to kill her. Miranda is going to die while I watch.

What did Gram's letter say? The crinkled page flutters in my thoughts as I experience a wash of intense pleasure. Dee *enjoys* watching Miranda suffer — *making* her suffer. He shows me a flash of what he truly wanted with her. Mary melds with Miranda. There's more punishment.

Dee's satisfaction increases as Miranda fades. Her heart squeezes in his unseen fist, her lungs emptying like bellows stomped by his heavy feet. Her soul tastes sweet to Dee, like

I hear Gram's voice then, apart from all the others: *Lay on hands.*

For the first time, there's an image in my mind instead of just words. *My grandmother in the kitchen of our house, a woman on the tile floor not breathing. Gram places her hands on the woman's chest, eyes closed, and . . .*

I press my palms over Miranda's heart and call on the spirits to provide whatever good energy they can. If Dee can hurt people using the spirits, I can help them, right?

A bright river of light floods out of me, and I beg her, "Wake up! Fight!"

I lift my hands and wait. That's all Gram showed me. I look over at Whitson's eyes, glassy and staring into the sky. Dee's cloaked followers don't seem to know what to do. Either that or their master's weakening has had an effect on them too.

Whatever the case, they are hushed, walling off the action on the stage again. I hear my dad barking commands somewhere not far off. We won't be isolated for long. Miranda's dad is wheeling, flailing, struggling against Dee while Eleanor grabs clumsily at his body.

And still Miranda lies there, peaceful, a sleeping beauty. I put my palm against her face and brush my thumb over the cursed mark. I want to tell her that I finally figured out how to use the spirits, and it's because of her. I want to tell her everything.

I press my forehead against hers. The touch feels so natural. If only I didn't also feel like my own heart is stopped in my chest, waiting to see if hers beats again.

MIRANDA

At first, there's nothing but darkness. My eyelids flutter, and it takes a universe-sized effort to see. I make out a face above me.

Grant.

A beam of light and hope zings through me . . . before I remember that he tried to kill me. He nearly succeeded. He isn't Grant anymore. He's Dee.

I drag in a ragged breath, and my lungs protest like I'm underwater. Raising my arms, I push against his chest as hard as I can. "No!" I shout. "Get away from me!"

I attempt to roll away from him, but his hands press me into place.

"It's me," he says. "For real. It's me."

I look up at him. Brown-black eyes. They aren't flat and black. They're worried.

"It's you," I say. "But where's . . ."

I turn my head to find Dad nearby, his arms flailing. "Help me up," I say, clutching at Grant's arm. I can tell my body what to do, and it mostly follows orders. Dee isn't controlling me, and I don't seem to be broken, just bruised.

Grant says, "It's Dee. Your dad said to put him back. He can end this. Miranda, I'm sorry."

"Don't be sorry." I know he's right. It's the same thing Dad was saying. I didn't want to hear it, but I understood it. I understand it now. Dad is gone. He has to stay that way. With Dee back inside him, he can leave and end this. The rules of the curse. Dad's going to use them to help me.

My heart feels like it's breaking.

I pause over Sidekick's body. He looks far too peaceful.

"I don't know if Sidekick's okay," Grant says.

"I'll find out after this is over," I say, cringing at the way my voice breaks. I drag in another shaky breath. "I have to talk to Dad. I can't know . . . not until afterward."

I get to my feet and stumble toward Polly, whose arm is around Dad. He's caught in a fit of mighty flailing. "Let go of him," I say. "Now."

Polly's expression is slightly dazed, and her protest is weak. "He can't keep the master at bay for long," she says, releasing him. She looks like she might fall down if a breeze hits her.

"They're not as strong because your dad is fighting him," Grant says. I look at him in question, and he adds, "The spirits just told me."

In this moment, that seems completely normal.

Dad's arms windmill, and I quickly have an arm around him, supporting him. "Dad," I say. "I'm here."

He goes still, and I'm trembling. I look at him and see my dad there in the eyes. My heart pounds, and it hurts with every beat. "What you were saying before — did you mean it?" I ask. "There's no other way?"

"Let me do this," Dad says. "Let me fix this for you. You walk me to the edge of the surf and I-I will leave this island. His curse means my body won't survive. He can't come back if I take him with me."

I want to cry. I want to hug him. I want to tell him how much this means. My father, the hero. Coming up with the plan to defeat a curse hundreds of years old. But there's no time.

"Okay. You hold on to him," I say, raggedly. My eyes burn with tears I can't afford to shed yet. "Keep him in there. I'll help you. I'll be right here the whole time."

"Yes," Dad says. His shoulder thrashes. "We have to go. Now."

Chief Rawling thunders onto the stage, shouting, "Clear this area." He has a host of uniformed helpers with him, and they scuffle with the cloaked figures of the returned — to them just townspeople — trying to get them off the stage.

"Grant," I say, "Dad and I are going to the water. Can you keep your dad out of the way?"

Grant doesn't ask questions, though he must have plenty. Instead, he yells, "Mom!"

Sara must be with the cops, because she's at Grant's side in an instant. She's no longer wearing her cloak. Even without that, I can tell she isn't under Dee's influence any longer. Grant must be right about the returned being affected by Dee's struggle with Dad, because the cops are making serious headway.

It gives me hope.

While Grant talks to his mom, I get my father's attention again. I want to talk to him about life instead of death. I grip my arm around him harder, hold one of his hands in mine.

"Those stories about us, our family. Dad, I know it wasn't your fault. I don't blame you for anything." I swallow a sob. "You understand?"

Dad's head nods, a quick jerk, then smoother as he gets better control of his body.

Grant hears what I say and moves to help when I slowly cross the stage with Dad. We're headed for the beach that gives Waterside Theater its name. The sour, rotten smell of the dead fish washing out of the sound stings my nose.

Dad talks to me as we go. I'll stay with him as long as I can. Just like I promised.

"This is for the best, sweet . . . my sweetheart," he says. "You are a good girl. Don't be afraid. You've always been strong. I'll see your mom again. It's not so much further. This will all be over soon."

"Miranda, this is your dad," Grant says. "What if . . ."

"I know. And it's his decision. But it won't hurt, will it, Dad? It won't hurt you?"

"It won't," Dad says, reassuring me.

Please, please, let that be true.

Grant manages his side of the support but says nothing more.

We stumble down a short flight of stairs at the back of the stage with Dad and curve around behind it. The rocky beach meets us, a long pier thrusting out over the water nearby. Stinking heaps of dead fish are stranded on sand and stone. The chunk of moon above reflects on the sound like a long mirror, fading into the pinprick lights from the shores of the outer islands in the distance. The sloshing of the waves drowns the shouts from the stage.

Grant says, "Miranda . . . ?"

"He's dead, Grant. He's right. It's not easy, but it's the right thing." It's also the hardest thing I've ever had to do.

"Right. Thing." Dad chokes out his agreement.

We have to hurry. Dee's soul may be confused, depowered for the moment. That won't last, though. I'm not even sure this will work, but Roswell's notes said the transition from death to life can only be made once. The boundary won't allow more than a single crossing.

"It's a good plan," Grant says. "He's brave."

I'm not surprised he figured it out, given a handful of minutes. Our eyes meet behind Dad's head.

"I learned from the best," I say. "I see that now."

Dad nods, not like he agrees, but like he's touched. "Thank you," he says.

The surf laps at the beach, the waves a few feet away. Slimy fish are slick under my shoes, and I have to be careful with my steps. Dad's body begins to flail again — Dee is resurfacing. Maybe he knows what's about to happen.

We will make it.

We careen over rocks and sand and fish, tripping into the water. I hold on to Dad as he jerks. "Grant," I say, "give me a sec."

Grant looks reluctant, but he steps back onto the shore, leaving me alone with my father.

"Dad," I say, "let's go." I take his flailing arm, fight to get his hand in mine. And together we walk forward into the surf.

"Miranda . . ." Grant calls a warning, but I already know. I only travel a few steps with Dad, coming to a stop with the water at my knees, splashing up my legs. I'm not far enough out yet for it to hurt.

"I love you, Dad." I squeeze his hand. He looks at me, and then Dee is there, flat and black, lip curling.

But the eyes give way to Dad again. His features calm. Even in the near darkness, I can tell it's him. He's coming through for

311

me, after all these years, and I don't want to let him. I want to hug him to me.

"I love you too," he says. "Always. Let go."

And I do.

Dad walks, keeps walking, until his head sinks beneath the waves. White foam breaks over the spot where he disappears, breaks all around me. He doesn't resurface.

Grant wades out to me and pulls me against him. I say my goodbye in the silence, wondering who Dad would have been without the curse, who I'll be if I make it through tonight.

"It's over," I say. "I think maybe it's over."

The shouts from back on the stage spike, frantically, reaching us.

"It's not over," Grant says.

"Something's happened." I palm tears off my cheek, and I'm not embarrassed by them. I'm not embarrassed by being a Blackwood. I don't care what anyone else thinks about us anymore.

Grants holds my hand tightly in his as we navigate through the dead fish shoreline and back up the steps to the stage. The reason for the noise becomes clear.

The bodies of the returned have wilted like so many flowers. They lay sprawled where they fell across the stage. The police officers are checking for pulses, for breath. Other townspeople join them, hovering over loved ones. The rest of the theater is quiet, the people still left in the audience not knowing what to do.

"It worked," I say, dully. "He's gone. And so are they. I did this."

I spot Chief Rawling then, kneeling beside a fallen form. Sara.

"Mom!" Grant releases my hand, moving through fallen bodies to reach his parents.

I follow, afraid the death isn't over. What if I made everything worse?

A wave of sound rolls across the stage. Sudden intakes of breath — gasp after gasp — are all around me as the returned stir back to life. Some sit up drowsily. Others stretch and climb onto unsteady feet.

I listen to their laughter, their confused questions.

"It's really her," someone says. More laughter. The buzz of happy conversation. Shrieks. I call out, "Polly?"

"Here," a weak voice says.

On the other side of the stage, Polly is touching her shoulders in confusion, like she doesn't know where or who she is. She reaches back to tighten her ponytail in a gesture I know well. She stops when she realizes her hair is down instead of up.

"They're really back," I say. But my beginning of a smile dies when I turn to Grant and Chief Rawling.

Sara is still unconscious.

Grant shakes his mother's shoulder, gently, as if she's breakable. He moves to check her pupils. Her eyes pop open.

"Mom, are you okay?" Grant asks.

In answer, Sara climbs to her feet, folding Grant and his dad into her arms. "I'm so sorry," she says, over and over. "I'm so sorry."

Grant shifts his head over her shoulder to meet my eyes. *We did it.*

I nod. *We did.*

I don't linger. They're a family. I need only to look over at Bone, sitting in shock beside his dead father, to remember that I don't have that. My family is gone now.

I squeeze Bone's shoulder as I walk past. My steps are slow as I approach Sidekick. I ease down beside his furry yellow body, prone like he's sleeping but too still for dreaming. I place my hand against his ribs.

I feel no movement, and part of me dies. Part of me follows Dad off the island, into the deep water, and meets the fate of the Blackwood curse.

At first, what's left of me believes the slight rise and fall beneath my fingers is wishful thinking. It's what I want but not reality.

It isn't, though.

Sidekick is breathing. His ribs lift against my hand, then fall, slowly at first, then more steadily.

I hold my own breath for a moment so I can better feel his, relaxing when he groans and wriggles against the pressure of my hand. *Belly scratch.*

"My good boy," I say. "Welcome home."

The missing are returned, the natural order is salvaged, and gentle waves embrace the shore. The time to mourn what we've lost will come, but not tonight. Tonight, the island is all around us.

And that's good.

GRANT

I've only talked to Miranda once since the night at the theater, and that was on the phone. Two days ago. The phone conversation felt like a blind date, not that I've ever been on one. It was frustrating and stuttering, like we just met and have nothing in common. Jokes were met with expanding pauses.

Toward the end, when the silence became too much to endure, too many dead fish and insects swimming between us in its gulf, I said, "I'll come by on Sunday?"

"Sure," Miranda said in a weird tone that I have analyzed over and over. I've come up with a thousand theories to explain it. At this point, I don't know what to expect.

But I still want to see her.

So why, when I knock at the front door of the Blackwood house, do I feel like I'm about to walk in and discover Dee sitting on the couch? Then again, if Miranda doesn't open the door pointing a gun at me, that's progress.

She doesn't.

"Um, hi," she says. She smiles at me, tentative. Nervous.

Sidekick bounds past and jumps up on me. Heavy paws land on my thighs, and I focus on petting his furry face. I've never been happier to see a dog in my life.

"I'm so glad he came through," I say, looking up at Miranda.

"Yeah. So . . ." she says. "You want to come in?"

"That's the plan."

I follow her over to the couch but decide not to give Sidekick the advantage this time. When Miranda sits down, I carefully select the spot right beside her. I leave an inch or two between us so we're not *quite* touching. Sidekick hops up on my other side and licks my hand until I pet him.

"You're not in jail," she says. "That's good."

I snort. "Because the feds had no freaking clue what to put in their report. They got out of here as fast as they could. And Dr. Whitson having your dad's body bag at his place . . . it was enough for Dad to close the case. But I'm sure he told you about that."

Her nod is tight. "He called."

"We went to Officer Warren and Delilah Banks's memorial services yesterday. Bone's not having one for his dad. He's going to live with his mom in Ohio."

"You know that wasn't you?" she says. "You didn't hurt them. It was him."

"I didn't kill them. But it's still hard. Knowing . . ." Knowing that if I'd learned how to cope earlier, maybe I could have stopped their deaths. I don't know if I'll ever get over that.

Miranda must sense I need to move on. "How's your mom?"

"She's atoning," I say. "Even though we keep telling her we understand."

"What about the spirits?" she asks.

"Much better." To my relief, if I don't want to see or hear them, I don't have to now. I have a feeling if they need me, need to tell me something, it'll be different. Here's hoping they don't need to for a long time. Maybe ever.

"Good." Miranda pushes her hair behind her ear.

I can't help it — I reach out and untuck it. That earns me the beginning of a flush in her cheeks. "I like it loose," I say. "It's nice that way."

"Loose women are the most popular, that's what I've always heard," she says.

I really want to kiss her again. "Miranda —"

"Wait," she says. "I have something for you." She leaps to her feet and hurries up the hall.

Screw waiting.

I trail her the short distance to her room, meeting her at the door. I walk forward, and she backs up with each step. We end up in her room, standing close, which is all right with me.

"What's that?" I ask, pointing at her hands.

"I wanted to make you something." Her head angles toward the small sewing table in the corner of the tiny room. It's set up so she has to sit cross-legged on the bed to use it. Scraps of fabric are discarded next to it.

"Please tell me it's not a gray cloak," I quip.

Miranda thrusts her hand out. I accept the fabric bundle from her and unfold it. The T-shirt is blue — Superman blue, really — and the block lettering she stitched on is made of a motley collection of fabrics. The words stack on top of each other — *Random Fact Boy*.

I grin. "I still think we could have come up with something better."

"Check the label," she says, sounding too anxious.

GWENDA BOND

I pull the neck down and take a look. Stitched in black thread, twined in script, are two more words — *My Hero.*

Miranda doesn't say anything, and it takes me a moment to figure out how to react.

"Best present ever," I say. "Up there with the Statue of Liberty."

"Really?" she asks.

"Really."

Her smile is real then, and finally I kiss her.

MIRANDA

I've spent the past few days convinced that Grant would decide the girl who put him through all this is damaged goods. Convinced that what's between us would turn out to be nothing without the constant threat of death and destruction.

I almost can't believe I was wrong.

Grant stops kissing me, and I wonder why. I chase him back onto the bed, but he holds up his hand.

"This is going to sound weird," he starts, "but . . . I just saw a glimmer in the air and heard a voice, and I want to know if what it said means anything to you."

I straighten. My immediate worry that it's another something terrible kicks into hyperdrive. "I thought you said they were better."

"They are — they're pretty much gone. But this voice, it just kind of showed up, just now. Bad timing. But do you know the song 'Heartbreaker' by Blondie?"

I swallow. "It was my mother's favorite song," I explain. "But it's not Blondie. A lot of people think that, but it's Pat

Benatar. It was on a double album with both their stuff, that's why."

"I love it when you talk nerdy." Grant reaches out and casually puts his hand against my neck, cradling it. I'm distracted, but not distracted enough not to notice how nice it feels.

"What did this spirit say?" I ask.

"This voice — I heard it once before, when I first came back. When we were at the cemetery at your mom's grave. I heard it say, 'Curse-bearer, curse-born child.'"

"Me," I say. "She was talking about me."

"But just now, when she stopped singing 'Heartbreaker' — which I'll have stuck in my head for days now, thank you very much, Miranda's mom — she said 'Curse-breaker, curse-broken child.'"

I trace a finger along the snake on my cheek. It's lightened to a pale pink. "Do you think? I still have this."

"I think we should take a drive and find out. A scientific test."

"Great idea," I agree. "Plus, I'm too freaked out to stay here right now."

Grant's forehead furrows with confusion. "Why?" He applies slight pressure against my neck.

"Um . . . my mom was watching us make out."

"She's gone now," he says.

But that doesn't matter. I want to know if it's true, if I'm free.

*

I convince Grant that Pineapple is superior to his mom's car, what with the plastic covering the window I smashed. And I asked him to drive, not wanting to take us both out if it turns out the voice from beyond the grave wasn't my mom's or wasn't right.

But I believe. I can feel the truth of what Grant said.

"I forgot to tell you," Grant says, "I'm doing senior year here."

"Congratulations. You're dating the school freak."

"Oh, I am?"

I feel myself blushing. *Why did I say that?*

Grant cuts the tension by laughing. "I am, I am. You think you're still the freak? After the way you saved everyone. I don't think so."

Oh boy, he's got a lot to learn. Small towns don't reclassify people. I'll just be the Blackwood freak who saved everyone. Of course, really that was Dad. I miss him. I miss the times we might have had together without the curse.

"This is going to be a good year," I say, hoping it's true. We both deserve one. "Assuming I survive the next five minutes."

We're heading out I-64 toward the new bridge, the Virginia Dare Memorial Bridge, not the site of my previous attempt to leave the island. We'll know whether I can make it over and keep breathing a lot quicker in the car than on foot.

"It's good luck that the bridge is named after Ginny the good," he says. "Did I mention I really like my present? You should go to fashion school. Or straight to *Project Runway*. *My Hero* could be your label."

He's talking to distract me. I appreciate the effort.

"Let's just see if I'm still cursed."

I feel an unfamiliar flutter in my stomach at the idea. If the curse *has* been broken by Dee's real, final death, then I could. I could go to fashion school. I could go on reality TV — and not be the villain, never say the words of infamy: "I'm not here to make friends." I could do anything I want.

"Ready?" Grant says as the bridge comes into view ahead.

"You sure you want to chance it in the car?"

He lets up on the gas, waiting for my answer. I take a moment to admire the nice view I have of the side of his face before looking ahead. The water sparkles on both sides of the road like a sea of diamonds.

"Don't slow down," I say.

AUTHOR'S NOTE

This story was inspired both by Roanoke Island's history and its present-day reality. As in most mash-ups of history and reality with fiction, I've taken some major liberties. Locations have been altered in many cases, and some have been invented. I also tweaked the structure of local law enforcement. And I hope it goes without saying that nothing in this story is meant to reflect on the real people living on the real island. Sources differ about the final tally of missing colonists, so some books may give a different number than 114.

On the historical side, I enhanced John Dee's role in the colonization effort. That said, Dee actually was the title holder for the land and was consulted by Sir Walter Raleigh in developing the route for the journey. In fact, I had the odd experience of finding some historical support for just about every outrageous leap. We really do know very little about the colonists and why they made the voyage. And it turns out that alchemy was a bigger influence in the early New World than we're taught in history class — at least, my classes tragically neglected the subject. I discovered from Walter Woodward's book *Prospero's America* that John Winthrop Jr., who was elected governor of Connecticut in the 1650s, actually did found a "New London" in America, intending it to be a great center of alchemy. He even used Dee's *monas hieroglyphica* as his signature. And it was recently discovered that a piece of Governor John White's artwork *did* hide clues to a possible location the colonists may have traveled to.

Of course, it's still unlikely that the majority of the lost colonists were alchemists who longed for immortality and world domination . . . or is it?

ACKNOWLEDGMENTS

This is a weird one, because it was my first published novel — but now it's also *this* novel, a different one, and not my first. So I feel like I should still thank all the people who helped me out originally, plus a couple new ones.

Like most first novels, this one wasn't born in a vacuum of just girl and computer. For looking at very early versions of this story, my thanks to Write Club (Melissa Moorer, Katherine Pearl, Christopher Rowe, and honorary member Melissa Schwartz) and the Left Door Workshop. Thanks are also due to the entire wonderful community at the Vermont College of Fine Arts' Writing for Children and Young Adults program, but especially to my last semester advisor, Martine Leavitt, and to my last workshop group (Kelly Barson, Kari Baumbach, Liz Cook, Pam Watts, Rachel Wilson, and leader Cynthia Leitich Smith) for comments on the beginning of this novel. Emily Moses was invaluable in offering insider theater dirt and gave me Dare County Night. I also offer many thanks to Holly Black, Sarah Rees Brennan, and Scott Westerfeld for help as I was finishing up. And, of course, thanks to the best agent in the world, Jennifer Laughran, for everything.

A few closer to home: George the Dog, poster boy for American Values, aka the original Sidekick, and Emma the Dog, LLC, no one's sidekick; my parents, who always believed I could do this; and to my husband, Christopher Rowe, for talking me down and reading more drafts than any person should ever have to.

I've been lucky over the years to have the support of more people than I could ever possibly name here. I appreciate each and every one of you. Dear readers, booksellers, librarians, and other book people: I love you. And I'll add here a thanks to Amanda Rutter, the book's original editor, who took a chance on a new writer, and to the fabulous Beth Brezenoff, as well as my ever-insightful editor on *this* book, Alison Deering, and everyone else at Capstone for wanting to give it a new life.

If you enjoyed this book, please consider leaving a review or telling a friend. To learn more about my other books, visit my website at www.gwendabond.com or sign up for regular emails at http://tinyletter.com/gwenda.

ABOUT THE AUTHOR

Gwenda Bond writes young adult and children's fiction. Her novels include the Lois Lane series (*Fallout, Double Down,* and *Triple Threat*), which brings the iconic comic book character front and center in her own YA novels, and the Cirque American series (*Girl on a Wire, Girl Over Paris,* and *Girl in the Shadows*) about daredevil heroines who discover magic and mystery lurking under the big top. She and her husband, author Christopher Rowe, co-write a children's series together, The Supernormal Sleuthing Service.

Gwenda has also written for *Publishers Weekly,* the *Los Angeles Times,* the *Washington Post,* and many other publications. She has an MFA in writing from the Vermont College of Fine Arts, and lives in a hundred-year-old house in Lexington, Kentucky, with her husband and their charming/unruly pets. She might have escaped from a screwball comedy. Visit her online at www.gwendabond.com or @gwenda on Twitter.